W9-BYB-536

"That university *is* your family."

Bo said it without derision or sarcasm.

Speechless, Max nodded, ran a hand through her thick locks. She was staring into the most beautiful pair of eyes on the planet.

"Someday..." Bo said, in a voice as gentle as a caress. "Someday, you're going to realize that there are other families happy to take you in and keep you in the fold."

Max swallowed thickly. That was how powerful a masterpiece Bo was. He made her want to agree with him, to believe that a man with everything—looks, connections, education, money, a good heart—could be interested in a woman who was...who had...who was nothing like him.

Somewhere deep inside her, in a place unrattled by things like physical masterpieces and all sorts of kisses, big and small, a teeny, tiny voice whispered a very small doubt: *this will end badly.*

But the rest of her... The rest of Max's entire being was hoping that wasn't true.

Dear Reader,

What would you do if you inherited a town? Would it change the course of your life? Would you want it to? That was the genesis of The Mountain Monroes series for me—take twelve siblings and cousins used to living the city life, give them a remote spot in Idaho and explore where they go from there. Which brings me to this last installment in the series...

Life as "the gorgeous Monroe" has made Bo's days easy in many ways, especially with women. But a painful failed relationship and his siblings finding true love have given Bo an epiphany—it's time to find the one and settle down. If only he could find a woman who sees him as more than a pretty face or one of the wealthy, influential Monroes. Enter Maxine Holloway, single mom, orphan and a woman who has given up on love. She's come to Second Chance for the holidays. Max refuses to succumb to Bo's charm. And besides, she doesn't believe she's worthy of a permanent spot in a family, much less the wild, warm Monroes.

I enjoyed writing The Mountain Monroes series, including the challenge of making each book connected yet stand-alone. Whether this is your first journey with the Monroes or you've been along for the entire twelve-book ride, I hope you love them as much as I do.

Happy reading!

Melinda

HEARTWARMING

A Cowboy Thanksgiving

Melinda Curtis

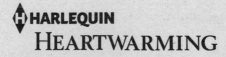

If you purchased this book without a cover you should be aware
that this book is stolen property. It was reported as "unsold and
destroyed" to the publisher, and neither the author nor the
publisher has received any payment for this "stripped book."

HARLEQUIN®
HEARTWARMING™

PLEASE RECYCLE
THIS PRODUCT IS RECYCLABLE

Recycling programs
for this product may
not exist in your area.

ISBN-13: 978-1-335-58463-2

A Cowboy Thanksgiving

Copyright © 2022 by Melinda Wooten

All rights reserved. No part of this book may be used or reproduced in
any manner whatsoever without written permission except in the case of
brief quotations embodied in critical articles and reviews.

This is a work of fiction. Names, characters, places and incidents
are either the product of the author's imagination or are used fictitiously.
Any resemblance to actual persons, living or dead, businesses,
companies, events or locales is entirely coincidental.

For questions and comments about the quality of this book,
please contact us at CustomerService@Harlequin.com.

Harlequin Enterprises ULC
22 Adelaide St. West, 41st Floor
Toronto, Ontario M5H 4E3, Canada
www.Harlequin.com

Printed in U.S.A.

Award-winning *USA TODAY* bestselling author **Melinda Curtis**, when not writing romance, can be found working on a fixer-upper she and her husband purchased in Oregon's Willamette Valley. Although this is the third home they've lived in and renovated (in three different states), it's not a job for the faint of heart. But it's been a good metaphor for book writing, as sometimes you have to tear things down to the bare bones to find the core beauty and potential. In between, and during, renovations, Melinda has written over thirty books for Harlequin, including her Heartwarming book *Dandelion Wishes*, which is now a TV movie, *Love in Harmony Valley*, starring Amber Marshall.

Brenda Novak says *Season of Change* "found a place on my keeper shelf."

Jayne Ann Krentz says of *Can't Hurry Love*, "Nobody does emotional, heartwarming small-town romance like Melinda Curtis."

Sheila Roberts says *Can't Hurry Love* is "a page turner filled with wit and charm."

Books by Melinda Curtis

The Mountain Monroes

Charmed by the Cook's Kids
The Littlest Cowgirls
A Cowgirl's Secret
Caught by the Cowboy Dad
Healing the Rancher

Return of the Blackwell Brothers

The Rancher's Redemption

The Blackwell Sisters

Montana Welcome

Visit the Author Profile page at Harlequin.com for more titles.

THE MOUNTAIN MONROES FAMILY TREE

Harlan Monroe
(deceased)

Darrell Monroe
(Oil/Finance)

- Holden Monroe
- Bo Monroe
- Kendall Monroe

Carlisle Monroe
(Hotels/Entertainment)

- Shane Monroe (twin)
- Sophie Monroe (twin)
- Camden Monroe

Ian Monroe
(Yacht Building)

- Bryce Monroe (twin, deceased)
- Bentley Monroe (twin)
- Olivia Monroe

Lincoln Monroe
(Filmmaking)

- Jonah Monroe
- Laurel Monroe (twin)
- Ashley Monroe (twin)

PROLOGUE

THERE WERE TIMES when twelve-year-old Beau-regard Franklin Monroe felt like he was on top of the world.

This wasn't one of those times.

It was Thanksgiving week, a time when the Monroes gathered. A time when the younger generation competed in the Monroe Holiday Challenge a five day event that culminated on Thanksgiving morning, followed by the crowning of this year's winner.

And this year's loser.

Sadly, for some unknown reason, Bo was often the year's biggest loser.

How could that be? Bo was athletic and large for his age. Everyone competing, except for his brother Holden, was younger than he was. He blamed it on his continuing growth spurts and clumsiness, a weak excuse at best.

But here it was. Thanksgiving morning. The last day of competition before the grand feast. And there was only one Monroe beneath

Bo on the leaderboard—his cousin Sophie. Something had to change.

Before he'd eaten breakfast, Bo had taken time to write in the small notebook his Grandpa Harlan had given him.

Run fast. Play hard. Pick myself up when I fall.

The notebook was a secret between his grandfather and himself. A way to be your own cheerleader, Grandpa Harlan had said. To create the life you want, he'd said. To get where you want to be.

Right now, Bo wanted to do better in the holiday challenge.

"What are we doing today, Grandpa?" Bo shouldered his way to the front of the pack, ahead of his two siblings and nine cousins. The sun was out in Philadelphia, but the cold air chilled his fingers and nose.

"There are six pumpkins hidden in the woods." Grandpa Harlan addressed all his Monroe grandchildren. "Each pumpkin you find and bring back earns you a point. One pumpkin has a leaf drawn on it. That one earns you two points. Got it? And…go!"

Bo didn't linger. He bolted into the woods.

But he wasn't fast enough to leave the pack behind. Holden tripped him. Cousin Shane elbowed him when he stumbled. Cousin Olivia knocked his cowboy hat off as he righted himself. And in the process, Bo careened into Cousin Sophie, who fell. Twin cousins Laurel and Ashley stopped to help her.

Bo ran on.

Finally, I won't be last.

Bo thrashed through the underbrush and tripped, falling on a pumpkin the size of a basketball hidden beneath the branches of a bush. Finally, his two left feet were good for something. And... Holy cow! This pumpkin had a leaf drawn on it with black marker. Two points! He wrapped his arms around the orange prize and stumbled back to Grandpa Harlan. If he hurried, he could return to the woods and try to find another.

His grandfather knelt next to Sophie, examining her scrapes, which were bleeding a little. Laurel and Ashley hovered nearby, sending Bo dirty looks.

Bo placed the pumpkin at their feet. "I found one." He danced around as if he'd just scored a league-winning touchdown. "I found one! I'm not last. I'm not going to get another loser trophy."

"Stop right there." Grandpa Harlan straightened and put a hand on Bo's shoulder. "You knocked Sophie down." His tone of voice didn't ring with approval.

Bo hurried to defend himself. "The only reason I bumped into Sophie was because Olivia pushed me." He tipped his cowboy hat back, tugged down his sweatshirt and tried to smile innocently. His mother always said his charm and good looks got him out of trouble at school. She considered them mixed blessings. But with a combined total of eleven siblings and cousins, Bo had to work with what little he had. "It's not my fault. Blame Olivia."

"But you didn't stop to make sure your cousin was okay." Grandpa Harlan helped a still crying Sophie to her feet. "As the Grand Poo-Bah of the Monroe Holiday Challenge, I hereby award your pumpkin to Sophie."

Laurel and Ashley cheered.

"But…" Bo's shoulders slumped. "I would have helped her up if I'd have known that was a rule." He glanced at Sophie's scrapes, which looked painful, and those tears of hers, which were real, and felt remorse. "I'm sorry, Soph."

"I won't reverse my verdict." Grandpa Har-

Ian softened his decision by righting Bo's cowboy hat. "I hope this is a lesson you take to heart, Bo. No matter what else goes on, people always come first."

Take it to heart? He'd never forget this feeling of letting Sophie down and being a failure.

Five of the competitors, including Holden, Shane and Olivia, emerged from the wood, each carrying pumpkins and wearing big smiles that said they hadn't come in last.

"I'm cursed." Bo trudged back to the house where he'd receive the biggest loser trophy served with his pumpkin pie. "I hate the Monroe Holiday Challenge. I'm done playing."

But he knew that was a lie. Because if there was a chance that he wouldn't come in last in the competition, he was going to take it.

As for the rest of his life?

He was going to try his best never to be last at anything else. Ever.

CHAPTER ONE

"GOOD NEWS, BO. We're bringing back the Monroe Holiday Challenge this Thanksgiving."

Bo Monroe had just taken a sip of his beer when his cousin Shane made his announcement. He nearly sprayed said beverage into the firepit in the backyard of the Bucking Bull Ranch. Instead, he managed to swallow and say in a choked voice, *"Why?"*

A steady stream of snowflakes fell with a soft pitter-patter on his straw cowboy hat. It was a week before Thanksgiving and snow had been falling in Second Chance, Idaho, since October.

Or so he'd heard. Bo and his dog Spot had just arrived from Texas for a visit and Bo had accepted an invitation to have a beer with Shane and Jonah after a family dinner. Spot, his Harlequin Great Dane, was hanging out with the rest of Shane's family indoors, probably curled up in front of the fire since the dog was a born and bred Texan, unused to temperatures below fifty.

"You want to know why we need to bring back a beloved holiday tradition?" Shane sat at Bo's right. He grinned from ear-to-ear, and considering he'd been in a near-fatal car crash a few months ago, it was good to see him smiling again. But not over this. "Because none of you want me to hold the Holiday Challenge crown forever."

Bo's competitive streak agreed. It was his pride that didn't want to compete.

"You've held the crown for over twenty years. I'm willing to let you hang on to it forever." Jonah shrugged deeper into his jacket in the chair to Bo's left. Born and raised in Hollywood, Bo's script-writing cousin hated the cold as much as Spot did. Jonah wore a blue parka, fur-lined hood up over his short red hair. "I hated those challenges. And most of us hated Olivia, Holden and you, Shane, for winning."

Bo nodded.

"But this time things will be different," Shane promised, sounding like a CEO at a shareholders' meeting, which was fitting considering he had been a CEO up until last January. In deference to the cold, Shane wore a thick, stylish blue jacket, a knit cap and gloves. He might be living on a ranch, but he was not, and never would be, a true cowboy. "We have to do this before we're too old."

Thinking of age and physical prowess, Bo sized up Shane, making a mental tally of his cousin's corporate softness.

I could take him... If I wasn't cursed in the challenge.

"I don't know about Bo, but I'm not up for a physical competition." Jonah stretched one leg toward the fire, groaning like it pained him to do so. "I pulled a muscle climbing the ladder to the hayloft."

"And what were you doing in the hayloft?" Shane teased.

"I was helping Emily move hay." Jonah tried hard not to smile but ended up grinning back at Bo, still riding his wave of post-engagement bliss.

Although Bo was happy for his cousin, that bliss stung a little.

Over a year ago, he and Jonah had been in love—or thought they'd been in love—with the same woman—Aria. They'd both lost her. A blessing of sorts, as it turned out. Jonah had quickly moved on, writing a script about the experience as a form of therapy before landing the heart of Emily, a diehard cowgirl and former rodeo queen. Bo had been picking up the pieces of his heart at a slower pace, taking into consideration Aria's last words to him...

"Look at us together. We're perfectly matched in the mirror," Aria had said in a voice that was as delicate and refined in tone as her polished good looks. "You may be an engineer, Bo, but you have no ambition, no life plan. And nothing to indicate you want a wife and family, except for those scribbles you make in your notebook every morning. And Spot, I suppose." She'd scratched his dog behind the ears before handing Bo his leash and dog dish, items she'd used while dog-sitting. "And even Spot has to deal with your long absences from traveling and working on an oil rig."

Spot had stared up at Bo with the same accusation in his big brown eyes.

Even my dog thinks I stink at relationships.

After that, Bo had taken a hard look at himself and realized that—on paper, at least—he looked like he wasn't interested in long term relationships or happily-ever-after. He was determined to change that impression.

"Listen," Shane said, voice rising above the soft hiss of falling snow and the crackle of flames. "I've been telling my boys about the challenge and they're excited."

Bo and Jonah exchanged looks and then simultaneously said, "No."

"I reject your rejections." Shane wasn't the type to give in easily. "The boys have come up with a list of games to play, ones with a cowboy twist." The boys Shane referenced were the ones he was going to adopt in January after he married their widowed mother, Franny, at New Year's.

"Are these games Franny approved?" Bo shook his head, dumping a bit of snow from his hat onto his shoulders. "Forget I asked. *I* need to approve the games. You all owe me that much."

Jonah gaped at Bo. "I can't believe you said that. You're actually considering playing?"

"Only if I have a chance to win." Or at least not come in last.

"It was never about winning," said Shane, the family's most frequent winner. "And this time, it won't be cut-throat. It'll be fun. We'll have teams of three instead of competing one-on-one—two adults paired with a kid. I bet that boy you're picking up tomorrow will enjoy it, Bo."

That boy was a relation of a friend of Bo's,

Nathan Blandings, an army engineer who'd been unexpectedly deployed overseas. Nathan had called a few days ago and, over a bad connection, asked Bo to host the young orphan for the week of Thanksgiving. Bo wasn't usually the man someone chose for such a job, him being a bachelor and all. Nor was he usually the man who accepted such a request, having an active social life. But he hoped the experience would give him perspective when it came to settling down and contemplating how to raise his own kids.

"Fine. I'll take Max." Hopefully, the kid was a budding athlete with the will to win.

"If only you had a significant other..." Shane began.

"Back off." Bo crossed his arms over his chest, trying not to look as wounded as he felt. "Not everyone finds love as easily as you two."

"Dude, we aren't the ones compared in appearance to underwear models." Jonah chuckled. "And yet, of the twelve Monroes who inherited Second Chance, everyone found love here, except you."

I'm even last in love.

Bo slumped in his folding chair. It was true. He couldn't go anywhere in town without seeing a happily partnered family member. They all had someone to confide in, to share private jokes with, to cuddle up with on a cold winter night.

And I have Spot.

Who was a bed hog.

Shane cleared his throat. "Bo, I know you attract a lot of attention just stepping into a room."

"Being too pretty is a curse," Jonah mocked mournfully.

Bo pressed his lips together to keep from sneering at Jonah.

"It's not all about physical attraction." Shane stared at the falling snowflakes dreamily, like a man staring at the woman he loved. "I saw something in Franny the moment we met. There was a sadness in her eyes. I had to find a way to chase those blues away, even if I didn't know why I was doing it. Turns out it was because she was meant for me. That's the kind of person you need to find."

Bo kept silent, not understanding how someone could be meant for someone else or how you'd know it instantly.

"If we're handing out love advice…" Jonah felt the need to chime in. "I was attracted to Emily from the start. She's my kind of pretty and my kind of talker. Admittedly, Em was mistakenly attracted to you at first." He clapped Bo on the back. "But she eventually fell for brains over beauty. Truly, it's what's inside that counts. Her values match my values, her sass can handle my sarcasm. *That's* the kind of person you need to find, Bo."

Although it was true that women were often drawn to, or in awe of, Bo's physical appearance, Bo found that to be a turn-off. He was more than a pretty face.

He shook his head, shaking off romantic notions, along with another dusting of snow. "That's enough, guys. I don't need love advice. I have a plan for love." As any good engineer would, once he applied his smarts to the situation.

His cousins stared at Bo as if he'd bought a ten dollar ticket on a two dollar ride.

"I'm getting my house in order. Literally." Bo warmed to his topic, leaning forward. "I made an offer on a home in Houston. And I want to find a place up here before I leave next weekend." Not to mention, he'd accepted a full-time job at an oceanographic oil company that offered generous health and retirement benefits. "I've got a life plan, one that is specific about the kind of life I want to lead and the woman I want by my side." There would be no more falling for complicated, high maintenance women or women with messy relationship histories. "I've got a clear vision of my future. When my plans are in place, I'll look for love. And mark my words, the next woman I fall for isn't going to be able to resist me."

His cousins' mouths hung open.

In awe, Bo assumed.

FRIDAY AFTERNOON, Bo stood in baggage claim at the Boise airport holding a sign with a name printed in bold, black letters: *Max Holloway.*

He scanned the approaching crowd for someone wearing an airline uniform and holding the hand of a young boy.

A little girl wearing a bright pink tracksuit and thick, round glasses ran up to Bo, brown, corkscrew curls straining the bands around her ponytails. "Hi." She tucked her thumbs beneath her purple backpack straps. "I love cowboys."

"Is that so?" Bo tipped his cowboy hat and spared a smile for the overly friendly girl before continuing his search for an escorted minor in the crowd.

"For Max Holloway?" A woman with light brown, curly hair and thick, round glasses wheeled a large, yellow suitcase to a stop in front of Bo's booted feet and set a car seat by her side. She wore blue slacks, a white button-down blouse and a blue blazer. So much blue. She had to be an airline employee of some sort.

But if she was, where was the little boy?

"I was expecting Max?" Bo stared at the little girl, who seemed nothing like a Max and too small to be traveling alone, much less compete in the Monroe Holiday Challenge.

"It's *Maxine*," the woman said in a no-nonsense voice.

"Okay." Max was Maxine and an adorable little tyke. Plans for the holiday challenge would need to be adjusted. Even the lines he'd written in his notebook this morning—*be positive, beat Shane*—seemed a stretch. Maybe he'd use this as an excuse to drop out or at the very least get paired with someone who could help him win. Smiling, Bo handed the woman his placard. "Do I need to sign anything before taking custody of Maxine?"

The woman gave him a disapproving once-over. The airlines had chosen her well. She didn't seem like the type to put up with drama—be it lost luggage or awkward transfers of minors traveling alone.

The urge to win her over surged within him, strengthening his smile.

"Right. You need identification." Bo took out his wallet and showed her his driver's license. "Are you looking forward to Thanksgiving?"

"Yes." The airline employee stared at him steadily through her thick glasses. Her eyes were the color of his favorite, oak-aged whiskey. She glanced at his ID. "Beauregard Franklin Monroe."

Beauregard...

What had his parents been thinking?

"Not everyone can grow into an old school name like Beauregard." Grinning at the little girl, Bo twirled an imaginary handlebar mustache. "But you can call me Bo." He tucked his wallet in his back jeans pocket, propped the car seat on the yellow suitcase, took possession of the little girl's hand, and then navigated through the sea of travelers. "Do you like dogs? Spot is waiting for us in my truck. You'll love him. I feel like ice cream before we make the drive over the mountain to Second Chance. What do you think?"

The little girl blinked up at Bo with eyes

the same color as those of her airline chaperone. "Don't I have to eat my vegetables first?"

"Of course not," he said cheerfully. "It's the holidays." That's what his Grandpa Harlan used to say, much to his mother's chagrin.

"Vegetables first," said the woman behind him. "Always."

Bo stopped just before the exit. He hadn't realized the airline representative was still tagging along. "Sorry. I didn't sign for her, did I?"

The woman wasn't carrying a pen. She didn't have a sheaf of papers. But she was frowning at him in the worst way.

"Mama, just once I wanna have ice cream before vegetables." The little girl smiled coyly. "Please…"

"Mama?" Bo took a step back, earning another frown from the woman.

"I think there's been a mix-up." The woman gestured from the little girl to herself. "Nathan said you'd take us in for Thanksgiving." At Bo's blank look, she added, "*Us*, as in two."

"No. Nathan said…" Bo trailed off, trying to remember.

My…(unintelligible)…needs a place to spend the holidays. Max is an orphan and…

(unintelligible)...can't spend with them. (Unintelligible)...you owe me.

Shane and Jonah were going to have a good laugh over this misunderstanding. They might even try to make a team out of them.

Not a chance.

Bo drew a deep breath, determined to make the best of things, such as they were. "To be honest, we had a bad connection and I'm not sure what Nathan said exactly." Bo forced himself to chuckle, although he felt like nothing was funny. "All I got was that some kid named Max needed a place to spend the holidays. And then came the email from Nathan with the flight number and arrival time, plus the name Max Holloway."

The woman straightened her jacket and righted her glasses, all the while keeping a close eye on her little girl. "Is that all?"

"Yeah. That was the gist of it." He forced another mirthless chuckle, a little ha-ha-ha that would never pass for Santa's ho-ho-ho. "It's all good. There's plenty of room in Second Chance for both Maxine and you." Whoever she was.

"That's Luna," the woman informed him in an exasperated voice, pointing at her daughter. "And I'm Max."

She was the orphan?

"And to think, I used to like surprises," Bo muttered.

"I like cowboys, and Mama likes books." Luna pushed her glasses up her nose. One of her ponytails was askew over her ear, as if she'd fallen asleep in Maxine's arms and shifted her head to-and-fro to get comfortable. Which was adorable but wouldn't help him win any reindeer games. "Are you a for-real cowboy, with a horse and everything?"

Bo drew back in mock surprise. "Miss Luna, I'm a Texan. Now, I'm currently horseless, but—"

"Well, shoot." Luna scuffed the sole of a little red, sparkly sneaker on the carpet. "You aren't a real cowboy. You just look like one."

"I'm a Texan," Bo repeated, feeling a frown crease his brow as he defended his adopted home. "Wearing boots and cowboy hats come second nature to me."

Luna eyed him up and down. "Do you have cows?"

"No."

"Do you live on a ranch?"

"No."

"You're not a real cowboy." The little thing had the nerve to look disappointed.

In Bo!

Except for Aria, Bo was never a disappointment to the ladies.

He swallowed the compulsion to explain his life plan to a pre-schooler. "Help me out here, Maxine."

"You're on your own, Beauregard." Maxine took possession of her daughter's hand and stepped around Bo, poised to take the lead. "Which way?"

CHAPTER TWO

"How do you know Nathan?"

"I met him working on an oil rig." The cowboy smiled, as if his statement explained everything, when it left Max just as confused as she'd been in the airport.

Maybe he's not being evasive on purpose. Maybe he's shy, like me.

Max noodled that theory from the front seat of the man's truck as he drove them out of the airport and toward the highway. Luna was strapped in her car seat in the back, sitting with Spot, the extremely friendly, ginormous Great Dane, whose black spots stood out on his white fur like buttons of coal on a snowman.

The sky was overcast. The deciduous trees were bare. The roads were lined with black slush, evidence of a previous snowstorm. Everything outside the truck looked washed out and dingy. The gloom, and their less than auspicious start at the airport, didn't bode well for the week. It was important that things went well for Luna's sake. The holidays were all about making Luna happy.

Max drew a deep breath and forced a chipper note in her tone. "Nathan mentioned your family had a place in the mountains."

"That might be an understatement."

"Really."

"You'll see."

She made a non-committal noise, wishing he'd say more.

"Spot is licking me," Luna reported, giggling.

Max turned to look. Sure enough, the dog lay across the back seat facing Luna, body long enough for his tongue to reach Luna's cheek. "Hey. Stop that."

The dog ignored her.

"Spot believes everyone's face tastes as good as ice cream." The cowboy flashed a smile Max's way. He must have noted her frown, because he tapped his shoulder and said with authority, "Spot, come."

The extra large dog pushed himself into a sitting position, faced forward and placed his muzzle on the cowboy's shoulder beneath his hat brim, earning a few pats.

"Stay," Max told the dog when he glanced

her way, because the last time Spot had looked at her, he'd jumped into her lap.

"You've got to say it like you mean it." Beauregard Franklin Monroe, or Bo, as he'd told her to call him, was a man of few words whereas Max was a woman of many.

She could already tell that they were oil and vinegar. Everything about the gorgeous man was movie-star perfection. His face had no bad side. His chin wasn't too round or too pointed. His nose wasn't too short or long. His dark brows and nearly black hair were thick and statement-making, as was the way his shoulders filled out a rust-colored button-down. Add a straw cowboy hat and worn brown cowboy boots, and he was a cliché lifted from the page of a romance novel.

Max allowed herself a small smile. She'd given up on romance and romantic fantasies three years ago during her divorce. It was the myth of family at the holidays that her heart stubbornly couldn't give up on. And her cousin Nathan knew it. He hadn't chosen Beautiful Bo as a last resort. There must be more to the cowboy than physical perfection.

"You must have a big family," Max mused aloud.

"Disgustingly large," Bo agreed. "Nosy,

caring and…competitive." He said this last bit kindly, as if doling out a warning. "But I love them and, for the most part, wouldn't have it any other way."

Max's heart clenched with envy. What she would give for a family like that.

Bo glanced in the rearview mirror, presumably at Luna. "Spot likes ice cream."

"Me, too," Luna piped up.

"Subtle, but ice cream isn't on the menu. We haven't had a decent meal since breakfast." And it was closer to dinner than lunch.

"Phooey," Luna said.

Bo spared Max a glance with dark gray eyes rimmed by eyelashes that were thicker than hers.

Was there no end to his perfection? She gave him a quick perusal but noted no faults, no warts, not even nose hair.

"You weren't kidding about vegetables," he said.

"I never joke about the importance of broccoli." But here she was, joking, the same way she'd joked the day she first met her ex-husband.

There's a red flag.

"In terms of jokes…" Max leveled her thick glasses, mentally shielding herself and her heart behind the armor created from being an unwanted orphan and being crushed by a disappointing marriage and a calculated divorce. "I'm not very good at repartee."

"Me neither. I've always thought it best to lay your cards on the table."

"Can we play cards?" Luna yawned. "Does Spot play Go Fish?"

"Spot is more of a cuddler than a card player." Bo reached up to pet the dog, whose muzzle still rested on his shoulder. "Why did you think I had a big family?"

Max was almost glad for the excuse to turn and look at Bo more fully. He was like a piece of artwork that deserved her full attention, a masterpiece she appreciated but couldn't afford. "On those rare holidays when Nathan isn't around, he arranges for someone with a big family to take me in."

"Does that make it less awkward for you?" Bo had a nice voice. Deep, with a tone that resonated unexpectedly inside Max. And he enunciated clearly without rushing his words, the way she'd been taught in public speaking. "Is it less awkward when you're taken in? By large families, I mean."

"In a way… I suppose…" Max wrinkled her nose, perplexed by the urge to divulge too much. She didn't like to reveal a lot of personal information during these holiday take-ins, not wanting to look pathetic. And yet, she didn't change the subject. "Do you know what happens when a big family gathers?"

"There's always noise and plenty of food." He patted his flat stomach.

I bet he has a six-pack.

She dragged her gaze away.

Do not think of him without a shirt on!

Max stared straight ahead, trying to regain her composure and hold tight to her secrets.

And failing.

"At big family gatherings, a person can get lost in the crowd, and temporarily feel like part of the group, even on the periphery." Which was where she felt safest.

Bo spared Max a glance that asked silent questions in a way that encouraged verbal answers, as if her secrets were safe with him. She'd already said too much, safeguards breached by the impact of his good looks.

Now's the time to change the subject.

"My parents died when I was young," she said instead, unable to stop the truth from tumbling out. "I bounced around to different relatives never really feeling…"

Shut up, Max, or he'll get the wrong idea.

Or the right one—that she and Luna were unwanted, even Luna by her ex-husband's family.

And didn't that sting.

"You had a feeling that you never really belonged?" Bo finished for Max.

"Yes." His insight made her overshare feel less like a raw confession.

"I'm sorry about your parents," Bo said solemnly. "That must have been tough."

It still is.

Hence her seeking temporary foster families for the holidays.

"I feel that way sometimes with my Monroe relatives," Bo was saying. "The not belonging part, that is. Two siblings. Nine cousins. And now their significant others, their kids, their in-laws."

Mr. Good Looking is single?

She glanced at his ringless left hand, heart beating a little faster.

Stop right now, Maxine Marie. Think of him like a fond cousin...

Max gulped. Bo was nothing like dear, sweet Nathan, who had a weakness for milk tea, mathematic equations and documentaries about scientists.

Unaware of her wayward thoughts, Bo

kept talking, scratching Spot behind one ear. "Like I said, I'm close to my family…but I'm just…physically far away most of the time. I stay with them when I visit Second Chance. I thought maybe I'd look for a place of my own this week. A vacation place."

This was interesting. Max enjoyed those house hunting shows on TV. Maybe she could be of assistance. That was her goal at the holidays, to be a help, not a burden. "What do you envision in a second home?"

"I have a long list about what I'm looking for and the life I want to lead. I refine what I want every morning in a notebook. Nothing as fancy as a journal."

"Lists? Affirmations?" She waved the idea aside. "I believe a person or place chooses you, rather than the other way around. You know what I mean? You walk in, and you just know that this is the person or that is the place." Max ignored the small voice in her head that suddenly whispered, *"This is my person."* The last thing she needed was to develop a crush on a temporary holiday host, especially an Adonis, who was clearly out of her league.

"How did we get to talking about houses and significant others?" There was something guarded about his expression, yet something vulnerable in his eyes when he glanced in the rearview mirror at Luna. He took an exit that headed east, directly toward some imposing, snow-covered mountains. "I don't usually talk about my personal life when I first meet someone."

"Me either. It makes me wonder what we'll talk about tomorrow." And the next day. Or the next holiday.

Don't even go there, Max.

Her hands were clenched in her lap, fingers tightly intertwined. She made an effort to loosen them. It was difficult, much like the energy she'd be exerting in a week's time when she boxed up the holiday memories of the family she'd never see again and left a little bit of her heart behind.

"I hope you weren't expecting anything fancy." Bo filled the silence between them. "We'll be staying at a cattle ranch."

"With *real* cowboys?" Luna asked sleepily.

"Yep," he said with a wry smile. "It's my cousin's fiancée's ranch. Plus, there are circles upon circles of Monroes in Second Chance. Lots of kids for Luna to play with. And tons of people to meet."

"And feed," Max murmured, vowing to stay busy in the kitchen and far, far away from Bo.

"Mama, Spot's licking me again." Instead of giggling, Luna sounded sleepy.

Somehow the large dog had moved without Max noticing. "Spot, sit." Max snapped her fingers a few times to capture the Great Dane's interest.

Spot ignored her, intent upon cleaning Luna's cheek and keeping her awake.

"Spot, sit." Bo repeated the command with better results. The dog returned its head to his shoulder, bumping his hat brim in the process. "You have to give a command like you mean it."

"I did," Max insisted, miffed although she'd never had a dog of her own.

Bo shook his head. "You said it softly, like you were melting into the background of a large crowd and didn't want to be noticed."

"Hey." Max bristled.

But before she could think of a retort, Bo apologized. "Sorry. I just meant you have to speak to an animal with conviction."

"I have conviction." How could she not? "I have degrees in art history, English literature and linguistics. And I've applied to a foresight program."

"Sounds like you're full of conviction," Bo allowed, although he scratched beneath his hatband as if unsure. "All those degrees… Do you have a career goal in mind?"

"I…" Her fingers knotted again. Why couldn't she think of a good answer?

"Mama likes school," Luna murmured.

Max untangled her digits, silently thanking her little girl for the save.

"Well…" Bo rubbed at the dark stubble on his chin. "I've never met anyone with more than two degrees, and they were all firmly established in a career after the second one. That's the goal of higher education, isn't it? To land a good job?" He spared Max a quick glance, hopefully not noticing her trying to hide her disagreement. "Help me out here. I'm working on the link between art history, English literature, linguistics and…foresight, was it? Are you going to teach at a university someday or work for some top secret government agency deciphering ancient texts to prove that aliens do exist and how they'll influence life in the future?"

Despite the tension, Max laughed, earning a grin from this unexpected cowboy.

Still, there were some things she didn't joke about, and the importance of her continued studies was one of them. A distraction and distance were in order. "I'm good at guessing holiday preferences. I'd say you're a turkey man."

Bo's gaze narrowed but didn't waver from the road ahead, which had dropped down to a two lane highway that wound its way through a thickening forest of snow-dotted pines. "Stepped over a line, did I?"

"Not at all." Max forced herself to smile through the lie and pursue a distraction. "I'm betting you're a turkey man. Mashed potatoes. No gravy." Simple food. Limited carbs.

"Wrong. You are so wrong." He chuckled. It was the first time she'd heard him laugh. The fake guffaw back in the airport didn't count. This sound was rich and layered, like the flavors in a nicely made pumpkin pie.

"I'm not wrong," she insisted, feeling like she was digging a deep hole and he was watching from a safe distance. "You've also got a big crush on apple pie. No pumpkin for you."

Bo made a sound like a buzzer. "Wrong again."

"I'm right. You like things easy. Straightforward. Women. Work. The place you live." He made lists, for heaven's sake. People who made lists were people of action, not contemplation. She was right. Max refused to let her convictions go. "And you're a Texan. Complications? Who needs them?"

He scowled. And that, too, was beautiful. "Has Nathan mentioned me at all?"

"Never. It's all right there." Her gesture encompassed him. Every gorgeous inch of Beauregard Franklin Monroe. "You're a message being sent out to the universe." And despite her best intentions, she was receiving all those messages.

Bo scratched beneath his hatband again, slowing for a turn. It was then she noticed the gadgets built into his dashboard. He had all the bells and whistles. There were more controls in his truck than she had apps installed on her cell phone. And he'd mentioned journaling, although he'd shied away from calling it as such.

Am I wrong about him?

Bo spared her another of his mischievous glances. "Maxine, why did you need a place to go for the holidays?"

"It's Max," she said in a thin voice wrought with frustration, a feeling that stomped all over her composure and made her want to give up trying to prove she was a clever woman of conviction and silently sit back and bask in the beauty and charm of Beauregard Franklin Monroe. But therein lay heart-crushing danger.

She cleared her throat and started over, trying to convince herself—and him—that she was just another someone passing through his life. "I told you why we're here. I'm an orphan. My parents died in a tornado twenty years ago." She still hated stormy weather. "I bounced around the family for years. Spent high school with Nathan's parents. He treats me like his kid sister, always inviting me to the holidays." Always insisting she come. "Things changed at the last minute and I…" Max swallowed thickly, surprised by the emotion welling in her throat. As an army engineer, Nathan could be deployed to dangerous areas. "I didn't want him to worry about us while he was overseas. It's why I agreed when he hooked us up."

"Hooked us up," Bo repeated slowly and with the beginnings of a smile.

"Not like that. Geez, don't live up to the stereotype of a brawny cowboy out to charm any and all females."

Bo laughed. "I get it now. You're the educated one, not me." He snuck her one of those sly glances, full of good humor and appreciation of the company, the kind that broke down her immunity to handsome men. "You like turkey, too, by the way. And when it comes to leftovers, it's turkey sandwiches with a layer of cranberry sauce and cream cheese. Oh, and pumpkin pie with extra whipped cream for dessert."

Max clasped her hands in her lap.

He was right.

And better than she was at keeping his private life private.

CHAPTER THREE

"Bo, YOU MISSED EVERYTHING." Five-year-old Adam greeted Bo when he parked his truck in front of the white, two-story farmhouse at the Bucking Bull and got out. Adam was a first grader, the youngest of the Clark boys who lived on the ranch. "Papa Shane and Jonah set up teams for the challenge."

"Of course they did." Bo scoffed, putting on his thick, shearling jacket and feeling like he was getting the short straw in the competition.

"'Cept you need to find a girl for your team," Adam went on, pausing his info dump to call to Spot. "Here, boy. Come on."

The Great Dane leaped from the driver's seat with the grace of a gazelle, took a beat to greet Adam and then sprang up the porch stairs before nudging the not-quite-shut door open and trotting inside.

"Softie." Bo moved toward the truck bed.

"For such a big dog, Spot don't like the

outdoors." Adam fell into step behind Bo. Despite the snow and the cold, the little cowpoke only wore a sweatshirt over his blue jeans and boots, not as bothered by the chill as Spot was. "Where's Max? He's on your team."

"She." Bo hefted that big yellow suitcase out of the truck bed. "Max is a she and she isn't going to compete in the challenge." He should take this for a sign and withdraw. With Maxine on his team, he'd come in last again, for sure.

But what if I didn't?

He silenced the hopeful voice in his head. He had a plan for this week, and it didn't involve chasing after pipe dreams of victory. He was going to find the perfect vacation home, one that any woman would step into and think it'd be ideal for a big family.

Besides, Maxine didn't need to suffer through the challenge. She'd had a tough enough life. Orphaned. Single mom. No place to go at the holidays.

A smile began forming on his lips.

Not that Maxine wanted his sympathy. She may not know how to bring a dog to heel, but she was a spitfire, refusing to back down when he challenged her. And when she realized he'd gotten her to say more than she wanted...

His smile spread.

"What's this about a challenge?" Carrying Luna, Maxine came around the truck bed, conservative black flats sinking into the snow.

Bo was going to have to find her a proper pair of shoes for the mountains.

"Max is a girl?" Adam stumbled back dramatically, pointing at Luna, beginning to catch on.

"Yep." Luna wriggled down from her mother's arms, curly ponytails an inch from breaking free of her hairbands. "I'm Luna and I'm a girl, too."

"You're Luna? Then who is Max?" Adam cried, clearly confused.

"Me." Maxine pointed at herself. Her glasses were fogging up and her wavy hair was haloed with snowflakes. She looked like a lost librarian, a sight that made Bo want to smile some more. "I'm Max. And you must be..."

"Adam." The little guy's eyes widened. "Holy haystacks. Papa Shane ain't gonna believe this." Adam raced up the stairs to the farmhouse and darted inside, slamming the door behind him.

Luna stared after him with a look of longing on her face. She was a cute little thing, the kind of kid he imagined snuggled up in a corner with a blanket, a pile of books and a big dog who hated the cold.

Spot peered at them from the front window, ears perked as if he'd return to Bo's side if only it were twenty degrees warmer.

"What challenge is Adam talking about?" Maxine tugged her too-thin jacket closed against the icy wind racing down the mountain.

Bo added a better jacket to the list of things Maxine needed.

"It's a Thanksgiving family tradition, kind of like a final championship except with less skill." Bo carried their yellow suitcase to the bunkhouse, which was a very small building next to the barn. "Forget about it. You're here to slink about in the shadows of the family, not vie for the limelight, remember?"

"That's not what I said," Maxine grumbled from behind him. "I'm good at games— charades, password, gin rummy. Come along, Luna. Follow Beauregard."

Beauregard?

"Just call me Bo," he said with a clenched jaw. Maxine wasn't cut out for the holiday challenge. She'd get elbowed back and shoved aside, fall and scrape her knees. How on earth was she going to help him win? He opened the bunk room door, set their bag down and turned on the lights. "Just so you know, the challenge has nothing to do with indoor games or mental acuity."

"All games involve strategy," Maxine said with a sniff, nose in the air.

Luna slipped past Bo and looked around, wide-eyed. "Mama, are we camping?"

"No, sweetie." But Maxine had lowered her nose and was taking an inventory of her own.

Bo sighed. "This is the ranch bunkhouse. Next door is the barn. On the other side of that is the arena. And the entire ranch proper is surrounded by woods. If you get curious, stick within sight of the buildings. I don't want to be sending out a search party for you in this weather." Bo gathered his things, stuffing his shaving kit in his suitcase, and rolling his sleeping bag.

"Are we displacing you?" Maxine continued to glance around, no doubt taking in the two bunk beds, small kitchenette and smaller bathroom.

"I thought Max…you…was…*were* a boy. I'll find a spot in the main house." Or in one of the small, summer camp cabins that he'd helped renovate last spring down by the lake. He often stayed at the Lodgepole Inn in the heart of town, but it had been fully booked when he called last week. "Don't worry about it."

Adam burst in, followed by Shane. "See? I told you. Max is a girl. A full-grown girl. That means, I don't have to share Cocoa with her." Adam crossed his skinny arms over his chest. He'd been given the short, squat brown horse as an early Christmas gift and was rather proprietary about him.

"Are you a real cowboy?" Luna's gaze darted to Shane, to Bo and then to Adam. "You're my size."

"Course, I'm a cowboy." Adam's eyes widened at the implication that he wasn't. "Been one all my life."

"I've been wishing for a real cowboy since I saw one on TV." Luna moved to Adam's side and took his hand in hers. She clearly had game, and sensed an opportunity. "Is Cocoa your horse? Is he fast?"

"Darn right, he is." Adam's chest puffed out with so much pride he didn't seem to notice a member of the opposite sex had a grip on him. "Davey says he's small and Charlie says he don't run straight, but he's mine and he's perfect. Do you want to see him?"

"Please." Luna glanced up at Maxine. "Can I?"

Maxine nodded and the two kids ran out the door, presumably toward the barn where Cocoa was in a nice, warm stall.

Bo thought now was a good time to make his exit, but Shane had closed the door behind the kids and stood in Bo's way.

"Welcome to the Bucking Bull." Shane greeted Maxine warmly, as if he'd expected a woman and a little girl all along. "I apologize for the bunkhouse being a bunkhouse. Let me talk to Franny, my fiancée. Her family owns this ranch. We'll shift people around. Special guests should stay in the main house."

"We'll be fine here," Maxine reassured him, adjusting her big, round glasses on her pert little nose. "We don't want to be any trouble."

Shane opened his mouth, presumably to argue with Maxine since arguing was what he did best, but Bo was quicker at the draw. "Trust me. If Maxine says she's fine, she's fine. She's here to soak in our family traditions." And blend into the background, whatever that meant. She wasn't the type of woman who'd ever fade into the background, and he wasn't sure she should try.

"I guess that answers another question." Shane studied Bo's face, grin unfurling like the Grinch about to steal Christmas. "Welcome to the Monroe Holiday Challenge, Max."

"YOU'VE GOT GUTS, GIRL. I wouldn't have agreed to do the challenge."

"Do I need guts?" Max asked Gertie, the elderly woman who'd brought her a glass of water.

They stood in the corner of the farmhouse living room where Max could get the lay of the family landscape. And what she saw worried her. Three cowboys under the age of ten ran around the house, taking Luna, Spot and a gray-muzzled, black Labrador with them. Two pretty cowgirls verbally sparred with Bo, Shane and a casually dressed, redheaded man as they finished dinner preparations.

Everywhere she looked there was noise and exuberance. Every time she offered to help with something, she was politely turned down, even by Gertie, who'd been shooed out of the kitchen herself.

Where were the uncles who were happy to have someone to talk to about politics or the economy? Where were the grandparents who appreciated Max's take on the latest *New York Times* bestseller? Where were the distant cousins who hadn't brought a date? The work friends who couldn't afford to go home for the holidays? The babies who needed rocking? The cooks who needed a hand in the kitchen? The puzzle just crying out for someone patient enough to assemble the portion with all that snow?

Max's gaze settled back on Gertie and her comment about the holiday challenge.

Do I need guts?

Max's gaze bounced toward Bo.

She was beginning to think she did, although perhaps not for the reasons Gertie had in mind.

"I have three degrees," Max said faintly to the ranch's matriarch, falling back on her best defense against feeling like an outcast.

"That's my point." Gertie gave a throaty laugh, seemingly not impressed by Max's education. The old woman had the look of a weathered cowgirl in her faded denim jeans, pink checked button-down shirt, and short, gray, flattened hat-hair. "You don't strike me as the type to take up the challenge. From what I hear, there's a lot at stake in terms of pride to the winner, bragging rights and such."

"Do you know what the challenge is?" No one seemed to want to tell Max.

"Near as I can tell, the games—plural—will be proposed and voted on tomorrow by the Monroes. You'll be having a vote, seeing as how you're part of Bo's team." She bobbed her chin in the direction of the children running past. "The problem is that my three great-grandsons get a vote, too, since Shane's adopting them. At their age, they'll want to do something wild. And you know, they can bounce back if they fall off a horse. But you..." Gertie gave Max an assessing look. "Have you ever ridden a horse?"

"I have." A lazy trail ride on a rutted, wooded path on a horse that had long since passed its prime. No steering had been required, since her horse had been content to follow the one in front of her. No stay-in-the-saddle skills either, since they'd walked the whole trip. Maybe this was her out. Now that Max knew a little more about the games, she'd much rather sit and watch than participate. "But I don't have boots, so—"

"We'll find you a pair." Squinting, Gertie glanced down at Max's black, no-show socks, the ones she'd worn with her black leather flats. Everyone had removed their shoes upon entering and all but Luna and Max were wearing thick socks. "Between we three Clark girls, there's bound to be a pair of boots that fit you, Max. And socks, too. Thick ones. Did you bring a pair of blue jeans?"

She nodded. "But—"

"Max, you're going to be the talk of Second Chance." Emily, a vivacious brunette, joined them. She was Adam's aunt, a cowgirl, and had enviably smooth, tamed locks, and an infectious laugh. "Not only have you agreed to take part in this cockamamie challenge, but you were brought to town by Mr. Bodacious, the most sought-after bachelor Second Chance has seen since... I don't know when." Emily laughed.

"Thanks?" Max tugged down her blouse, feeling over-dressed in her casual work clothes. "To be clear, Bo is just a friend of my cousin's. We're not dating." But she'd wondered what those perfectly shaped lips of his would feel like pressed to hers.

Off-limits, Maxine Marie.

She sighed, trying to shift her thoughts away from chiseled good looks and imagined kisses that would never be.

The kids and dogs ran past again, heading for the stairs. Luna didn't even look at Max. Unlike her mother, Luna had no qualms about joining the main group as if she belonged. Her budding confidence made Max feel even more out of sorts.

"Max." Emily's eyes sparkled. "You must have an adventurous streak."

"Not in the slightest," Max admitted without thinking. "The biggest adventures I take involve diving into the racks of the university library. I'm a graduate assistant."

Gertie and Emily stared at Max as if testing the weight of her words. And then they both laughed.

"I'm so glad you've got a sense of humor." Emily grinned, despite the fact that Max hadn't tried to be funny. "You're going to need it."

"Why is that exactly?" Max asked uneasily.

"Because you're on Bo's team and…" Emily leaned in closer, as if sharing a secret. "…Bo has never won the holiday challenge. Ever. They say he's jinxed and is his own worst enemy."

That poor man.

Max had the urge to hug him before she remembered that a man as attractive as Bo had no need for her sympathy. Women prob-ably beat a path to his door.

"Every game has a strategy." *And I have three degrees!* Suddenly, things didn't seem so bleak. Bo needed a strategic thinker on his team. Maybe Max could be his coach rather than a participant.

"Dinner!" someone called from the kitchen at the back of the house.

The kids and the dogs came thundering back down the stairs, crowding Gertie and Emily. Again, Luna passed Max without ac-knowledgement. Again, Max felt she didn't belong, not even on the periphery of things.

Max drifted toward the small folding table, the one set up for the children to eat in the living room. If she moved Luna to one side, she'd be able to squeeze in.

Bo appeared next to Max, took her arm and steered her toward the kitchen. "You're not sitting at the kids' table."

"How did you—"

"You told me you like to exist on the out-skirts." They reached the kitchen and took their place at the back of the buffet line. "But there are only four chairs at the card table and there are four kids."

"Oh, but Luna—"

"Won't like it if you take the place of one of the boys at the table. She and Adam are best friends already and she worships his older brothers, Charlie and Davey."

Max's head was spinning with all the new names and faces. But the fact remained. She didn't do well in boisterous groups. And everyone here was boisterous.

"Why so glum?" Bo's hand was still on her arm, warm and guiding. "What's wrong with you? I thought you wanted to spend the holiday with my large family."

"But they're all so—"

"Talkative?"

"Yes. And—"

"Loud."

"Uh-huh. That's not my wheelhouse." Max tried to smile. "In fact, I've been thinking about this challenge of yours. I'm very good at designing game plans. I can be part of your team on the sidelines. A… A…consultant." An assistant to direct the efforts of all those muscles.

"Your wheelhouse is bigger than you think." Bo glanced down at her with those beautiful gray eyes of his. "What sports did you play in school?"

"Yoga?" Max hated this feeling of being

inadequate. Because if these challenges were anything like physical education classes in school, she was going to be the one who tripped over the ball and fell on her backside. Max wanted Luna to have a good holiday but that didn't mean she wanted to fail at activities this cowboy bunch could complete easily.

Bo continued to stare at Max as if she'd grown a second head and was harmonizing Christmas carols with herself. He blinked and washed a hand over his face. "Do you dance?"

"Doesn't everybody?" At home, where no one could see?

He nodded briskly. "Good. At least, you're coordinated."

"Oh." She wasn't. The beat eluded her. She danced to a drum all her own.

Bo looked at her sharply, requiring another quick recovery.

"I mean, oh, check out the lasagna in that buffet. It smells as delicious as it looks."

Bo mumbled something that sounded like he was in trouble.

But it felt like Max was the one mired in difficulty, committed to a week in the mountains where she had no place to comfortably fade into the backdrop.

CHAPTER FOUR

"WE NEED TO let Maxine bow out of the competition," Bo said as he, Shane and Jonah were closing up the barn later that night. "She's nervous. She only agreed to play because it was the polite thing to do when Shane welcomed her to the ranch."

Bo felt oddly protective of the woman and her little girl. He'd tried to set Maxine's mind at ease all through dinner, to no avail. All she'd wanted to talk about was the challenge, and there wasn't much to say about what this year's competition would be like. That hadn't stopped Shane and Jonah from recounting stories of Bo's numerous failures.

"Don't use Max as an excuse to bow out of this." Shane scoffed as he topped off Cocoa's water trough. "At least, wait until we've voted on the games tomorrow before you chicken out. You don't even know what the challenges are. Max and Luna could be a huge asset."

"Chicken out?" Bo huffed.

"Yeah." Jonah scratched a small gray pony behind the ears. "Give them some credit. Luna's got spunk and Max seems really smart."

Bo had every confidence in Maxine's smarts and Luna's pluck. It was their physical prowess and safety he worried about. "I'll cobble together a team without them." There were enough Monroes in town to fill two slots.

"Nope. We called around this morning." Jonah laughed, the sound grating on Bo's nerves. "Although not everyone has committed, the ones that have don't want to be on your team. You have the stink of defeat, cousin."

"Sometimes, you have to play the hand you're dealt." Shane sounded an awful lot like Grandpa Harlan. "You chose Max last night, so maybe you should stay the course."

"But I didn't know she was *Maxine*." Bo drew a deep breath. "Look, we're cut-throat. We play to win. And she's…" He wasn't exactly sure how to categorize Maxine. With those glasses, that frizzy, curly hair and her conservative clothes, she looked like a college professor, but no academic had ever sparred with him the way she did.

Or looked as sweet with snow sparkling in her hair.

"She could get hurt," Bo insisted. "They both could."

"They're all you've got," Jonah summarized for him. "Unless you'd like to sit this year out."

Bo scowled.

"I thought you'd be unable to resist redemption." Shane nodded toward the door. "Evening, Max."

Bo spun around.

Maxine was staring at him, hesitating at the barn door with her hands tugging the ends of her thin jacket closed. He had no idea how much she'd heard but he could tell by the look on her face that she'd taken whatever comments reached her as a personal affront.

"Where's Luna?" He rushed over to Maxine and hustled her toward the bunkhouse.

"She's inside frosting Christmas cookies with Gertie and the boys." Maxine gave him a dirty look.

"You're not competing. Don't argue. Trust me when I say you'll thank me for it later." He finally got her inside the bunkhouse and closed the door behind them.

"Winning is important to you and your ego.

I get it," Maxine said imperiously, pacing in the tight quarters. "But be honest with yourself. The reason you don't want us on your team is you don't think we can help you win. Safety has nothing to do with it."

Bo set his jaw. "You wouldn't say that if you talked to my sister or female cousins about their sprains, strains, scrapes and contusions."

"If that's the case, why would Shane be so keen to bring it back?" She gestured to the chair at the table and waited for Bo to take a seat before sitting on the bunk nearby. Maxine had that determined look to her—head high, steady gaze amplified by those big glasses, lips set in a stern line, long wild curls tumbling every which way in the most confusing manner.

Confusing to him anyway, because despite his best intentions, he found himself talking. "The competition started with my grandpa Harlan. He used to take his twelve grandchildren on trips. Mostly just him, a motor home and all of us. I never felt so close to family as I did on those vacations."

Something akin to longing passed over Maxine's face, reminding him she didn't have family she'd consider close, except for Nathan.

"And then when we got together for Thanksgiving one year, Grandpa Harlan created the family challenge." To tire them out, he'd said, so they'd sit still at the dinner table. "At first, there were team competitions—football and soccer games. But it quickly morphed into individual events. And then they were individual events spread across the days we were together."

"And you didn't win," she said quietly, not asking.

"Not once." Bo nodded, though it tasted bitter to admit. "You'd think, with a combination of mental games and physical challenges, that I'd be in the running sometimes."

She neither confirmed nor denied his assertion, which prodded his pride. "We'll bow out of the competition. If the family is as large as you say, you'll probably be able to find teammates who'll help you do better."

Not likely, if what Jonah said was true. "Thank you. I'll sleep better tonight knowing you and Luna will be safe."

"Please." She rolled those big eyes and then shoved her glasses back in place. "We both know you'll sleep better because you won't be worried about coming in last."

He grinned, giving up on the argument. "Now, see. That's what I like about you. Even though we just met, you know me well."

Bo knew her well, too. And by the look in her eyes, he could tell she was disappointed in him.

Truth be told, he was disappointed in himself, too.

"MAMA, THERE ARE cowboys outside and it's not even breakfast." The morning after their arrival in Second Chance, Luna stood in her pajamas at the bunkhouse window, peering out the frost-ringed panes. She waved her hand excitedly. "And there's Spot."

"Cowboys?" Max lay on the top bunk, content to watch her daughter from her warm sleeping bag. Without her glasses on, Luna was just a comforting blur outlined against a square of light. "You mean your cowboys? Adam? Bo?"

Bo, who didn't think Max could cut the mustard when it came to the holiday competition (he might be right). Bo, who prioritized winning like some professional athlete (understandable since he'd always come in last).

Bo, who made her pulse pound with wanting, her imagination run wild and her heart pang to comfort him (which made her exit from the competition that much wiser).

"No, Mama. These are new cowboys." Luna ran over to the door and let Spot in, shutting the door behind him.

The dog circled Luna excitedly, and then put his paws on the bottom bunk and extended that big head for Max to pat.

Luna returned to the window. She gasped. "Mama. There's a cowgirl outside. Look, Mama. Look. She's just my size." Luna gasped again as Spot joined her, adding reverently, "She has boots and everything."

"Happy Almost Thanksgiving." A cowboy's face and hat appeared in the window, a man whose features Max couldn't make out without her glasses on. He waved before turning away. "They're still in their pj's, Mia. Let's check out what Gertie's got going for breakfast."

Breakfast. Coffee. Max should be helping.

"We overslept." Max sat up too fast and hit her head on the ceiling. "Ow. What time is it?"

It was quiet in the bunkhouse, isolated as

it was from the farmhouse. She hadn't heard anyone get up this morning.

"It's time to meet a cowgirl, Mama." Luna ran to the suitcase on the floor in the corner and rifled through it, tossing items behind her. "Where are my clothes? Where are my cowboy boots?"

"You don't have cowboy boots." Max climbed down from the bunk and found her glasses on the small table. She put them on. The world came into focus. Outside the window, the sun glistened on fresh snow. Whoever had been outside was gone now. "Honey, stop throwing stuff everywhere." Max bent to pick up the discarded clothes, although hindered by Spot, who was determined to rub against her like a cat teasing for affection. She straightened. "Spot, what are you doing?"

The big dog sat next to her, practically on her feet, shivering.

"He's cold, Mama." Luna stroked his long back. "Feel."

Max did. The dog's fur was chilly and his paws wet. "Spot is cold. He needs a sweater." She'd never seen a Great Dane wear a sweater, but then again, she'd seen few Great Danes in her lifetime.

"I have a sweater." Luna dug into the yellow suitcase once more. When she found her red and green holiday sweater, she held it up to him. "He'll look so pretty."

"I'm afraid that sweater is too small, honey."

Luna pivoted, returning to the suitcase. "Your tops will fit him." She hauled out Max's maroon, zippered Missouri State sweatshirt. It had a bear on the back and looked like it might fit the dog, who easily weighed over a hundred pounds.

But still, Max hesitated. "I don't know. Spot might not like it." And Bo would frown, for sure.

The big dog sniffed the sweatshirt, tossing it with his nose and making Luna laugh.

"He likes it, Mama. Put it on," Luna commanded, handing the sweatshirt to Max.

Max shook it out and unzipped it. "I tell you what. We'll give it a try. And if Spot doesn't like it or it doesn't fit, that's that."

"Okay." Luna slung her arm around Spot's shoulders. "Hold still, Spot. We'll get you warm."

Surprisingly, Spot allowed them to put the sweatshirt on him, including zipping it up. The sleeves didn't reach his paws and the waistband hung down a bit below his ribs. But overall, it was a better fit than Max had imagined. Not to mention, the maroon color went well with Spot's white and black fur.

Max stepped back to take in the dog's reaction. Spot sniffed at the sleeves, and then hopped up on Luna's bunk, curled into a ball and sighed contentedly.

"He likes it!" Luna clapped. "We have to get dressed and show Bo. He'll be so happy that Spot is warm." She dug through the suitcase again, further demolishing all of Max's careful packing.

A few minutes later, the trio crossed the ranch yard toward the main house, feet sinking in the snow. Max held Luna's hand. Instead of running to the house, Spot trundled next to them as if he was no longer bothered by the cold.

"Our sneakers are going to be wet before we reach the front porch," Max noted, already feeling damp on her toes.

"We need boots, Mama." Luna swung Max's arm happily, as if this was a done deal.

"I don't think it's smart to buy boots for one holiday." Max kept them on a budget. Clive was always late with child support payments after the holidays. And then Max remembered what Gertie had said last night about borrowing boots. "Maybe Adam has an old pair you can wear. After all, he's going to share Cocoa with you while you're here."

"Cocoa likes apples." Luna smiled sweetly, suitably distracted. "Can we go to the store and buy some?"

"Maybe. Let's see if anyone's going to the store today." Second Chance was rural. She'd only seen one store when they'd passed through town—a general store. And the Bucking Bull Ranch was a few miles north of town.

They climbed the front steps and knocked on the door.

Adam flung it open. "Why are you knocking? You should be running in to get pancakes before Davey and Charlie eat them all."

Spot trotted past him, prancing a little as if showing off his new wardrobe.

"What is Spot wearing?" Adam scurried after him. "Dogs don't wear clothes."

"He likes it," Luna called after her beloved cowboy.

They hung their coats and kicked off their wet sneakers, leaving them with the broad collection of boots beneath the various cowboy hats hanging in the foyer. People were everywhere—adults standing around drinking coffee, kids bouncing around excitedly.

"I saved you breakfast." Bo waved them toward seats at the dining room table like a ground crew bringing an airplane to a gate. "It wasn't easy with this crowd."

"I'm sorry we overslept," Max said.

"Don't be sorry. And don't listen to Bo." Gertie poked her head out of the kitchen and harrumphed. "Those cakes are hot off the griddle. Sit yourself down and butter those up while I make more. No one goes hungry at the Bucking Bull."

While Max took a seat, Luna went to stand next to a little girl with dark curls sitting on a cowboy's lap at the dining room table. "Are you a cowgirl?"

The little girl nodded, mouth full of pancake.

"This is Mia," the cowboy said. "I'm Tanner. And that's Quinn." He nodded toward a little boy beside him who drank so deeply from his glass that he gave himself a milk mustache. "You must be Max and Luna."

"Maxine," Bo corrected. Apparently, he wasn't ever going to refer to Max by her nickname.

"You can call me Max. Are you a Monroe?" Max asked Tanner, because he looked like a less intense version of Bo—not as muscular, not as sure of himself, not as picture perfect.

"More or less." Tanner gave her a small smile.

"Enough to be invited to the challenge," Bo grumbled, placing a mug of coffee in front of Max.

"And smart enough to refuse," Tanner countered, not missing a beat. "We appreciate the invitation, but we prefer enjoying the company and spectacle to participating in gladiator games."

Finally. Here was a man Max could stand with on the periphery. She beamed at him before helping Luna into a seat next to her new cowgirl friend, Mia.

Spot trotted through the dining room and into the kitchen.

"Was that…" Bo edged his way around the table and into the kitchen. "Why is my dog wearing a sweatshirt? He is not a doll or a plaything."

"He was cold," Max said with a straight face. "Tell Gertie not to bother with the dishes. I'll do them after I eat."

"You won't," Gertie called from the kitchen, where something sizzled. "You're company. Guests don't do dishes at the Bucking Bull."

Max sat back, frowning. "I'm happy to help."

"Let her pitch in, Gertie. Maxine is determined to earn her keep." Bo spoke from the kitchen, tone turning incredulous. "What have they done to you, boy? Come here and let me take that off."

Spot pranced out of the kitchen, still wearing Max's sweatshirt. Tail wagging, he continued his escape across the dining room, and into the living room.

Bo returned to his seat next to Max. "Texans don't have dogs who wear clothes."

"You might want to rethink that." In between cutting Luna's pancake, Max snuck a quick glance at Bo, drinking in all that ruffled masculinity and trying hard not to smile because she was the cause of his upset. "You're good at rethinking. After all, you rethought having Luna and me on your team."

"Because the games have been rough and tumble in the past." Bo's defense rumbled through the room. "I should get some thanks for that."

"No one who participates will require medical treatment." Shane refilled his coffee mug from a decanter on the sideboard. "The reputation of the games has been blown out of proportion."

"Or not." Bo leaned over to whisper to Max as Shane headed toward the living room and Luna chatted with her new friend. "Admit it. You're over me removing you from my team. You're happily thinking of moving to the background with Tanner."

He was right, of course. Max's cheeks flushed hotter than the steaming pancakes Gertie brought in on a plate. "What's wrong with that?" she whispered back. "You didn't want us on your team."

"Guilty as charged." He straightened, keeping his voice down. "Underappreciated are those who make the tough decisions."

"Please." Max rolled her eyes. "It was a calculated choice, one that placed too much value on physical prowess. Your muscles will only get you so far."

"What are you two whispering about?" Gertie asked, although her gaze took inventory of every plate at the table.

"I was wondering if anyone had a pair of boots Luna could borrow," Max fibbed with a smile. "Adam said she could go riding later."

"After the chores are done," Gertie confirmed. "There are probably a pair in the mudroom, along with thicker jackets and such. Franny never throws anything away.

Feel free to poke around the top shelves and take what you need for yourself, too."

Max thanked her, half expecting Bo to continue their banter after Gertie's return to the kitchen. But Spot ambled in, seeking to make peace with his owner. And then Shane called for Bo, and he left the table, taking Spot with him.

Which was fine. It gave Max much needed breathing room.

Rather than moon over him, she took in the antique furniture in the dining room—the large table made of dark wood, the matching chairs and sideboard. A horseshoe hung over the back door, which led to a pine tree–lined yard complete with a firepit circled by chairs, ones currently folded and blanketed in snow.

At the front of the house, doors opened and closed. Feet pounded up and down the stairs. From her seat, Max could see the photographs crowding the fireplace mantel—yellowed pictures, black and white photos, shiny color portraits. This was a home that created spaces for family to gather and showcased its history. It was a home that made Max's heart ache with longing for what she didn't have.

"First time at the Bucking Bull?" Tanner asked, interrupting her reverie.

Max nodded, as a door slammed above them. "There's a lot of activity." There seemed no place for her to settle into and no person for her to settle in with, although she had hopes for Tanner.

He shrugged. "Just wait until the rest of the family shows up. It gets so loud you can't hear yourself think."

"And the kids run wild, don't they, Daddy?" Squirming in his lap, Mia glanced up at her father.

"Yep."

"I want to run wild," Luna said, eyes sparkling with interest. "Can I, Mama?"

"We'll see." Max had no idea how wild the Monroe children could be. She wanted Luna to be happy, but she wanted her to be safe.

"She'll be fine," Tanner promised, as if reading Max's thoughts. "There's always an adult around. And the kids all look out for one another."

That was reassuring.

But it begged the question: *Who was going to look out for Max?*

CHAPTER FIVE

"WE'RE GOING INTO TOWN, Maxine," Bo called from the foyer of the farmhouse, blowing in along with a gust of chill air. "Shake a leg."

Spot trotted past Max to bestow love on Luna by way of slobbery kisses. He'd won the wardrobe battle, at least for now, still sporting Max's sweatshirt.

"We're taking a drive?" Max had been heading to the door, carrying the boots and jackets she'd found in the mudroom. She slowed, dropping a small, black cowboy boot to the floor. "Why?"

Bo picked up the boot and plucked its mate from her grasp. "Because I said so."

"Only parents are allowed to use that line." Max readjusted her load. "And you are not my daddy."

"Sugar or otherwise," Bo murmured with a half-grin.

"Stop it," Max said aloud, although she

meant the command for herself and her suddenly rapidly beating heart.

Behind Max, Tanner dumped a puzzle on the card table the kids had used for dinner last night. The pieces were large and colorful. His daughter, Mia, eagerly climbed on a folding chair beside him.

"A puzzle." Luna ran to the table. She wore blue jeans and a pink sweater with matching pink bands holding her two thick pigtails. "Can I help?"

"Sure." Tanner pulled out a chair. "It's a horse puzzle. Do you like horses?"

"I love Cocoa," Luna said staunchly, rising to her knees and straightening her glasses. "I'm going to ride him later. Did you bring a horse to ride, Mia? I bet you have a horse of your own."

While the two girls babbled on about horses, Max touched Bo's arm. "I should stay." Her hand fluttered toward the girls, but her gaze stayed on Bo as if he were a much-longed-for gift and she stood on the outside of a store window, looking in and wishing. "After this, there'll be horseback riding." Max couldn't allow Luna to ride without being present to ensure her safety. And it was the perfect reason to keep her distance from Bo, who frowned at her.

"There won't be riding until after lunch," Tanner said, not looking up from the task of turning puzzle pieces face-up. "They need to clear the snow from the arena so the kids can ride safely. Shane and Jonah can't get the snowblower running. I heard Emily and Franny make a pact. They're determined not to take pity on their fiancés and help them troubleshoot." He chuckled. "There's always something breaking down on a ranch and those two city slickers need to prove themselves, I guess."

"See? We have plenty of time." Bo's frown righted itself into a winning smile. "Let's go, Maxine, before they enlist me to help."

Max dug in her heels. "I've only just met Tanner. It's too much of an imposition to ask him to watch Luna."

"How long are you going to be gone?" Tanner asked, still bent over the table.

"Two hours, tops," Bo reassured him.

"We ought to be able to finish a couple puzzles and make a visit to the henhouse during that time." Tanner nodded. "Head on out, Max. The girls will be fine."

"I'll watch them, too." Gertie came in from

the dining room and sat in her rocker. She reached for a pair of knitting needles and a ball of chunky, harvest-orange yarn. "Go on. You won't get an opportunity to see Second Chance much after those games start."

"We'll be fine, Mama." Luna propped her elbows on the table, surveying the pieces with hawk-like intensity. She loved puzzles.

"I'm being dismissed," Max murmured.

"Look at that face…" Bo marveled in a near-whisper. "Luna won't even notice you're gone." Without further commiseration or ado, he steered Max toward the bench by the door. "Put your boots on and let's go."

Max moved slowly, reluctant to leave. Puzzle solving in a quiet house was one of the activities she'd imagined as part of her holiday.

"Look at this." Mia showed a puzzle piece to Luna.

"That's a horse's butt." Luna giggled.

Mia tapped the puzzle piece. "Look at the ribbons on her tail, silly. Don't you think it's pretty?"

"Oh." Luna stopped laughing and adjusted her glasses. "It is pretty. Mama braids my hair sometimes. Can we braid Cocoa's tail?"

"Braiding manes and tails takes hours," Tanner said in a no-nonsense tone of voice.

"And you'd have to ask Adam, because Cocoa is his horse."

"He'll let me do it," Luna said in a bossy tone.

"Luna," Max warned. "Be nice."

"She's as nice as they come." Bo fidgeted, pointing toward the door. "Come on."

But something about braiding a horse's hair struck Max as odd. Just look at how Bo had reacted to his dog wearing a sweatshirt. "Do cowboys want their horses to look pretty?"

Tanner smirked. Bo shook his head. And Luna...

"Shush, Mama." She waved Max off. Like a too-busy boss.

And she was only four!

"Dismissed," Max murmured again, slipping her feet into cowboy boots that were stiff and unyielding but had room for her to wiggle her toes. "And here I thought she'd need me until her teenage years."

"Yeah, yeah. Kids grow up so fast. Or so I've heard." Bo held her borrowed jacket, so that all she need do was slip her arms inside. "Let's roll. I could use a second opinion on this house hunt."

Max shrugged into the green jacket, which was thicker than the one she'd brought. "I take it you have no mechanical skills and don't want to come to Shane and Jonah's aid on the snowblower."

Bo's mouth dropped open. And then he shook his head. "Why can't you take this invitation in the spirit it was offered?" He opened the door, waited for Spot to bound past, and then ushered Max through and down the steps.

The cold was bracing, more eye-opening than caffeine. Everywhere around them there was snow—on the ground, on the vehicles, on the trees and rooftops. It was beautiful, completely different than the scenery from the busy Boise highway.

"Was there an invitation, Bo? I don't recall being asked." He'd told Max to come. Her steps slowed.

Across the ranch yard, there was activity in the barn. Voices and laughter filled the air, but no snowblower engine hummed to life.

"I have an ulterior motive for bringing you along, Maxine." Bo opened the back door to his truck and whistled. Spot bounded over and jumped in. "I owe you a sweatshirt. I don't think Spot will be happy if I take yours off him. He hasn't run around outside this much since we left Texas." Bo walked around

to the passenger side and opened the door, in-
dicating Max should get in.

Max settled her booted feet in the snow,
crossed her arms and raised her brows. The
wind teased her long locks. But she refused to
play Bo's game. "I still haven't been asked."

Bo grinned, and Max could have sworn
her knees went weak. But she didn't collapse,
and she didn't give in to that charm. She held
her ground.

There's hope for me yet.

Hope that she'd return home next week
without a broken heart.

"Maxine," Bo said gruffly, standing on the
running board and raising his cowboy hat
with one hand. "Would you like to take a
ride with me into town? Maybe check out a
couple of vacation houses that are available
and allow me to reimburse you for a sweatshirt my dog borrowed and has no intention
of returning?"

Oh, that smile. He was devastatingly charming when he wanted to be.

Max hid her dreamy sigh beneath a huff as
she came around the front of his truck and
climbed in. "I'd be honored."

A few minutes later, Bo was driving them
slowly down the snow-covered drive toward

the main highway, Spot's muzzle on his shoulder. "I've been thinking."

"Should I be worried?" Max faced him, stroking Spot's ears as an excuse to take in Bo's classic profile.

"You need to be more assertive."

Her hand fell away from Spot's silky ear. "I am assertive."

"Nah." Bo shook his head. "If you were assertive, you'd find a place to spend the holidays on your own. And if you had that confidence, you'd stay at home, just you and Luna, and create traditions of your own without ever spending time on the fringe of another family's holiday."

Max opened her mouth to argue, but found she had no defense. Nevertheless, it wasn't a good idea to give Bo the last word. They may have met less than twenty-four hours ago, but of this, she was certain. "Why are you so antsy to find a vacation home?"

He scoffed. "I'm not antsy. I'm driven. I wrote down a list of goals to keep in mind this morning."

Sensing there was more to the story, she waited for him to say more.

"I'm thirty-six," he admitted after a moment. "And it's time I settled down."

Max took her time pondering that statement. She'd known plenty of women who wanted to settle down, but never a man. Weren't men who were ready to settle down supposed to be unicorns? Rare and mythical creatures?

Finally, she said, "Don't you want to shop for a vacation home with whoever you marry? Your wife could hate what you choose and then you'd have to start all over again. With a new list," she added.

A small crease appeared in Bo's forehead, just beneath his hatband. And then he shook his head, shaking off that frown and replacing it with his resting confidence face. "I've put a lot of thought into this blueprint. I'm sending a signal to females everywhere that I'm not a bachelor drifting through life without purpose. I have a plan to move forward—a nice house in Texas, a cozy place up here, a great job with benefits, charities I regularly support, and so on. I'm settling down, buying furniture and crockery sets."

"You're nesting," Max pointed out smugly. "That's what women do when they're getting ready for kids. Are you planning to adopt? To be a single dad?"

"No." He swung his head around so abruptly

that Spot recoiled into the back seat. "You're putting the cart before the horse. What I'm saying is… What I'm telling you is…" His voice lost its bluster. "I'm ready to fall in love…again."

"Again?" That was the most important word in that sentence. Max should know. She'd studied linguistics. He'd tacked that word with a cadence that emphasized rather than minimalized. "Are you freshly out of a relationship?" He didn't look as if he'd recently suffered from a broken heart.

"That's none… You are the most confounding…" Bo brought the truck to a stop where the gravel drive met the two lane highway that led to Second Chance. He turned his face her way. "If you must know, I was in a relationship that ended long enough ago that I'm over it and recently enough that I'm trying to learn from my mistakes."

Max found it hard to believe that any woman would let Bo go. Yes, he was a handful. Yes, he had a habit of being bossy. And presumptuous. And sarcastic. And was a bit full of himself. But he'd admitted making mistakes in the relationship. And if a man could be judged by his family and his dog, Bo was a keeper. Plain and simple.

Not that she planned on telling him that.

But that didn't mean she didn't want him to tell her more. Because she did. "And your mistake was…"

"Thinking that my life wouldn't change if it included a wife and kids." He made a sudden right turn onto the highway, looking a bit troubled. "That made me sound like a naive bachelor."

Max grinned. "Which you were, apparently. Past tense. No shame in that."

He grumbled something she didn't catch. "Anyway… You could make me feel better by telling me what you learned from your relationship with Luna's father."

Could she? Max shook her head.

"It's not embarrassing if it's a lesson learned." He snuck a glance at her. "You have three degrees. You must like learning. And here is someone who wants his next relationship to succeed. Give me pointers."

"Seriously?"

"Seriously." And then he fell silent, waiting. And driving. And basically, looking like a million bucks.

They continued to head north—she thinking about her failed marriage and he…waiting for her to speak.

It was the silence that finally got to her. "Fine. We weren't on the same wavelength when it came to the important things."

"Important things like your values, your dreams, your…"

Max knotted her fingers in her lap. "Everything."

"It couldn't have been everything. You had a child together, which implies something clicked. Maybe you even got married…" He looked to her as if seeking confirmation.

"We were married." After an intense but brief courtship. "But things fell apart after I'd given birth to Luna and finished up my second degree. Clive was shocked that I wanted to pursue a third area of study."

A silence fell between them. An awkward silence. One where Max could just imagine what Bo was thinking, except all she heard in her head were Clive's words.

Why do you need a third degree?

What do you mean you might get a fourth?

And finally…

Are you going to be a college student forever?

"I have an inquisitive mind," Max said in a small voice. As defenses went, it was weak.

And she knew it because Clive had laughed when she'd said it to him.

And Clive's voice… It just kept on coming at her.

You're a wife and mother now, he'd said the first time they'd talked about her continuing her education, as if she'd give that up.

We all have to grow up sometime, he'd said, tossing his hands in frustration when she hadn't.

You pursuing a third degree won't help me with the academic selection committee at Yale, he'd said before walking out the door one night.

You only think about yourself, he'd said when he'd presented her with divorce papers.

"I'm a good mom," Max said with more heart, building steam. "And what I learned from my marriage was that your spouse should accept you as you are, including the path you've chosen through life."

"Truth." Bo nodded. "And also, ouch. If we were at a bar, this is where we'd order a round of shots and toast the scars of failed relationships."

"I don't drink," she said, breath ragged.

"Fair enough." He reached over and squeezed her clasped hands. "Toasts are symbolic. There's no law that says your glass must contain alcohol. Or that you ever have to forgive someone who's done you wrong." He slowed to take a curve. "Of course, my grandpa Harlan would say you should forgive if only because hurt and grudges are heavy burdens to bear."

"It sounds like your grandfather had a good therapist."

"Maybe." Bo put both hands firmly on the steering wheel. "He was married four times."

"Geez. Four times?" Max drew a deep breath and loosened her fingers. "I've only been divorced once, and it made me determined not to risk marriage again."

"Never say never, Maxine."

She shook her head. "I'll leave the optimism toward love and goal setting for romance to you unicorns."

Bo chuckled. "I'm very serious and very real, Maxine. But speaking of lists... I have a list of what I'm looking for in a property." He opened the center console and plucked a folded sheet of lined paper from a stack of the same. He handed it to her. "Care to take a look?"

"And peer into the inner mind of a unicorn? Absolutely." She unfolded the paper and smoothed the creases, reviewing his wish list, which was titled My Vacation Home. "You aren't asking for much. Just grand views, an open floor plan, set away from the highway and move-in ready."

He glanced at her with that sly smile of his. "Don't forget my large master bedroom and three car garage."

From what she'd seen of the town on the drive to the ranch, his list was pie-in-the-sky impossible. The homes here were older and smaller than she'd seen in Boise. "I thought this was a vacation home. Why do you need a three car garage?"

"A man needs room for his snowmobile and ATV."

"You don't want much," she said, heavy on the sarcasm.

"Just perfection."

She rolled her eyes, and then pushed her glasses higher up her nose. "Nothing is perfect."

He chuckled and patted his chest, which she took to mean Bo thought he was perfect, while Spot took his gesture as a signal to place his muzzle on Bo's shoulder.

Man, they were adorable.

Max forced herself to look away, to acknowledge that there was beauty up here everywhere—the wide-open, blue sky, the snow-covered pines, glimpses of a broad valley leading to the jagged Sawtooth Mountains. "Are we meeting a Realtor?"

"No. Funny story." Bo slowed the truck and signaled a left turn. "My grandpa Harlan was born in Second Chance. About a decade ago, he came back and, according to some accounts, thought the town was dying. So he bought up just about every business and house in town, then turned around and charged a one dollar a year lease to folks who wanted to stay."

"Rent for one dollar a year? That sounds too good to be true." How she wished she'd been a resident back then. She'd have more financial freedom now. Max sighed. What was the use of wishing? She'd never been one to win the lottery or so much as a business card drawing for a free lunch. "What's the catch?"

He made a turn onto a narrow driveway cut between a thick grove of pine trees. The ground was covered with undisturbed snow. Bo stopped to put the truck in four wheel drive.

Spot put his front paws on the center console, as if on alert. Not that there was much to see beyond a deep layer of snow on the drive and thick stands of snow-covered trees on either side.

"Grandpa Harlan passed away earlier this year. The catch is that his twelve grandchildren, including me, inherited the town. And at the end of the year, we're going to decide what to do with it—sell, develop or raise the lease terms." He shrugged, as if inheriting a town and determining its future was no big deal.

"We live in different worlds." Max laid a hand on Spot's shoulder in case the dog lost his balance or decided her seat was preferable to his in the rear. "I guess those deals your grandfather made were a good thing for residents while they lasted. Is someone living in the house we're going to look at?" She didn't want anyone to be displaced.

"No. Despite the great lease terms, a lot of folks just up and left. This is one of the abandoned properties."

"Doesn't it bother you that the terms 'abandoned' and 'move-in ready' are probably mutually exclusive?"

Bo chuckled. "I hope you're wrong."

The road turned, revealing glimpses of a house ahead through the trees.

"It's a log cabin." Max couldn't hide her

surprise. "I suppose that makes sense in the woods. But...did you know we were coming to see a log cabin?"

Bo frowned. "Shane left out that little detail." And Bo didn't look happy about it.

Max reviewed his written list of requirements once more. "Maybe we should go on to the next one because..."

They pulled into the clearing, and everything came into perspective.

There were no trees behind the cabin to the east, nothing but the snow-covered cabin accentuated by the sweeping scene behind it—a miles-long meadow stretched across the valley toward a thick, pine-filled tree line and the Sawtooth Mountains. The same picture postcard vista Max had been admiring occasionally from the highway on the drive up yesterday.

"I'll take that dollar lease," Max whispered reverently.

"Get in line. Grand view? Check." Bo turned off the engine. "But it looks smaller than what I wanted and there's no garage."

"For the price you're paying, you can build a garage."

"That takes time."

"Are you for real?" Max gaped at him.

"Building takes time, but so does finding the right woman."

"There is that." He grinned at her. It was the kind of grin that made a woman feel like she was in the running to be Mrs. Beauregard Franklin Monroe.

That is, if a woman was naive.

When it came to romance, Max was no longer naive.

They got out, footsteps crunching in the foot-deep snow. Spot bounded ahead, full of energy. He reached the front door before they did. It took a few minutes to find the key, which was underneath an empty flowerpot buried in snow to the right of the uncovered porch landing. The door needed a big shoulder push to get it open. Once it was ajar, Spot rushed in, nose to the floor. He ran from room to room.

Not that there was much to explore. The living room and kitchen comprised one half of the cabin, and two bedrooms and a bathroom the other. It was sparsely furnished and nothing like what Bo had on his list.

"You wanted open plan living," Max noted anyway, trying to look on the bright side. If she was the one house hunting, she'd have made compromises for that view.

"It's small. And the floor isn't level." Bo tested the floorboards, rocking back and forth, creating all sorts of creaks and groans in the wood. "Makes me wonder about the roof."

Max drifted into the bedroom in the back, coming to stand before the window where the view of the valley was unobstructed. She set her palm on Spot's broad head when he sat next to her. "This isn't bad."

Bo joined them, turning his head to-and-fro to take in the sights. "It's amazing."

They stood together, admiring the view. They didn't speak, and on some level, words didn't matter. Not when they were both appreciating the same thing.

Max's imagination drifted…

If I took his hand…

She tensed, shifting away from him and Spot.

I'd make a total fool of myself.

She returned to the living room. There was an old, upright piano in a corner and a cross-stitched sampler hanging over the mantel. The pine cabinets in the kitchen had brass knobs, tarnished where hands had worn the surface smooth. An oval footstool sat before a burgundy wingback chair, positioned to capture the light from the window and the warmth from the fire. It was a cozy home, designed to appreciate the out-of-doors, a place where time slowed and the people inside these thick, log walls were what really mattered.

Spot padded past her to stand at the front door, staring back at them as if ready to be let out.

"A few more minutes, Spot." Bo came to stand next to Max, glancing about the room. "This place reminds me of my grandfather. He made his mark on the world, but he was essentially a simple man." Bo pointed to the cross stitch. "He used to say *People come first* all the time."

"It's nice that you remember. I don't recall things my parents used to say to me when I was a kid—their stories and history, sayings and such." And suddenly, that absence of knowledge was a gaping void, a missing part of herself that she longed desperately to fill. "I wish I'd valued what I had back then."

"How old were you when they died?"

"Ten."

He swore softly. "Don't be so hard on yourself. Everything was still about me when I was ten. I can't imagine what being orphaned would have been like for you."

Unbidden, the bad memories came tumbling back. The roar of the tornado broken by the sound of nails giving way and boards breaking free. The sharp cracks and loud bangs as the roof caved. The long hours waiting for help, crying out until she was hoarse. The two days she'd spent in a shelter with a neighboring family, unable to believe her parents weren't going to walk through that door at any moment. The whispers of her grandparents. The whispers of various aunts and uncles. The solemn sit-downs as she was passed from one home to the next.

It's not that we don't love you, Maxine...

But they didn't love her. If they had, they would have kept her. The same way Clive would have stayed if his love was true.

"Oh. Hey, none of that." Bo drew Max tenderly into his arms.

At first, she didn't understand why.

And then she realized she was crying.

CHAPTER SIX

BO WAS A sucker for tears, the heartfelt kind.

The kind that trailed slowly down Maxine's cheeks.

Why is she crying?

Bo didn't know. He held her gently in his arms, as if she'd break if he brought her closer.

He wanted to draw her closer. He wanted to press a soft kiss to the top of her curly-haired head. He wanted to see her roll those big brown eyes at him and then adjust the set of those large glasses of hers on that pert little nose, because her biggest expressions upset the balance of her frames. But most of all, he wanted the world to go easy on one Maxine Holloway—orphan, disappointed in love, single mom and without a family for the holidays.

Bo ran a hand over her long locks. The strands were weighty and unruly, a bit like Max herself—strong and particular. "Don't cry, honey."

She sniffed. "I'm not crying."

That made him smile, as did the fact that she didn't try to move away.

"Must be me who's having leaky waterworks," he teased softly, allowing silence to descend.

The cabin didn't offer what he was looking for, but it had something more—peace. It settled over him, like a beloved, familiar blanket. The view was awe-inspiring. The cabin unpretentious and cozy. No one would be lost in a house this size. Everyone would be together. Close. Like him and Maxine.

They stood like that for a few more minutes. He stared at the view and realized he'd never be able to look over the valley and not think of this intriguing woman who wanted to be called Max—a name that in no way matched her spirit. "What is your middle name?"

"Marie," she mumbled into his chest.

He smiled. "Maxine Marie. If that isn't a home run in the name game, I don't know what is."

She snuffled and eased away from him, righting her glasses and swiping at her cheeks with both hands. "You have got to be kidding me, Beauregard Franklin. Your name implies refinement, heritage and gravitas, while mine—"

"*Maxine* says you're one tough cookie," Bo cut her off. "But *Marie* counters that with softness." Finally, a name that fit, a name that clicked into place for him. "*Maxine Marie*. That name says something."

She blushed. "I bet you say that to all the girls."

And just like that, the tears were behind them and they were back to the sparring ring.

He liked that she'd never been speechless or stammering at the sight of him. She'd never fawned or flattered as if his good looks made him a cut above her. "Come on, Maxine Marie. After we see another house, I'll buy you a cup of coffee and take you shopping for a sweatshirt."

It took a few minutes to lock up and get back in the truck. Bo turned the heater on full blast because despite wearing Maxine's sweatshirt, Spot was shivering. That meant Maxine had to be cold, too, even in her borrowed coat.

They were silent for much of the drive to the next place. Unlike the quiet that had fallen between them on other times, this felt companionable, as if they knew each other so well there wasn't need to fill the air with small talk.

Bo found the turn easily. This time, the property was on the western side of the highway, butting up to the mountain range that separated Second Chance from Boise.

"No view here." He parked in front of a two-story house that was surrounded by tall pines. "It's not worth seeing."

"It has a two car garage and more space than a little cabin." Maxine hopped out without waiting for him, holding the door for Spot to follow. "Give it a chance."

This time, Spot let them blaze a path through the snow to the house rather than leaping ahead.

Bo found the key at the bottom of an empty clay pot on the covered porch and opened the door. Immediately, the smell of animal assailed him. "Whoa." He covered his mouth and nose with one hand. "We should go. I don't want to disturb whatever is living in here." Something had claimed territorial rights and might feel threatened enough to attack.

Spot sniffed and backed outside, also happy to leave whatever was inside.

"Good idea." Maxine retraced her steps

to the farthest end of the porch. "Besides, the only thing open about this floor plan is the animal community living inside. That's a shame. It showed such promise outside."

"It showed no promise. There's no view." Bo locked up and dropped the key back under the flowerpot, making a mental note to tell Roy, the town handyman, about the wildlife trespassing.

A few minutes later, Bo held the open door to the Bent Nickel Diner for Maxine to enter.

You would have thought he'd escorted the Queen of England to tea.

The restaurant was nearly full, and almost everyone was a local he recognized. Conversation died about the time the door closed behind them.

"Who've you brought?" Rail-thin Roy was the first to greet them. He wore blue coveralls beneath a thick brown jacket. "A new Monroe?"

"No." A twinge of unease settled between Bo's shoulder blades. He didn't like the way folks in the small town thought everything that went on was their business, especially when it came to his business. "This is Maxine. She's here for Thanksgiving." And then he grasped her hand, having spotted an empty table in the back.

"Is this the woman who landed the most sought-after Monroe?" Ivy rushed forward. She ran the diner with Bo's cousin Cam and enjoyed having the latest news. Although, to be fair, she was also one of the most nurturing women in town. "Coffee and pie on the house for you, Maxine. Well done."

"Oh, no." Maxine dragged her feet, slowing Bo down. "I didn't land anything…or anyone. Bo is a friend of my cousin's."

"Blind date?" Roy piped up, trailing along behind them, scuttling ahead of Ivy.

"No. We were looking at houses," Maxine explained, possibly meaning well, but her comment only inflamed the gossips.

There was another flurry of chatter.

Bo guided Maxine into the booth with her back to the room. He sat across from her and frowned at their entourage—Ivy and the elderly Roy—trying to encourage them to vamoose by telling Roy about the animal trouble in the house they'd just left.

No such luck.

"I'll get right on over there." But Roy's feet remained stationed next to their booth. "Why are you house hunting with someone you just met? That's odd."

"You're looking for a home together?" Ivy's

smile grew. She gave Roy a side hug. "That's adorable."

"But…" Maxine said weakly, cheeks turning red in the sweetest way.

"Don't bother trying to enlighten them," Bo muttered, having been part of the gossip train in Second Chance before. It was best to sit quietly and let their imaginations run their course.

Roy rested his hands on the table. "Is Maxine a mail order bride? Haven't seen one in these parts since after the war."

"We had mail order brides in town?" Ivy's interest was diverted. "When?"

"I'm not a mail order bride," Maxine tried to explain, but Ivy and Roy were deep in history and ignoring her. "Bo, do something. *Say* something."

And although he normally was a staunch defender of his bachelor status in Second Chance, there was something about Maxine's exasperated tone of voice that made him believe now was not the time to do so.

"In theory, we were together," Bo allowed, if only to rile Maxine a little.

Her mouth formed a small O.

"House shopping," he added.

Behind those thick glasses of hers, Maxine's eyes narrowed. "*Beauregard* seems to think that owning his dream vacation home will pave the way to him landing his dream girl."

Bo barely stopped himself from laughing. Unlike most women he'd dated, Aria included, Maxine had game and wasn't afraid of using it on Bo.

Conversation in the diner fell into a lull. Presumably, folks wanted to hear what was being said between Bo and his supposed date.

Maxine's brown eyes flashed, and she drew herself up in her seat as if preparing for battle. "Does anyone know of any houses around here for a confirmed bachelor who wants a move-in ready house with a view? Something his yet-to-be-found wife will like?"

Suggestions were tossed out quicker than snowflakes blew in a snowstorm.

"And…" Maxine raised her voice, doubling down on whatever punishment she thought she was dishing out to Bo. "…Bo also wants a man cave big enough to store snowmobiles and the like."

A blizzard of comments erupted.

Bo gave Maxine a round of soft applause, not that anyone noticed. The patrons were too busy coming up with housing suggestions and debating their choices with each other. "Do you have siblings, Maxine? Because you have teasing honed to an art form."

"I'm an only child. And that wasn't teasing." She lifted her chin. "That was self-defense. You were hanging me out to dry."

He shook his head. "You're tough. It would take more than that to rattle you." Initial blush aside.

"Honey, listen to your cousin over here giving out compliments," Ivy called over the lunch counter to where Cam was cutting slices of pumpkin pie for someone. "Isn't that sweet?"

"Bo isn't sweet," Cam teased, shaking a can of whipped cream. "And... Maxine, is it?" He waited for Maxine's nod of confirmation. "Bo needs to try harder because Maxine could do so much better than him."

"Hey." Bo gave his cousin a dirty look. "Whose side are you on?"

Cam laughed. "Love, obviously."

"Love," Bo muttered.

Maxine leaned forward, brown eyes sparkling. "I take it back. You're not turkey and mashed potatoes. You're dark meat, baked sweet potatoes and cranberry dressing."

Bo wasn't going to give away if she was getting closer or not. "And for dessert?"

"Pumpkin pecan bread pudding."

Bo tipped his hat back and smirked. "Wrong again."

"I'll figure you out," Maxine promised. "Just you wait and see."

He smiled, looking forward to the wait.

"ROLL OUT THE red carpet." Bo set down his coffee cup. "Hollywood royalty has arrived."

Having just finished a slice of delicious pumpkin pie Max turned from her enjoyment of the orange and brown Thanksgiving decorations in the diner to see whom Bo referred to.

The bell above the diner door tinkled. A petite redhead walked purposefully to the lunch counter, as if she'd done it hundreds of times and one specific stool was her regular seat. She was followed by a tall, handsome cowboy—like really handsome, Bo's kind of handsome. The pair's faces were familiar, yet Max couldn't immediately place them.

That's because I'm still muddled after being in Bo's arms earlier.

Now there was a memory to tuck away the

next time demoralizing images from her past hit the replay button.

"Hey, Hollywood," Bo called out. "Don't you greet family anymore?"

The couple veered toward them, polished smiles gracing their suddenly very familiar, very famous faces.

"You're…you're…" Max stammered. She gulped and pushed her glasses up her nose. "Ashley Monroe." One of her favorite rom-com actresses. "And Wyatt Halford." One of her favorite action movie stars. Max thought she might faint.

"I'm Ashley, Bo's cousin." Ashley touched Max's shoulder. "And this is my husband, Wyatt. We're all just somebody with a craving for pie, you know."

Wyatt curled his arm around Ashley's waist as Bo introduced Max as Maxine.

Several things dawned on Max at once. First off, she was in the presence of Hollywood royalty. Second, they were related to Beauregard Franklin Monroe, whose grandfather was named Harlan.

Harlan Monroe, business tycoon and famous philanthropist.

Max, you idiot.

Somehow Max managed to comment on the weather without falling over from shock.

When the couple left them and made their way to the lunch counter, Max scooted out of the booth and slid in next to Bo. She grabbed his blue checked shirtsleeve and pulled him close enough to whisper, "You didn't tell me you're one of *those* Monroes." No wonder her cowboy host could afford a fancy truck and a vacation house. In fact, he could probably afford a ten car garage.

"I don't know what you mean." Bo did a bad job of hiding that smile of his.

"Those Monroes. *Those Monroes*," she said furtively, yanking on him in frustration. "The famous Monroes. The obscenely rich Monroes."

"I'm not obscenely rich." Bo's expression dropped from mischievous to sincere. "In fact, I've been unemployed by the family since January thanks to my father, who couldn't inherit any of my grandfather's wealth last January unless he cut me and my siblings loose financially. Same goes for my uncles. They disowned my cousins. The fortune my grandfather left us is what you see here—lots of property in the middle of nowhere and one dollar a year leases."

"If Nathan were along, he'd be in so much trouble," Max muttered, sitting back, and taking in the clean but run-down diner, the assortment of patrons and the very famous couple sitting down to have coffee and pie. "Nathan never said a word about you being rich and famous."

"That's because he met me on an oil rig where we both worked as engineers. He sees me like the man I am, not the family I come from," Bo said testily. "Come on, Maxine. Don't tell me you're intimidated by someone with a different background than yours."

"I'm not." She sat back and clasped her hands in her lap, feeling one hundred percent intimidated. She snapped her head around as his words finally sank in. "You're an engineer? You went to college?"

"Yep." Bo stared at his empty coffee cup. "You kept assuming I was a working cowboy."

She had.

"You shouldn't judge a man by the slant of his cowboy hat."

She elbowed him. Just a nudge.

"You're a Texan," Max stated, trying to remember the few details he'd given her about himself. "Don't tell me you're a rocket scientist working for NASA in Houston." He'd made that joke about her three degrees and the study of aliens.

"Okay, I won't." Bo gave her that sly smile that gave her stomach butterflies. "I'm an engineer in the oil industry, obviously. And just like Nathan when he's not called up by the National Guard."

Max drew a deep breath. There was a lot to process here, but she couldn't allow Bo the upper hand or she'd never hear the end of it. She reached for the only defense she could see, slim as it was. "I'm still one-up on you education-wise. Me having three degrees and all." That gave her comfort, small though it might be. She was spending Thanksgiving with the world renowned Monroes. Never had she wanted to evaporate into the fringe of a gathering the way she did now. "It'll be fine. They're all just a bunch of somebodies who put their pants on one leg at a time and crave a slice of pumpkin pie during the holiday season." Real people, just like Max and Luna.

Oh, who am I kidding? They're nothing like me and Luna.

Her gaze was drawn to Ashley and Wyatt once more. They were just so beautiful, so put together. She ran a hand through her thick, hard-to-tame locks. She glanced down at her worn, borrowed boots, thinking about her balance-challenged checking account. And then she stared at the talented, famous couple once more. She'd enjoyed each of their last movies and privately swooned over Wyatt's dashing good looks.

Bo leaned closer. "I never did understand how it took Wyatt so long to be acknowledged as one of the sexiest men in Hollywood."

"He deserved it long ago," Max murmured. She gasped and pushed Bo's shoulder with her own. "I will not apologize for being a fan."

"I'm okay with that just as long as you don't start fan-girling." Bo smirked.

"As if." Max needed to get a hold of herself, or she'd be an annoyance to her Monroe hosts. She nudged Bo with an elbow once more before returning to her original seat. "We should get going. They've probably cleared the arena of snow by now and Spot is probably getting cold in the truck."

"Good point."

Neither one of them moved.

"I like you, Maxine." Bo's gentle gaze took in her wild hair, large glasses and no-frills wardrobe. "You're different."

She sighed, aware of the fact.

And ruing it.

WHILE MAXINE HEADED over to shop for apples and a sweatshirt at the general store, Bo settled up their bill.

"Maxine is nice," Ashley told him from her nearby counter seat. "Not exactly what I'd say is your type. But nice."

"Don't get any ideas about romance," Bo said gruffly, thinking of a list he'd made outlining the woman he wanted to fall in love with next. "She's here because of a misunderstanding."

Ashley tossed her trademark long red hair over one shoulder and gave Bo a superior look. "I'm married to the love of my life because of a misunderstanding."

Wyatt raised his coffee cup, a smug grin on his famous face. His cell phone and sunglasses lay on the counter, items as trendy as the international film star himself. "Here's to misunderstandings."

"God bless 'em." Cam gave Bo his change. He may not wear a chef's jacket much anymore, but he still held himself as tall as his award-winning reputation. "Ivy and I had nothing but misunderstandings the first few weeks we knew each other. But somehow, we worked it all out."

"We have no misunderstandings and no future." Bo tucked his wallet in his back pocket. "I get it. Shane or Jonah told you I was looking for love."

"Shane," Ashley confirmed with a nod.

"In my case, Maxine announced it to the entire diner." Cam grinned.

Had Bo been pining for his Monroe branch of the family? Now that he was here with them, he couldn't remember why. "I'm not looking for love with Maxine. I haven't completed my love-plan preparations yet, so I'm not even searching. I just enjoy talking to her." And wondering how it would feel to have her turn her face up to his when he held her in his arms.

Bo frowned.

"That's when love strikes." Ashley leaned over and planted a quick kiss on Wyatt. "When you aren't ready."

"Spare me the cheese." Bo rolled his eyes.

"Yep, love hits when it's the most inconvenient." Grinning, Cam whisked away Wyatt's and Ashley's empty pie plates and tucked them into a tray beneath the counter. "You should know this, Bo. When love appears, it lands on you like a ton of bricks. In a good way, of course."

"That's not what this is," Bo insisted, crossing his arms over his chest. "I have a timeline and a plan for love, and I'm sticking to it."

"Like the plan you've made to win this year's holiday challenge?" Cam teased.

"Maybe." Bo pushed his cowboy hat more firmly on what undoubtedly his cousins thought was his very thick skull. And then he walked away.

Their laughter followed him out the door.

"I'M WORRIED ABOUT YOU," Maxine told Bo as they drove toward the Bucking Bull on the steep, slushy driveway. "You've been quiet since we left town."

"I'm fine." He'd been mostly silent since he'd exited the diner, worried that his teasing while they'd been there was sending the wrong impression to Maxine, since it seemed to be sending the wrong impression to his cousins.

And me.

Things weren't going according to his plan. He didn't want to be attracted to Maxine. She was everything that he didn't want. Stubborn, with a complicated romantic history, and a life that wasn't anywhere near where he was building his own. It was time to put her firmly in the friend zone.

"Did your family touch a nerve regarding the holiday challenge?" Maxine stroked Spot's ears. His big dog rested his broad head on her shoulder.

If Bo wasn't careful, Spot was going to spend the night in the bunkhouse. Since Bo was sleeping on the couch, that would free up much needed legroom. But still, it was unsettling…both that his dog was falling for Maxine and that Bo was envious.

"Spot." Bo tapped his shoulder. "Come."

Spot gave him a quizzical look but kept his muzzle on Maxine's shoulder.

"You know, winning isn't everything." Maxine turned her head his way, mirroring Spot's curious gaze.

Her unfashionably large glasses should have been a turn-off. They should have hidden those marvelous, expressive, brown eyes of hers. But they didn't. It wasn't fair.

"Winning may not be everything, Maxine, but losing is to be avoided at all costs." Bo needed to spend less time thinking about Maxine and more time focusing on the challenge. Or he should, once they decided tonight what the exact challenges would be. And knowing Shane, it wouldn't be a simple run through the woods hunting hidden pumpkins.

"That's not what's bothering you," Maxine said in a tone that softened her words. "And… slow down. Please."

"I'm going five miles an hour." In four wheel drive. Up a hill. In slushy tracks made by other vehicles.

"I know, but we need to talk without an audience." Maxine laid a hand on his arm. It was a soft touch, a friendly touch, but it was a touch that reminded Bo of how delicate she felt in his arms. "Remember me? I'm Max and I'm just here through the holiday. I'm sorry about crying on your shoulder earlier. That was inappropriate. And I apologize for what happened in the diner. Those people are probably expecting a wedding invitation from you soon. But I promise you, you and the rest of this town will forget me when I'm gone. And when I leave, rest assured I won't be mooning over what could have been with one Beauregard Franklin Monroe."

"Are you…" He brought the truck to a full and complete stop. "Are you friend-zoning me?"

She didn't remove her hand from his arm. She didn't blink or blush. "I'm just stating the obvious. I didn't want you to think I was falling for you."

Maxine *was* putting him in the non-romantic zone. She'd beaten him to the punch!

As usual.

He pressed his lips together. This woman. She was frustrating. And he was sure she was frustrating him for all the wrong reasons. She was an enigma he could spend years puzzling over. And that was puzzling in itself.

"Work with me, Beauregard." Maxine withdrew her hand, smiling slightly, as if she'd just won a tennis set and was confident that she'd win the match.

Her words made no sense to him. No woman had ever shuttled him into the friend zone. Did he have food stuck in his teeth? Bad breath? Zits? Body odor? This entire conversation had blindsided him.

Bo passed his palm over his arm where she'd touched him, feeling her lingering warmth. "My mood has nothing to do with you."

"Exactly what I was thinking." She nodded.

He was sure she agreed just to agree. Just as he was certain he had to correct her. "I'm not talking about…"

That was when it hit him.

This.

This confounding feeling that he enjoyed Maxine's company and could enjoy it for years to come.

Just not as a friend.

Gritting his teeth, Bo pressed the accelerator. "I'm cranky because I didn't find a house today."

What a lie.

"Did you expect it to be easy?" She chuckled. "Come on. You know everything worth having in life is worth a little effort."

Like her?

No, not like her. This confounding, complicated woman could not be who he wanted.

"I made a list. I have a plan." The words sounded childish. But he wasn't going to back off. "I thought long and hard about what I wanted my future to look and feel like." About who he wanted to come home to every night.

And it wasn't a prickly woman who argued with everything he said and made him want to hold her whenever she felt blue.

CHAPTER SEVEN

"MAMA, YOU'RE JUST in time."

Still reeling from a cryptic conversation with Bo, Max parted ways with her holiday host as soon as he parked the truck at the two-story farmhouse.

She'd only been trying to reassure him that she wasn't setting her romantic sights on him. But he'd sent her mixed signals and hadn't agreed that friendship was the way to go. A man as good-looking as Bo was had to have discouraged his fair share of women. Could it be that he had trouble letting women down easy? Could it be that he wasn't used to women declaring they weren't interested in him that way?

Whatever it was, Max wanted to put some space between them. She found her daughter in the barn with two other little girls, all three of whom were being watched over by two cowboys—Tanner, and a man who introduced himself as Finn, the fiancé of Bo's sister, Kendall.

Luna, Mia and Lizzie, Finn's daughter, were about the same age, and were about to attempt to braid a small black pony's tail. Since Luna had no interest in the apples Max had bought, she put them on top of a nearby shelf and came over to watch.

"Adam wouldn't let us braid Cocoa's tail," a pouting Luna informed Max. She'd found a small, straw cowboy hat somewhere and with it looked no different than the little cowgirls standing on either side of her.

Tanner had assembled the items the girls needed and was instructing them in the art of horsetail grooming, which seemed to involve long, slow brush strokes while holding the tail away from the horse's rump.

"This won't last long," Finn predicted, scratching at the dark beard on his chin around what looked like a deep scar on his cheek.

"I don't know. Luna enjoys playing with hair." At least, she enjoyed trying to braid Max's hair.

Finn grinned at Max. "You've not spent much time on a ranch or farm, have you?"

What was he trying to tell her? Max peered over the stall door. "Luna, step back, please."

Too late.

Three little girls squealed.

Before Max realized what was happening, Tanner had dropped the pony's tail and swept the little cowgirls back to a safe distance from the fresh manure.

"Ew." Luna shivered and danced around with the other girls. "I don't want to braid no more."

Mia and Lizzie agreed.

"I guess you'll be wanting to ride now?" Tanner did a bad job hiding his grin as he let them out. "We can saddle up and join the boys in the arena."

There was a chorus of assent.

Finn and Tanner set about saddling ponies for the girls, working with practiced efficiency. Max was tasked with finding riding helmets in the tack room. And meanwhile, the three pre-school females got out the apples she'd bought for Cocoa.

Max stroked a palomino pony's soft neck as Tanner finished saddling him. "I thought Luna was going to take a turn on Cocoa."

"There's no need for that," Tanner told her. "The Clarks began offering trail rides last summer. They expanded their stable. Trust me. There are more than enough mounts for the dozen or so kids that will be around this weekend."

"She'll ride this little girl all weekend." Finn tightened a girth strap on a brown pony. "Bluebell."

"Bluebell isn't Cocoa," Luna said matter-of-factly, curls smashed beneath her helmet, glasses slipping down her nose. "But she's mine and I love her."

"That's nice, sweetheart." Movement outside the barn caught Max's attention.

Bo was talking to Jonah on the front porch of the house, shaking his head. He pressed his cowboy hat more firmly on his head and went inside without so much as looking toward the barn.

Toward me.

Max drew a deep breath, telling herself that was for the best.

Meanwhile, Spot joined them in the barn, stopping a safe distance away from Luna and her brown pony. He sniffed the air and whined a little.

Max took pity on him and moved to his side, giving him some loving strokes. "Horses and ponies make me nervous, too, Spot."

"Not me, Mama." Luna wrapped her arms around the little brown pony and gave it a squeeze. "Cowgirls love horses."

"Cowgirls love horses," Tanner agreed. He caught Max's eye and winked. "Just not manure."

Max laughed with a feeling of relief. She'd spend the rest of the week here hanging around Tanner, Finn and their daughters. She felt no unsettling attraction to Tanner, and Finn was engaged. Together, they'd keep each other company on the perimeter of Monroe activities.

Problem solved re her attraction to Bo.

In no time, Tanner and Finn finished and helped the girls mount. Then Tanner led Mia's and Luna's ponies toward the arena, while Finn led Lizzie's pony.

Franny's three boys and Tanner's son, Quinn, were playing a game of red light/green light on horseback in the arena. Emily stood at one end of the arena calling out instructions. The snow had been removed and the ground was dark and slippery looking. But Emily wasn't keeping the green light on long enough for the riders to pick up much speed. She paused to help the girls line their ponies up with the boys at the far end of the arena.

"Do you want to ride Bluebell?" Luna asked Adam. "We can trade."

"No, thanks." Adam patted Cocoa's neck. "A cowboy is only as good as his horse."

"You're a good cowboy." Luna pulled back on the reins at Emily's direction.

From where Max stood, Luna looked just as competent as the other young riders.

Unexpected tears filled her eyes. She glanced at Finn and Tanner to see if they noticed.

Both men were beaming, attention fixed on their kids, too.

Max gave a sniff, trying not to blubber. "I guess I'm not the only parent to be overwhelmed at how quickly my little girl is growing up."

Finn nodded.

"It seems like just yesterday that Mia took her first steps." Tanner tugged the brim of his black cowboy hat lower over his eyes and cleared his throat. "She's been learning liberty horse training. My son, Quinn, doesn't care as much about riding and horses as he does about roping. But Mia... It's like she was born to be a horsewoman like her mama. God rest her soul."

"Same here. Lizzie's been harping on about getting a horse to replace her pony," Finn admitted, scratching his beard. "I keep telling her to wait until she's five. I wish I could put her off longer, but she rides like she does everything else."

"Without fear," Max said, earning nods from the two men. "I'm glad we're only here until next Friday. Then it's back to city life."

"Where Luna will probably find something else to be obsessed with," Tanner predicted.

"Something else to keep you awake at night," Finn added knowingly.

"I suppose if it's not one thing, it's another." Max spotted Bo on the other side of the arena.

He climbed the fence rails and said something to Luna, who nodded and sat taller in the saddle.

And much as Max didn't want to think about Bo's handsome face or his broad shoulders, she couldn't help but dwell on the kind habit he had of watching out for her little girl.

THEY CAME BY TWOS.

At least, that was how Bo noticed his family members wander into the farmhouse Saturday night at the Bucking Bull.

First there were the couples—Jonah and Emily, Wyatt and Ashley, Bentley and Cassie, Olivia and Rhett. And then there were the newly formed families—Cam, Ivy, R.J. and Nick; Sophie, Zeke, Alex and Andy; Kendall, Finn and Lizzie; Laurel, Mitch, Gabby and the twin babies; Ella, Noah and Penny; Holden with Devin, and a very pregnant Bernadette. And of course, the hosts of the Monroe Holiday Challenge, Shane and his Clarks—Franny, Davey, Charlie, Adam and Gertie.

Most of them crammed into the living room, spilling into the dining room, taking up the couch and filling chairs, finding space to stand or sit on the floor. The others, the ones who had never participated in or seen the challenge before—Maxine and Luna, Tanner and his kids—stood near the front door. Everyone had come to enjoy the spectacle that was going to be the feature of the next few days.

The opening ceremony of the Monroe Holiday Challenge had arrived.

Not everyone had signed up to play. There were five teams so far. Their members were written on sheets of paper and taped to the living room windowpanes. Bo was Team Bo and the only team of one. None of his relatives had asked to compete with him and he'd been too proud to ask. The stink of defeat, as

Jonah had mentioned, was real and it was only a matter of time before he would be forced to withdraw.

Regardless, Bo held his head high from his place in the living room corner, with Spot leaning against his leg. And if his gaze drifted toward Maxine and his mind drifted along with it, so what?

What if Maxine and Luna joined me and I didn't come in last?

A pipe dream, he was sure.

What if Maxine saw me as more than a friend?

That last thought rankled.

He'd never been on the receiving end of a friend-zone declaration before. Aria had ended things completely with no option for friendship. And with other women he'd dated, Bo had been the one to voice the sentiment that things weren't working out. He should feel relieved. Those conversations were challenging to initiate and difficult to end. Someone's feelings usually got hurt.

In this case, mine.

And wasn't that mind-bending? Maxine had drawn a line in the sand without ever sharing a kiss with Bo. Forget his plans or his timeline about not dating until the new year. Her reiteration that she wasn't going to be long in his life made him feel short-changed. Not because of the boundary she'd verbally made, but because there was a delectable chemistry between them, one he recognized and she was determined to ignore.

His gaze connected with hers. She turned to Tanner with a start, color blooming in her cheeks.

Or maybe, like him, she found it hard to ignore temptation. Maybe, like him, she was setting attraction and love aside until the time was right. Not, like him, to get his house in order, but to—

"Attention, everyone." Shane tapped a flip chart with a list of game names written on it, severing Bo's train of thought. "As you know, the Monroe Holiday Challenge is finally back. Tonight, we're going to vote on the games to be played. Thanks to everyone who contributed an idea. And for those who haven't yet declared their playing status—"

"Hold the phone." Gertie got to her feet. "I've been hearing a lot of stories about how physical this competition can be. And my great-grandsons have been crowing about the stunts they want to pull. This sounds more dangerous than riding bulls in the rodeo."

Gertie should know. The Bucking Bull raised and sold bulls to the rodeo circuit for eight-second rides.

There were murmurs of agreement. Jonah reminded everyone that he'd pulled a muscle recently, to which even Emily, his fiancée, groaned.

"For safety's sake," Gertie continued, talking like she'd forgotten to put her hearing aids in. "I think all games should err to the conservative side. Maybe there should be two categories—one for younger cowpokes without any risk of injury, and one for team events where only adults do something foolish." Gertie sank back down into her rocking chair. "That's it. I've said my piece. Y'all can discuss."

The volume in the farmhouse increased, but the particulars were lost to Bo as the voices built louder than upset chickens in a too small henhouse.

Bo kept silent, stroking Spot's back over Maxine's soft sweatshirt, waiting for the right time to gracefully withdraw.

He caught Maxine's eye once more. She had Luna propped on her hip. Her teeth were worrying her lower lip. And in her eyes...

"I'm sorry," she mouthed.

And if that wasn't the theme of the day, Bo didn't know what was.

"All in favor of dividing the challenges into Gertie's categories, including multi-person events," Shane shouted above them all, raising his hand.

The majority of the assembled raised their hands.

"If you do that, what about Bo?" Maxine called out. "Who's going to be on his team?"

"I don't have to play," Bo said, trying to hide his disappointment.

"Wise move given your track record." Holden, Bo's older brother, could be a complete pain. He stood behind his petite fiancée, arms cradling her large, pregnant belly. "Since Bernadette is due soon, we're not competing. I know some of you see this as an opportunity one less contender on the leader board—"

Bo heaved a weary sigh. Why did Holden always have to make things about him?

Holden smiled at Bo "—but my absence from the games means my son, Devin, can play on Bo's team." Devin, who was a freshman in college and had spent much of the summer taking tourists on trail rides.

"Thanks." Bo felt a weight lift from his shoulders.

"Sorry, Uncle Bo. I don't want to compete." Devin got to his feet, the spitting image of Holden at that age. He picked his way toward the door, taking Bo's hopes with him. "You guys are too intense. I came here for the holidays to relax and stuff myself with turkey and pie."

Shoulders heavy once more, Bo sought solace from Spot, cradling the dog's white, velvety face in both hands. "You'd be on my team if there was a dog challenge, wouldn't you, buddy?"

Spot tried to lick Bo's chin.

"We're not competing either." His cousin Sophie laid her head on her husband's shoulder, looking inordinately happy the challenge was behind her. "I guess now's the time to announce that Zeke and I are pregnant."

Several minutes were lost to congratulations, including Bo's, during which time others officially backed out until there were only the original five teams that had been posted on the windows—Jonah and Emily, Wyatt and Ashley, Olivia and Rhett, Shane and Franny, plus Bo.

He was still reluctant to withdraw. The

fact that there were fewer teams this year increased Bo's odds of not coming in last.

Postponing the inevitable, Bo picked his way to the kitchen for a glass of water while the children with permission to compete were divvied up to the teams.

I'll compete next year, Bo told himself, making a mental note to add it to his life plan later. Writing things down always made him feel more committed. This morning, he'd written, *Win this thing*.

While the four competing teams voted on what the events would be, Bo ate a frosted sugar cookie that was shaped like a Christmas sock. It had an excess of red sprinkles that fell to the floor when he took a bite. Spot licked the floor clean.

Bo couldn't quite believe the challenges that were voted in. For the kids, there'd be scarecrow stuffing and gingerbread house decorating. For the full team, there'd be Western-type events—a roping competition and a horse-drawn skier pull. The final event would be held on Thanksgiving morning and involve all team members riding in a sleigh parade. All sleighs had to be decorated by each team and would be judged by non-competing Monroes.

As events go, these are tame.

Maybe it wasn't such a bad thing that he was missing the competition this year. Still, he didn't rush to withdraw. Instead, Bo ate another cookie, listening to Shane calling for volunteers.

"Excuse me," someone called out.

Spot's ears perked. His head swiveled around. And then he trotted off.

Bo knew that voice, too. "Maxine?" What was she up to now?

He left the kitchen and stood at the back of the dining room crowd, unable to see anything.

"I can't believe we're doing this, but…" Maxine sounded exasperated. "Sign us up for Team Bo."

"What?" Had someone talked her into it? Bo pushed through family in the dining room and stepped over various kidlets sitting on the floor of the living room. He came to a stop near the windows, separated from Maxine by Gertie in her rocking chair, who was wielding a needle on something that looked like a bright orange hat.

Maxine balanced her daughter on one hip while writing her name and Luna's beneath his. "There. Done."

Spot stared up at them adoringly, a feeling

Bo shared but was reluctant to show because he was certain participating in the challenge went against all of Maxinc's holiday rules. He had questions and objections. But all he could get out was one word. "Why?"

"Why not?" Maxine said briskly, handing Shane the felt-tip pen. She hitched Luna higher on her hip. "It sounds like fun."

"We like games." Luna twirled a finger in her cloud of curly hair, morning pigtails long since gone. "And there are horses. And cowboys."

Bo spared the girl a grin before capturing Maxine's full attention with a touch to her shoulder. "But…it's not on the fringe. You'll be front and center." Not overlooked or relegated to a quiet corner. Bo thought about her tears today when she'd told him about being orphaned. And her admissions of a childhood filled with upheaval, being passed from one relative to the next. He didn't want her to be crushed—emotionally or physically—in the challenge. "It may be scarecrow stuffing and gingerbread house decorating, but it's still a competition."

"I know," she said simply, shrugging. "I usually enjoy just supporting and watching what goes on at someone's family gathering…"

Wishing she was a part of the family, he bet.

"I don't want to take someone else's lime-light or their place at the main table…"

Because that would risk rejection. Something she'd had entirely too much of.

"…but despite there being dozens of Monroes here…" Maxine glanced around the room. "…there seemed to be an empty place that needed to be filled."

At her words, something inside of him shifted, something he wasn't ready to name.

"You won't regret it," he promised her, grinning and hoping that was true.

"There, now." Gertie put her hands inside the orange knit cap she'd been finishing, stretching it this way and that. And then she handed it to Maxine. "I made you a hat, Max, and none too soon. You'll be out in the weather with the rest of these Monroe hooligans. You'll need to keep a level head if you're going to help Bo work himself out of last place."

"*She'll* need a level head?" Bo scoffed.

Gertie grinned up at him. "Indeed, she will."

"Are you having a good time, Luna?"

"Yes, Mama." Swaddled baby doll under

her arm, Luna rolled over in bed and snuggled deeper in her sleeping bag. She'd had a big day on the ranch and had almost fallen asleep in the shower earlier.

Max sat at the small table in the bunkhouse and sipped her hot chocolate, still unable to believe she'd joined the holiday challenge and still nervous about participating.

It had all started with a feeling that had come over her while she'd been standing with Tanner in the foyer.

"No one is joining Bo's team," she'd said half to herself and half to the cowboy next to her.

"Can't say as I blame them," Tanner had said. "From what I hear, Bo was really good at tripping himself up."

"Still…" Max's heart went out to him. Last she'd seen, Bo's expression had looked defeated. She'd been selected last for enough playground games to know how that stung. Not to mention, the last time she'd played any sports, her face had gotten in the way of a soccer ball. She knew a bit about humiliation on the field. "Why don't you and Quinn join him?" She flashed Tanner a bright smile.

Quinn, a cowboy of about five or six, shook his head.

"You don't want to play with the other boys?" The trio of Clark boys who lived here on the ranch, including Adam, who was about Quinn's age.

Quinn shook his head again. "We've got work to do at our place. Right, Dad?"

Tanner had hastened to reassure his son that he could compete if he wanted, but it was clear to Max that the boy had been influenced by the hard-working values Tanner apparently held dear.

And then Luna had tugged on the neck of Max's sweater and said, "I want to be on Bo's team."

That was all it took for Max to volunteer. But she hadn't done it just for Luna's sake. Admittedly, her own feelings were involved. The easiest to acknowledge was being a help to Bo. The hardest was extending her time near him without making a romantic fool of herself.

Max sipped her hot chocolate, hoping the next few days would be as smooth and gentle as her drink. Scarecrow stuffing? Sleigh decorating? How intense could the competition be?

Someone knocked softly on the door. She got up to answer.

It was Bo and Spot.

"Can we come in?" Neither waited for her assent.

Spot hurried inside and hopped up on Luna's bed, curling into a ball that took up half the lower bunk.

Bo brushed past Max, carrying a small plate of frosted sugar cookies. He sat at the table and set the cookies down in front of him. "We need to talk."

"Do we?" With a sigh, Max closed the door. "Luna's already asleep. We have to keep our voices down."

"Okay." Bo peered inside her mug. The man had no boundaries. "Hot chocolate?"

She rolled her eyes, then pushed up her glasses. "Subtlety is not your specialty. Do you want some?"

"That would be great." He bit into a liberally frosted, Santa shaped sugar cookie. "Now that we're alone, you can tell me the real reason you volunteered for the competition."

"The real reason?" Max frowned.

Do not admit the truth.

Max busied herself with making him a cup

of instant hot chocolate, using the small microwave to heat a mug of water and dissolving a packet of hot chocolate mix in it. "I told you. Luna wanted to do it." She could feel Bo's inquisitive gaze on her, sense the tension in the stiff set to his shoulders. "I never want Luna to feel that she should hold back if she wants to join in."

"So…it wasn't pity?"

"Please." Max scoffed softly. That had been a part of it, too, but the smallest of parts. "Unlike me, Luna fits in here."

"You fit in," Bo said gruffly, settling back in the chair. "Your problem is that you look for differences to push you to the fringe of things."

Did she? Had she since she'd arrived? She had.

Max nodded. "You might be right. Still—"

"Luna comes first."

"Yes." She'd walk through fire for her daughter. Max set his mug of hot chocolate on the table, feeling the press of emotion at the back of her throat because few people asked about her guiding principles when it came to her daughter and for whatever reason, she wanted this man to understand. "Luna will never know what it's like to be an afterthought. I don't want her to learn how to hold back her tears because she's waiting for the other shoe to drop. She shouldn't have to walk on eggshells wondering when the next moving day will come." She shouldn't have to store important possessions in her suitcase for fear she'd leave something dear to her behind in the next move.

Max drew a ragged breath.

On the bed, Spot sighed, as if commiserating.

"Maxine…" Across from her, Bo ran a hand over the back of his neck. "Doesn't that imply you need to stop borrowing other people's family at the holidays?"

Her throat closed. Why did her throat close?

She nodded, clearing it enough to say in a hoarse whisper, "Just not yet."

"What are you waiting for?" Bo voiced the question softly.

But it reverberated inside of Max as if he'd shouted, shaking the foundation of defenses she'd built up, demanding she face some of her own inner truths. The reason she kept pursuing college majors. The reason she couldn't bear to spend Thanksgiving and Christmas with just her and Luna.

Clive's sneer drifted into her mind's eye. *Don't admit it. Not now. Not with Bo.*

She didn't want to see derision on Bo's face.

"Is it because you're applying for another degree?" He sipped his hot chocolate, letting the question hang between them. "I suppose you'll be moving if you get accepted."

"Actually, all my degrees are from, and will be from, Missouri State." No moving required.

Bo studied her, gray gaze cataloging every blink and breath. "It's all making sense now."

She didn't want to hear whatever sense he was making of things. "Yes. Now you understand why we volunteered."

He opened his mouth as if about to argue, but closed it again. He nodded and moved the plate of cookies to her side of the table. "My grandfather would have liked you. You put family first."

"Like you don't?" She'd had more than her share of sweets today. She took a cookie anyway. She did so admire a frosted Christmas tree–shaped cookie.

"I haven't put family first lately. And I want to." He drummed his fingers on the tabletop. "Jonah and I used to be close. My older brother... My kid sister... We used to be better about keeping in touch. They're all landing here. And where family is..."

"So goes the heart." Max laid a hand over his, quieting those restless fingers. She let her touch linger, soaking in the warmth of his skin, the strength of his hand beneath hers. Reluctantly, she drew her palm back, but slowly, because touching him was like a dream and she knew how painful broken dreams could be.

He stared at his hand.

Make light of it, Max.

She turned the cookie plate, spinning it slowly so the remaining cookies were out of reach. "You confuse me, Beauregard."

"Maybe you and I need to write things down. For clarity." Bo lifted his gaze to hers, smiling slightly.

Max drew an easier breath.

"I'm glad we cleared the air." Max's tone didn't quite hit the tease she was striving for. "Regardless, you should be happy we volunteered to be on your team. We can be your secret weapon."

His smile broadened. "Have you ever been someone's secret weapon?"

"Never." But she'd hold the memory of being his close to her heart forever.

CHAPTER EIGHT

THE FRONT DOOR slam was a jarring alarm.

"I'm up." Bo jerked to a sitting position, eyes shut against the sudden glare of light. He tried to move his legs, which were bent at an uncomfortable angle because...

Spot grumbled on top of the sleeping bag, protesting Bo's efforts to free the legs that the dog was lying on.

"It's Bo!" a little voice cried.

"And Spot," said another.

"Boys, shhh."

Bo pried his eyes open. It was dark outside, and the house was quiet except for the pitter-patter of little stockinged feet.

Two shoeless, identical twin boys scrambled into Bo's lap, bouncing on him like a new couch cushion.

"Oof." Bo was knocked down. But the good news was that the twins had upset Spot, who relinquished his place on Bo's legs. "Dudes, did you eat too much sugar this morning?"

"We had eggs," said Alex, scratching his cowlick.

"And bacon," said Andy, rubbing his tummy.

Bo turned his head toward their mother. "Sophie, why are you here so early? No one's up yet."

His art- and antique-loving cousin made her way gingerly across the living room. "Zeke works here, remember? He has the early shift today and the boys couldn't bear to be left behind." Sophie sat carefully in Gertie's rocker. "They were afraid they'd miss today's competition. And since I had morning sickness, I thought bringing the boys here would be no trouble. There are always kids up and running around."

"Maybe in another hour." Bo struggled back up, gently tumbling boys toward his feet. "The coffee hasn't even begun brewing." Or at least, he couldn't smell it.

"Ugh." Sophie pressed a hand over her mouth. "Don't talk about coffee…or food. The boys' breakfast nearly did me in."

Said boys were trying to tickle one another, checked shirts bunching above their waists.

Bo sighed. "Alex? Andy? If you get off me and promise to be quiet, you can play video games on mute."

The twins slid to the floor, giggling. Spot removed himself from the room, going to sit in the dining room and staring at them with his chin raised as if offended at rambunctious, early risers. Maxine's sweatshirt, which Spot still wore, was twisted nearly as badly as Alex and Andy's shirts.

"I'm against video games," Sophie said, albeit weakly, since her hand still covered her mouth. "We don't have them at home."

"An hour or so here or there won't ruin them." Bo got up, working out the kinks in his back and neck. "If you let them play, I'll get you some crackers. And then you can lie down on the couch while I supervise." He rummaged around beneath the television, bringing out the game console and selecting an age-appropriate game.

"Are those your pajamas?" Alex sat cross-legged in front of the television as the screen came to life.

"Yep." Sweats and a T-shirt. The old farmhouse could be chilly, but not as nippy as the bunkhouse. Bo had meant to ask Maxine if she'd been warm enough in there with just one space heater.

"My pj's have superheroes." Andy sat next

to his brother. "Alex tries to take mine but his have cartoons."

"We share everything," Alex said.

"Not without asking," his twin replied.

"You should always ask before borrowing." Bo handed each boy a controller, which ended the argument.

"You're going to make a good husband someday." Sophie drew shallow breaths. "I had my doubts. You seemed stuck in the rut of bachelorhood forever. But look at you now."

Bo thought about Maxine and her determination to live her life in educational limbo. "All it takes is a wake-up call, I guess." He left her in charge, not that he could head right for the kitchen and those crackers he'd promised her.

Spot needed to be let out. Then let back in. The coffee machine needed starting, and Spot needed to be fed.

All the while, Bo fantasized about having a place of his own in Second Chance where he could sleep in undisturbed.

He brought Sophie her crackers, along with a glass of water. She'd already taken up residence in his sleeping bag, but she sat up to eat. He took her place in Gertie's rocker and stared

sleepily at the video game the boys were playing, wondering if Maxine was awake.

He'd spent too much time last night thinking about Maxine. He wanted her to be happy.
And he wanted to help her be happy. It just
wasn't his place—her friend-zoning had
made that clear.

He reached for his notebook and a pen he'd
left on the end table.

Ask Maxine what she wants to do.

*Win today's challenge. Find a place to
call my second home.*

A place Maxine approves of.

Bo washed a hand over his face. He didn't
write that last thought down. Sleep depriva-
tion was toying with his thoughts.

"Help." Andy had pressed something and
frozen the game.

Bo placed his notebook on one knee and
took charge of the controller, pressing a few
buttons to get the game back up and running.
And then he ripped the page he'd written the
day's intentions on and folded it neatly into
a small square.

"…and then I fold it like this." Grandpa

Harlan had folded and creased the paper enough times that it was small enough to fit in his shirt pocket. He gave it a pat once he'd tucked it away. "And once it's here, it reminds me what needs doing—not just today, but on the road I take to the future I envision."

"You want to make Maxine happy?" Sophie interrupted his recollection of the past, clearly having seen Bo's scribbles. "That's sweet. Does she know you put her on your daily notepad?"

Bo shook his head. "Maxine isn't a believer in affirmations or daily intentions." Perhaps that was why she was stuck in a rut.

"Just because you approach things differently doesn't mean you aren't compatible," Sophie said, misinterpreting the context of Bo's remark. "Just look at me and Zeke. I love reading thick, dusty books on art history. And he likes watching online videos about horse training. But we both like to learn."

"You're assuming she and I have interest in each other." If he'd known his cousin was going to peek at his notebook, he'd have written *Friend Zone* on his sheet of paper. "Maxine is timid and needs prodding to find happiness." He hadn't thought of it that way until that moment. But it felt right.

Sophie chuckled, wrapping his sleeping bag around her shoulders. "No timid soul would enter the Monroe Holiday Challenge."

"Not if they knew what they were walking into." But those holidays Maxine spent with others… She didn't know what she was walking into there, either. And there was her admission that she didn't want to get married again. "Hey, Sophie. You were married before. I never heard you say you didn't want to get married again."

Sophie gestured to the boys and put a finger to her lips, signaling him to be more circumspect with tiny ears around. When she answered him, it was in a whisper. "People can be cruel to each other. Some marriages end so badly you're scared to get involved again. If that's where Max is emotionally, you need to go slow."

"Slow isn't exactly the Monroe way."

"But the path to love isn't the same for everyone."

"I get that." It made complete and total sense to him. "But how do you know that it's love?" He'd been blinded into thinking he was in love before, fooled by his competitive nature, misled by a woman who didn't want to be alone and only let go of one man when she had another firmly in her clutches. "I recognize attraction. I just don't know if I can trust what I'm feeling to be real."

Sophie's opinion mattered because she'd met Zeke last winter and married him in April.

"Well, with Zeke, I couldn't stop thinking about him." Sophie's eyes glistened with emotion. "And I always wanted to ease his pain. He was working through a lot when we met and I just… I just wanted him to be happy, whether he chose to be happy with us or not."

WHEN THE SUN finally came up for Day One of the Monroe Holiday Challenge, the air was crisp, clear and bright.

It was midmorning by the time the five teams were fed and assembled, along with family members who'd agreed to judge and those who wanted to watch. Every Monroe in town was present, from the youngest— Laurel's five-month-old twins—to the oldest, Bo's brother, Holden. All told, there were nearly forty people present.

"I can't believe I overslept again," Maxine complained to Bo as things were being set up in the barn's breezeway. Maxine had her orange knit cap pulled so low the brim almost touched the frame of her glasses. Her brown curls spilled out from beneath the cap and spread in a wind-tossed tangle over her shoulders. In cowboy boots, blue jeans and a thick green jacket, she looked capable of taking anything and anyone on, including him.

"You're just cranky because you didn't get to help make breakfast or do the dishes afterward," Bo told her. "You know, it's okay to be a guest. It's not like anyone expects you to earn your keep."

She smirked at him. "It's what I do."

He let that comment slide because he liked that about her. He also liked that she looked ready to compete this morning. She'd even talked a little smack with Ashley earlier when his cousin had told Bo he was going down. But when he looked deep in Maxine's whiskey-colored, darting eyes he detected more than a trace of nervousness.

"Last chance to back out and just be a spectator." Bo hoped she wouldn't take the out but he was prepared to put her well-being first if she happened to have cold feet. "Last chance," he said again when she still hadn't answered. He smoothed a lock of hair over her shoulder. "Maxine?"

She blinked up at him. "Let the games

begin." Her words sounded hollow. She glanced at Luna, who stood with the other younger contestants and Spot, who'd decided his role in life this week was to be Luna's sidekick. "Don't worry about me. I've been in competitions before, more than once."

"Spelling bees and academic decathlons—" or whatever it was that people with three degrees considered competition "—are nothing like this."

Maxine smirked again. That seemed to be her default expression when she was nervous. "I still had to get up in front of people and perform. And I still had to worry that I wouldn't disappoint my class or team or school."

"Fair. But we're in this now. You're Team Bo for the next five days." Maybe longer if he was patient and played his cards right. "I won't quit on you if we lose or pass you on to another team."

She looked him up and down. "Did you make notes this morning about your intention to win?"

"I did." The folded paper rested in his back pocket. He chose not to tell her she'd made it to his daily list.

Maxine gave him a brisk nod. "Although

I don't ascribe to the practice, we can use all the help we can get."

"Agreed." He smiled at her. "I have a good feeling about our odds." And he wasn't sure he meant this competition.

"Well, that makes one of us," Maxine muttered.

"Welcome to our first challenge—the turkey wrap and rope." Holden stood in the middle of the ranch yard, acting as emcee since Shane was competing. Like Bo, he wore a cowboy hat and a shearling coat. But his stance was that of a leader, something Bo had neither aspired to nor been able to pull off where his family was concerned. "One member is going to wrap another of your team members with burlap feed bags, held with clothespins. Once your judge declares the turkey to be adequately wrapped—feet to shoulders—the third team member will attempt to lasso the turkey."

"I'd like to try roping," Maxine told Bo, chin set at a determined angle.

Setting aside her happiness for a moment, Bo took a second to consider her slight frame and academic background and weighed it against his goal of making a good showing. Now that the first event was upon them, the urge to win was becoming more pressing. "Have you ever roped before?"

"No, but I think I'd be good at it."

"Why?" He couldn't disguise the doubt in his voice. Their competition was lining up, most having already determined who was doing what.

"After years of yoga, I'm stronger than I look." Negating that claim to strength, Maxine pushed her glasses up with both hands. "I'm quite good at throwing balled up paper in my office trash can."

Everything inside Bo tensed at the thought of putting their chances of winning in such naive, inexperienced hands.

"I'll remember your skill if basketball becomes an event. But for now, there's strategy to the competition." Bo took Maxine gently by the shoulders and turned her to face his cousin Olivia and her fiancé, Rhett. "Look at that cowboy. See his big belt buckle? Rhett won that in a roping competition."

"Be afraid." Olivia grinned ferally back at them, like the multi-decorated racing boat champion she was. "Be very afraid."

Maxine gasped.

"I told you we don't mess around." Bo shifted Maxine's shoulders until she faced

Emily and Franny, who were coiling lariats at each team's station. "See those two Clark cowgirls? They spend their days roping stray bulls while on horseback."

"It's all in the wrist," Franny told Maxine.

"And it's all fun and games." Emily laughed. "That is until someone like Bo loses for the umpteenth time."

Bo made a reactive sound in his throat, low and growl-like.

But this wasn't about him.

He angled Maxine toward Ashley and Wyatt, who were holding a heated debate about who should rope. "Those two may be actors, but they've been practicing their riding and roping skills for months in anticipation of filming a Western movie next year."

Maxine turned to face him, frowning slightly. "Your point is that we're both overmatched in the roping department?"

"Yes." Bo drew himself up. "And unlike you, I've actually tossed a rope a time or two." Back when he was a kid. "I have a better chance of roping you than you do of roping me."

Maxine tsked and laid a hand on his shoulder, looking calmer now than she had before he'd highlighted the competitive field. "You're getting nervous. Apprehension stiffens muscles. Which is why I should rope."

She had a point.

Bo drew a deep, calming breath. He still wasn't convinced she should toss the rope. "If it's strategy you need to hear, I'd be a bigger body for Luna to wrap in burlap. It'll take her longer." They were running out of time to argue. Contestants were taking their places.

"Fair enough. We do it your way." Maxine's hand fell away but her eyes flashed. "This time. I like winning, too, you know."

"I haven't forgotten. Charades, password and gin rummy."

"You're incorrigible," Maxine muttered, but she was smiling.

"I'm ready," Luna called to them, holding a burlap bag and shaking it repeatedly, as if it was a beach towel and she wanted to remove all the day's sand.

Spot sat next to her wearing Maxine's sweatshirt and a doggy smile.

His team's optimism lifted Bo's spirits.

"Here." Bo plunked his cowboy hat on Maxine's head, pressing it down over her orange knit cap. "This will protect your face from the lariat when I lasso you. No arguing. I'm team captain, and I say you'll be the turkey."

"Gobble. Gobble." Maxine went to stand with the other turkeys fifteen feet away while Bo picked up the stiff lariat. She showed Luna how to wrap her up and fasten the clothespins.

Bo had never felt so positive going into a competition.

We could win.

"I see you haven't lost your competitive spirit." Ashley stood next to Bo, grinning as if she fully expected to take him down the way she'd threatened earlier.

Granted, Ashley held her rope with more confidence than he did, but that just might be her acting.

I can only hope.

"Ashley, I'm older now and more aware of the strategy involved in these reindeer games." He nodded toward Shane and Franny, who'd decided to let young Davey try to lasso one of them instead of his more experienced mother. "You win by making smart decisions, not coming out to have fun."

Ashley's laughter filled the air. And then she kissed him on the cheek. "I love you, Bo, but when it comes to the holiday challenge, beating you is all that matters."

MAX KNELT IN front of Luna one more time before the turkey wrap and rope started. "Now remember. You wrap me up tight, like you wrap up your baby doll at bedtime." Max had thought a lot about technique last night and that was the best metaphor she could come up with for her little girl.

"Swaddle, Mama." Grinning, Luna pushed her glasses up her nose. Spot took the opportunity to lick her cheek, making them slip again. "I *swaddle*."

"Yes, you do. And you swaddle really well." Max smiled at Bo's cousin Cam from beneath Bo's hat brim. The cook from the Bent Nickel Diner had been assigned to judge when Max, the human turkey, was fully wrapped and could be roped. "Be kind to us. We're new."

Cam laughed. "Rookies or veterans. The challenge and its judges make no allowances for either."

Her smile stiffened. She avoided intense competitions like this in her everyday life. What if she and Luna let Bo down? He'd said it would be okay if they didn't win, but would it be?

"Judges, are you ready to pronounce turkeys wrapped?" Holden called out and at the nod of the five judges, added, "On your marks…"

"Remember to wrap me up to my shoulders, honey." Max got to her feet, putting heels and knees together, plastering her hands to her sides. "We have to be smart about this."

"Get set…" Holden raised his arm.

Max spared Bo a glance. He was looking as stiff as the loops of rope he was holding. "We've got this," she told him, hoping it was true.

"Go!"

Someone whooped. Someone else hollered. A whole lot of people applauded and cheered the competitors on.

Watched over by Spot, Luna pinned two corners of a burlap sack to the seams of Max's jeans at her calves. And then she wrapped the sack around Max one and a half times, pinning the end on the calf of Max's other leg. One more bag and Max's knees were covered.

Max carefully lowered herself to her knees to make it easier for Luna to wrap the rest of her.

"Great idea, Maxine." Bo still looked tense. His competitive resting face was more what she'd call resigned-to-lose face.

She was struck by the longing to kiss that pessimistic expression away.

The wrapping continued. The cheering continued. Luna's little cowgirl friends, Mia and Lizzie, jumped up and down, clapping and shouting encouragement.

"I did it!" Luna pinned the last burlap bag at Max's shoulders.

"Rope this turkey," Cam told Bo. He took Luna's hand and led her a safe distance away, calling Spot to follow.

They were the first ones done. The other contestants were struggling with falling clothespins and unraveling burlap—even Franny, who was wrapping Shane.

It was then that Max realized her error. With her legs wrapped, she couldn't get back up without putting Luna's wrap job at risk. But maybe it was a good thing she was kneeling? She'd be a smaller target. "Bo, rope me already."

"Give me a second." Bo twirled the rope over his head in slow motion, handsome face drawn in concentration. "Duck your head. I don't want to hit you in the face."

She did. The lasso bounced off the crown of his cowboy hat with a resounding *thunk*. "I'd be easier to rope without your hat on."

Max shook her head from side to side, but his hat was stuck on her head and not going anywhere.

"Safety first, Maxine." Bo coiled the rope and threw again, missing Max completely.

"Be a good cowboy," Luna called to Bo.

"Relax and take your time," Max said in a soothing voice.

"Rope this turkey!" another Monroe judge cried from behind Shane.

Franny backed away. "Lasso Shane, Davey. You can do it."

"Now's the time, Bo," Max murmured, willing Bo to victory.

Franny's oldest son, who couldn't have been more than ten or eleven, began twirling his lariat with more skill and speed than Bo had exhibited.

"Rope this turkey!" called another Monroe judge behind Olivia, drawing young Charlie a safe distance away.

Two contestants threw rope—Davey and Rhett, the roping champion. Rhett's rope fell first, dropping around Olivia and falling cleanly to the ground.

Olivia whooped. "That's my man!"

A blink later, Davey's rope dropped over Shane's head, hooking over one shoulder.

Franny and Davey ran to Shane, hugging the burlap-wrapped turkey.

Thunk.

Bo's rope bounced off the cowboy hat on Max's head again.

"So close." Bo snapped the rope back again.

"Try again," Max called. *Hurry.*

"Rope that turkey!" The last two judges cried in unison.

And then quicker than Max could say, "Happy Thanksgiving," Emily had roped a wrapped Jonah and Ashley had roped a similarly wrapped Wyatt.

Almost immediately after that, Bo's lasso fell loosely around Max's shoulders.

His expression fell with it. "Fifth place."

In other words, last.

Four teams were unified, hugging and laughing as they recounted what they'd done.

Bo turned away, shoulders slumped.

And even though Max understood his disappointment, even though she knew she and Luna had carried their share of the load, she couldn't help but feel that his turned back was just another in a long string of abandonments.

CHAPTER NINE

"Bo, take this."

This happened to be one of his cousin Laurel's twin baby girls.

Bo accepted the pink bundle and stared into a very suspicious little face. "Don't even think about crying, Grumpy Face. Here. Look at the pretty doggy." He pointed at Spot, who had followed him when he'd walked away from the roping debacle, needing space.

The red-haired, blue-eyed tyke stared at Spot without a change in expression.

"If you think Hazel has a grumpy face, you should take a look at your own." Laurel fussed with Hazel's thick, fuzzy blanket.

Spot extended his nose toward Hazel, sniffing as if he'd caught wind of food crumbs in her blanket folds.

Hazel giggled and pushed Spot's big black nose away with both hands.

Bo smiled, the sting of losing eased by the

balm of baby laughter. "You must smile all the time, Laurel."

"It's easy to smile when things go a baby's way." Laurel's red hair fluttered from beneath a teal knit cap. "Or a Monroe's way. I thought you were mature enough not to take this competition so seriously."

"I probably would be if I had at least one win under my belt. Don't hold a little moping against me."

Spot extended his sniffer toward Hazel once more with the same giggly result.

"I won't hold your poor sportsmanship against you, but the rest of your team might." Laurel gestured toward the breezeway where the activity had turned to preparing the stock for a ride down to the meadow.

And there was Luna. She looked fine. She stood at a stall with Mia and Lizzie, chattering as they looked in on a pony.

But Max...

It took Bo a while to find her. She'd walked toward the back of the barn, lingering in the shadows as if she wanted to be forgotten.

Or as if someone had betrayed her trust.

Bo swore.

"Not in front of the baby, Bo." Laurel frowned. "If you're looking to settle down with Max, why would you put her through the family challenge? And why would you treat her as if losing this event was her fault? She rocked it."

"She and Luna were awesome. I just needed a minute to collect myself." He blew out a breath, jiggling the baby a little. "I'll apologize. But everyone needs to slow down on assuming Maxine and I have something going on. She's not interested in me like that." And wasn't that like admitting another demoralizing loss?

Laurel's mouth dropped open. "What is she? A nun? Every single woman you've ever met has been interested in you."

"She's different." In too many important ways to count.

Laurel laughed a little. "Doesn't it just figure that you're ready to get married and the first woman who catches your eye is immune to your charm?"

"Go, Hazel. Laugh, laugh, laugh." He spoke in baby talk. "The situation with Maxine is about as funny as Shane resurrecting the holiday challenge and me thinking I could win."

"Look." Laurel plucked Hazel from Bo's arms. "If anyone can charm a woman into dating, it's you. Go on. What are you waiting for?"

Bo took in the way Maxine's hands were clasped and her gaze focused on her feet. "It's too late. I blew it."

Maxine looked about as demoralized as he'd felt a few minutes ago.

"Bo, the least you can do is make her feel appreciated by her team captain."

His cousin was right. And what Bo needed was a surefire way to make Maxine smile.

He lifted the baby from Laurel's arms and held her as if she was a flying superhero, horizontal to the ground. And then he hurried toward the barn, making engine noises that were incongruent to beings with capes.

Not that Hazel minded. She squealed in delight.

It might have helped that Spot trotted next to her, letting out a single, excited, "Woof!"

Maxine turned at the racket they were making. The guarded, icy look in her eyes melted at the sight of Hazel.

Bo stopped within touching distance of Maxine. "I'm over losing." He righted the baby, propping her on his hip. "It took a happy baby to knock me out of my funk." He stared into Maxine's whiskey-colored eyes.

"That was un-sportsman-like conduct. I owe you and Luna an apology. You should expect better from your team captain."

Hazel kicked her feet and expressed her displeasure that the hijinks had ended. She let out a long shout.

"A baby!" Luna appeared in front of Bo, grinning. "Abracadabra, baby, be happy!" She waved an imaginary wand.

Hazel lurched toward the little girl, reaching for her glasses.

Bo and Maxine moved quickly to prevent any damage.

Laurel appeared, reclaiming Hazel and spinning her around. "Come on. Let's go see what trouble Hope is getting into." She spared Maxine a glance. "You were awesome today."

"Thanks." Maxine had her hands clasped in front of her again. She wouldn't look at Bo. "I'll be honest. I don't want to go through that again." She drew a deep breath and met Bo's gaze levelly. "You walking off like that… without looking back."

"It hurt you," he said in a soft voice only meant for her, not any of the people scurrying about saddling horses and ponies. "*I* hurt you. I'm so sorry." Bo took her clasped hands, aware that all around them, gazes swung their way. He worked his thumbs into the knots she'd made of her fingers, easing the tension in her hands. "I've never been a team captain before. I won't make the mistake of walking away from you again."

His words fell between them, heavy with import.

And although Bo knew better than to promise such a thing out loud, silently he added, *Ever.*

"Mama, look at me. I'm a cowgirl."

Max smiled at her baby girl, snapping a photo with her phone. Sitting on top of Bluebell with cowboy boots and a riding helmet on, her little pumpkin looked every inch the budding cowgirl.

They were getting ready to ride down to the cabin-dotted campground located in a meadow bordering the highway. That was where the sleighs for decorating were being delivered.

Max checked the picture she'd taken, pleased that it was adorable. "We'll win the next round, won't we, Luna?"

"You bet, Mama."

"And we'll have fun doing it." Because Bo seemed to have had a change of heart about winning and losing, particularly how he reacted to losing. His apology meant a lot to Max. He'd said they were a team and that he wouldn't walk away again. And even if a small part of her doubted that promise, a larger part of her hoped it was true.

"Adam, wait for me." Luna gave her pony a gentle kick that sent her mount forward at a leisurely pace in the direction of the arena. Adam and the other boys were already there on their horses waiting for the rest of the Monroes to mount up.

Spot came to stand next to Max, leaning into her in a not-so-subtle plea for affection. Just in time, too, since Max was nervous about riding. "Maybe you and I should drive down the hill."

A few others had, including Laurel, her husband and her adorable babies.

"Spot's going to stay with Gertie in front of the fire." Bo brought a sweet-looking palomino horse over to Max. "You're not backing out of riding, Maxine. This is Butter. She's fifteen, if she's a day, which is ancient in horse years. She won't be bolting anywhere. In fact, she can't see well enough to do more than follow the tail of the horse ahead of you."

Max stroked the mare's velvety nose, and

then the white whiskers beneath the mare's chin. "She's darling."

"It's the closest you'll get to a horse with training wheels." Bo still had hold of Butter's reins. "Get on up. I'll hold her until you're ready."

"Thanks." Max did just that. Once in the saddle, she accepted Bo's help to slide her booted feet into the stirrups. "I'm sorry we had a poor showing earlier." Although he'd apologized for the aftermath, Max hadn't commiserated on the outcome.

Bo scoffed, tipping the brim of his hat back and looking up at her with an almost smile. "It was my fault. Thanks for not rubbing my lack of roping skill in my face."

"What happens on Team Beauregard stays with Team Beauregard." Max stared down on Bo's handsome face. She bet more than half the female population wouldn't notice the disappointment in those warm gray eyes. Or the small scar near his right ear.

"Wait here while I take Spot indoors. And then I'll collect my horse and we can go." He called Spot and jogged across the yard, disappearing inside the house with his big white dog, only to quickly reappear without him.

"Can we go?" Davey called out, seemingly to no one in particular.

"Not yet," Shane called from inside the barn. He led a dark horse out.

"Those kids won't wait much longer for the adults to get moving." Bo went into the barn, returning a few minutes later with a big brown horse that tossed his head and jingled the bit in his mouth. He led him next to Butter. "This is Rabbit. He likes going fast. We're going to use him for the skiing challenge day after tomorrow."

"Skiing?" Max grimaced. "I'm afraid the one time I tried to ski, I fell every few feet going down the bunny slope. Why couldn't it have been a sled pull?"

"It's not traditional skiing, remember?" Bo swung into the saddle, an action that had the horse prancing and Max worrying. Bo spoke to the horse softly, too low for Max to hear. But he wasn't just giving Rabbit verbal instructions. He shifted in the saddle, working the reins back and forth until the horse calmed.

Bo gave Rabbit's long neck a pat and continued his conversation with Max as if everything was under control and always had been. "One of us will be on horseback in this race. One of us will be towed behind while on skis, carrying a pumpkin. Luna will be waiting on the far side of the meadow. She'll make the base of the snowman while we ski across. Then we put the pumpkin on top of the snowman as its head."

Max took a moment for the details of the competition to sink in. "What warped mind came up with this challenge?"

"That would be little Adam, Luna's favorite cowboy." Bo grinned. "My grandfather would label him a holiday challenge genius."

Max shook her head. "This can't be an event. Where are they getting all the skis?" Not to mention ski boots that fit the competitors.

Rabbit tossed his head and pranced a little, expressing impatience to get on with it.

Bo walked him in a tight circle before returning him to a place next to Max and Butter. "There's a guy in town—Egbert. He rents fishing equipment in the summer, and snowshoes and cross-country skis in the winter." Bo gestured for younger riders to head out ahead of them. "Weren't you listening to that part of the discussion last night?"

"No." Max must have missed that detail when she'd been agonizing over Bo having no one on his team. "Is this a large pumpkin the skier carries? I assume so since it's the size of a head."

"I guess?" He shrugged those broad shoulders, seemingly unconcerned with logistics or the activity itself. "I haven't seen any pumpkins."

"And Luna's supposed to make the body of a snowman to put this pumpkin on?" Doubts flitted through Max's mind. What if the snow wasn't soft? What if Luna couldn't make the base big enough? "Maybe I should make the snowman. Luna can ride the horse."

Bo frowned. "Someone's got to make Rabbit go, go fast, and go in the right direction. Not to mention, stay on." As if to prove his point, his horse tossed his head and leaped sideways. It took Bo another moment to settle Rabbit down.

"Luna isn't riding that horse," Max said firmly. "But the snowman... It's just that she's so little compared to the other kids, except Adam. I don't want to pressure her about making a snowman, which should only ever be fun."

"Maxine, your daughter has the heart of a champion. And besides..." Bo grinned. "She only needs to make a base for the pumpkin.

We're being judged on speed, not the quality, height or strength of the snowman."

That was a relief.

The party set out at a walk in clusters of two and three. Max held on to the reins, but it seemed more like a formality than anything. Butter plodded along in a rut made by the tires of vehicles coming up and down the driveway.

The snow on the ground and blanketing the trees was a crisp white. The wind scattered bits of snow from tall tree branches, occasionally making it look like it was snowing. The children rode in front, their laughter filling the air, mingling with adult voices and the occasional deep chuckle.

This is what all holidays should feel like.

Warm and encompassing. Sparkly and fun.

Don't get carried away. You're not one of them.

Them. The wealthy, famous Monroes who lived lives completely different from hers.

"This is fun, isn't it?" Bo reached over and poked Max's shoulder with a finger. "Riding in the midst of a big family."

Had he read her thoughts? Did he know how tempting this situation was for a woman with no strong family ties? "You know it is."

"Of course it is." Bo chuckled. "Admit it. A part of you wants to be back at the house with Gertie, cleaning or making lunch or something that is divorced from the action."

"Riding or doing housework, both options have their benefits," Max said staunchly. "I'd have a good time either way."

Instead of arguing with her, Bo chuckled.

His cousin Olivia brought her horse even with theirs. She had brown curls similar to Max's but hers were short and crushed beneath a straw cowboy hat. "Hey, Bo. What's this I hear about a *plan* to fall in love?"

Max sucked in a lungful of cold air, momentarily rendered speechless by Olivia's bluntness.

Bo took it all in stride. "Considering your career and love life have been all over the place, I don't think you should tease a man for taking a more controlled approach to his future."

Behind them, Shane laughed and was immediately shushed by Franny.

"You may be an engineer, Bo," Olivia said in a voice that rang with a command and confidence Max envied. "But you're smart enough to know that love doesn't follow an instruction manual."

"I never said it did." There was color high in Bo's cheeks, although that might be attributed to the chill temperature and brisk wind. "You'll apologize to me next year when I find the woman of my dreams, especially when you realize I only found her because I wrote things down and directed my intention toward making my dreams a reality."

Max wished herself back at the house. The conversation was too personal. And not just for Bo.

Olivia's gaze connected with Max's. "Well, from what I hear, you didn't plan on hosting Max."

"That was a…" Bo faltered.

"Misunderstanding?" Max finished for him.

"No." Bo held up a finger, frowning while Wyatt and Ashley laughed at some private joke.

Olivia was determined to prove her point. "Bo, the person of your dreams is never the one you dream about at night."

Bummer. Max had dreamed of kissing Bo last night. It had been a pleasant dream, and she'd woken up late, still in the fog of a happily-ever-after.

"The person you're meant to be with is the person who shows up," Olivia continued, tossing a smile over her shoulder to Rhett. "The person who has your back in good times and bad."

"The one who forgives you when you make a mistake," Bo said, sounding like he was pointing out that Olivia had made her share of errors by calling out something specific.

"Exactly." Instead of taking offense, Olivia beamed. "Take my advice. Ditch those plans, Romeo."

"Thanks for weighing in, cousin." Bo sat tall in the saddle, taking the ribbing the way he'd taken the lack of Monroe team members the night before, with a quiet air of class. "Now's a good time to remind you that this morning's fifth place contestants get first pick of the sleighs to decorate."

"Sweet," Max said happily. "And there's our silver lining."

Bo grinned at her.

"Do these sleighs get hitched to horses or reindeer or...?" Max couldn't remember that detail.

"We can hitch our sleigh to whatever we want, which makes choosing a sleigh a tactical decision."

Olivia scoffed. "Are you trying to make me nervous? I know you. In the end, you'll just pick the biggest sleigh since it will stand out the most." She leaned forward in the saddle to catch Max's eye once more. "I hope you bring some design ideas because I've seen where Bo lives. If he has his way, he'll decorate the sleigh predictably and sparsely—with red ribbon and pine boughs."

"Not to mention jingle bells," Bo added darkly, obviously having been pegged correctly.

"Thanks for the tip," Max said crisply. "But I think you'll find Bo has a more strategic approach to the competition this year."

Max was going to make certain of it.

"WE'RE NOT TAKING that small sleigh." Bo had a hard time keeping his voice down as he argued with Maxine, blaming their disagreement on Olivia's prediction of his preference in sleighs. "Haven't you ever heard of the phrase *go big or go home*?"

Maxine rolled her eyes, then adjusted her glasses. "Didn't we just have this conversation with Olivia on the way here? Do you want to be predictable? Or take on such a large task?"

They stood among five sleighs Shane had procured. They'd been placed on the side of the meadow nearest the drive, flanked by a small lake and the cluster of cabins Bo had helped refurbish last spring. The rest of the Monroes stood with the horses at the gate, giving Bo, Maxine and Luna time to look at their options alone.

"I just want to win," Bo mumbled, passing a hand over the curve of the largest sleigh he'd ever seen. "Doesn't this sleigh look like a winner?"

Who knew where Shane had gotten five sleighs on such short notice. Who knew where he'd have gotten more than five if more Monroes had been interested in joining the challenge. Shane wasn't saying. Not that Bo cared.

What he cared about was the large, well-preserved sleigh with bright red paint. It had two bench seats and gleaming silver rails. It was better than a similar sleigh with only one bench and chipped green paint. It was superior to the other two sleighs that looked like they'd barely seat a driver, one of which Maxine wanted. And it was leagues ahead of the sleigh that was nothing more than a sled, looking like it had been cobbled together with boards recycled from wooden pallets.

"I like this one," Luna called from the

sleigh Maxine preferred. Someone had stenciled Santa's face on the side.

"Are you going to take all day?" Jonah called.

"Do we need to set a time limit on decisions?" Shane shouted next.

"Bo." Maxine took her hands from her jacket pockets and placed her warm palms on his cold cheeks. "Today is Sunday. There are daily challenges between now and then, plus you'll probably want to tour homes. That all takes time. The bigger sleigh is going to require more decorations. I've been in the general store. There aren't a lot of decorations to be had in town." She rubbed her palms back and forth over his cheeks, as if trying to warm them. "Choose wisely based on our resources and skill set."

She was right. Didn't mean Bo was ready to agree with her though. If he did, she'd pull away. And he didn't want her to stop touching him.

"Do you have previous experience decorating sleighs?" he asked her.

Maxine shook her head. "Do you know the criteria judges are going to use to choose a winner?"

Great question. "No clue."

"This one," Luna called out again, bouncing up and down on the seat of the small sleigh.

"Pick a sleigh already." Davey sounded put out.

Laughter filled the air, taking Bo back to days when he was Davey's age and had looked forward to each family challenge as a chance for victory and glory. Why was it that when he looked into Maxine's eyes, victory and glory didn't seem as important as the ability to make her smile?

"We're a team." He smiled down at Maxine. "I will take that smaller sleigh on the recommendation of my chief strategy officer."

"Good." Her hands fell away, but her gaze stayed trained on Bo's. "Beauregard, I feel the need to remind you that you have plans in the new year. Plans that don't—"

"Let's take one day at a time, Maxine Marie." Because it was becoming apparent to him that winning her affection would be a slow campaign up an icy slope. "Luna, you can make the announcement about the sleigh we chose."

"It's this one," Luna cried and not from the sleigh Maxine favored. Unbeknownst to himself and her mother, she'd climbed into the low sleigh without much siding that looked like it had been built from a wooden pallet.

"Finally!" Adam shouted.

"Wait." Bo rushed over to lift Luna and put her into the small sleigh Maxine wanted. "We want this one."

"Too late," Jonah called. "There are no backsies. No do-overs. No flubs and scrubs."

"Come on, man." Bo gritted his teeth until his jaw popped.

"Sorry, Charlie." Charlie guffawed the way young boys did, as if they'd never heard anything more hilarious in their life.

"Don't you like my choice, Bo?" When Luna blinked those big innocent eyes he couldn't hold a grudge, even though Bo felt hamstrung by her choice.

"It's more like a sled than a sleigh," Bo said with a sigh. A homemade sled made by someone who had no clue what they were doing. His engineering brain loathed it.

"That's why I like it," Luna said brightly.

"We'll make it work." Maxine drew Bo toward their choice. "There's nothing in the rules that says we can't add siding, right? Or anything to make this more interesting?"

"Rules?" Bo set Luna back down in their cheaply made sleigh. "What rules?"

"Right?" Maxine hooked her arm through his. "That's the spirit."

"I love it." Luna climbed out of the ramshackle sleigh and nearly fell face-first in the snow. "And I love Mama and Bo."

Aww. Bo felt all the feels, the warm snuggly feels that he assumed parents felt for their children.

Had he been mad about the mix-up? Bo felt none of that frustration now. There was just himself and Maxine and Luna, staring at opportunity, snubbing their noses at jokes made at their expense. They were united in this challenge. And perhaps that unity would extend past Thanksgiving.

What about my life plans?

With a slow shift of his arm, Bo brought Maxine closer. "Rules?" he said gently. "Who cares about rules? They're more like guidelines anyway."

Kind of like his life plans were turning out to be.

CHAPTER TEN

"WHAT DOES IT say about our sleigh choice that you and I could lift it into and out of my truck bed?" Bo scowled as they set down their wooden sleigh in a small shed near the bunkhouse.

"It says advantage Team Bo." Max dusted her hands off on her jeans, found Bo's hand and gave it a squeeze. "It says go with your gut and create something unique in this elements-protected environment."

Bo frowned, staring at it.

Poor Bo. Reality had set in. He hadn't wanted to pull their sleigh behind him on horseback for fear it would fall apart. And it needed serious structural work that couldn't be completed without tools and materials. So they'd ridden back to the ranch proper, and then driven his truck to collect it.

The other teams had left their sleighs in the snowy meadow underneath canvas tarps.

They planned to decorate them there, covering their work each night.

"I know Luna pulled a fast one, but I'm sure we can turn this lemon into lemonade." She squeezed his hand once more.

"Lemonade?" Bo slipped his hand free, placed one foot on the bench seat and pressed some of his weight on it.

The wood cracked.

"Careful." Max grabbed a handful of his shearling coat and drew him back. "If it breaks, we'll be building a sled from scratch."

"At this point, that might be a better plan." Bo removed his cowboy hat and rubbed a hand over his dark hair.

Max's hands itched to do the same. That was unwise. Look at the sparks she'd set off between them when she'd caressed his cheeks in the meadow.

She shoved her hands in her coat pockets. "Count down the days, Bo."

"Until what?" Bo mashed his hat back on his head. "Our defeat?"

"That's enough of that talk. You may have lost a few competitions when you were younger. But that was then." She spotted a bench nearby and dragged it closer. "Have a seat and let's brainstorm our way out of this."

Bo sat next to her, frustration radiating from him like a steaming pot of pasta.

Max's stomach growled, earning her a sharp look from her team captain. "We should hydrate and eat." She hadn't had any cookies today. Or pie. "I always think better on a full stomach. And then we can approach this problem with a fresh perspective."

Bo grunted, not moving, returning his gaze to the sleigh. "It's not safe for one person, let alone three."

"All right. If we aren't going to eat..." Her stomach protested that statement. "...feel free to get out all the negatives so we can start anew."

"Structurally unsound. Possible wood rot. Too small. Too unwieldy. Too homely." He wasted no time dumping on their sleigh. "If we had a few days, some wood and paint, we might be able to turn it into a lawn feature, one that doesn't look bad under a soft spotlight at night."

"Please, don't stop there," she told him when he paused to take a breath. "That's the first positive idea you've had for it."

"Positive? Show me the positives. From an engineering perspective, this looks like a total tear-down." Despite that one bright note, he sounded gloomier and gloomier by the minute. "The runners are bent and flimsy. The more I look at it, the more I believe it was someone's oversize sled, not a sleigh. And it's been ridden hard, probably crashed a time or two in the snowbank."

"Are you done?" She shrugged deeper in her jacket, hoping so. "You're drifting into the past, like you did earlier when you turned your back on me."

He blinked at her, really seeing her instead of that stupid sleigh.

"Okay, Scrooge. Now that we've listed everything about our sleigh's Christmas Past and Present, let's talk about its future."

"It has one?" Bo frowned, rubbing his jaw.

"Unless you want to withdraw from the competition, it has to have a Christmas Future, and a bright future at that." Max paused until Bo nodded, then she added, "Paint is a must." She preferred something along the lines of Santa Claus Red, if there was such a color.

"If you want paint, we'd need to heat this shed because you can't paint when the temperature drops below fifty degrees."

"Right." Good thing he knew that. "They had paint at the general store." The store had a wide variety of goods from chainsaw lubrication to nasal spray.

"Limited paint colors, but yeah." Bo nodded, still talking in that distant way, as if half his brain was wrestling with the sleigh structure. "Mack sells a little of everything at the general store."

"Lights are also a must," Max told him. "I saw some pretty strands of lights that were battery-powered. We need to buy them before someone else does."

"I suppose I'll need to straighten the rails and shore up the frame," Bo said with a resigned sigh, possibly signaling the end of his doldrums.

Now was the time for levity. "We can play to your traditional sensibilities with some red ribbon and pine boughs."

He smirked. "Hardy-har. Olivia would applaud that suggestion."

"She'll applaud us when we win." And if that wasn't over-promising, Max didn't know what was.

"Miss Optimistic." Bo turned on the bench, angling so he faced her, grinning as if they'd selected the big sleigh he wanted, not this piece of junk. "How did I get so lucky to have you on my team?"

"I believe you mentioned that you owed my cousin Nathan a favor." Max played it cool, but her heart was pounding because the most handsome man she'd ever met was looking into her eyes as if he had kissing on his mind.

She drew a slow breath and reminded herself that she was Maxine Holloway, the orphan no one kept around. This moment... That look... It was all as temporary as her entering the Monroe Holiday Challenge on an annual basis.

"We need to get organized," she managed to say to the man who planned his life down to when he was going to find a woman to love. "To repair the sleigh, I mean."

"Organize..." Bo murmured, his gaze dropping to her lips.

My lips!

"Oops." A petite blonde stood in the open shed doorway, somehow managing to sneak up on them while walking in inches of snow. She backed up a few steps. "I'm interrupting."

"No." Max rocketed to her feet, trying to remember the woman's name. "Elle, is it?"

"Ella." She wore a navy stadium jacket and fur-lined snow boots. Her blond bangs peeked out from beneath a blue knit cap. She fussed

with them, brushing the hair from her eyes. "I was married to Bo's cousin Bryce."

"Oh, that's right." Max scanned her memory for the details. "Except you divorced and now you're with…" A tall, silent type.

"Bryce died a couple years ago." Bo waved Ella inside. "Come in out of the wind."

"Right. Sorry." Max sat back down on the bench, mortified that she'd flubbed such an important detail as Ella's widowhood. "There are just so many Monroes to keep track of."

"It's okay." Ella's soft smile confirmed that she wasn't upset over Max's poor recall. "I stopped by because Mitch…" Her smile broadened a little. "I remember when I was new to the family. Mitch is married to Laurel and runs the Lodgepole Inn. He's been working on getting places in town declared as having historical significance to protect Second Chance from being developed as one of those soulless, luxury retreats."

Max nodded, acknowledging this information with a small, "Oh, I met them." Laurel and Mitch toted around those adorable twin baby girls, the ones that made Max long for another baby of her own, one with hair a deep walnut brown and eyes a soft, caring gray.

Ella turned to Bo. "Anyway, Mitch told me you'd discovered a log cabin. And when I checked the town map, there wasn't a cabin listed in the location he referenced, which might not be odd, except that since Grandpa Harlan bought up the property, it should have been listed there."

Bo and Max nodded slowly, the way people do when they don't really understand the point of the information being imparted.

At least, in this we're a team.

"And I'm confusing you. Sorry." Ella held up a hand. "Let me start over. When I came to Second Chance in January, I started to do an assessment of all the properties so that the family would know what everything was worth. And almost first thing, I discovered that a cabin that was supposedly in town wasn't in town. There was just an empty lot." She caught her breath. "So when you found a cabin that wasn't supposed to be there—on paper, at least—it made me wonder if that's the missing cabin. You know, if it had been moved."

Bo tipped his cowboy hat back. "That might explain the wonky floors."

"Why is this missing cabin so important?"

Max wondered aloud, thinking that she'd seen a few abandoned, one room log cabins on the drive up.

"Well, it turns out that the original cabin in town was where Harlan was born." Ella stuck her hands in her jacket pockets, looking a bit uncertain and teary-eyed. "It would be nice to know if the moved cabin was his cabin. For me, at least. He was always kind to me, even after Bryce died."

"It felt like Grandpa Harlan inside." Bo recalled the thought. He stared into Max's eyes. "And I'd like to know, too. Everyone who had a lease with him also signed a non-disclosure agreement. If they know, they can't tell us until January."

Ella nodded. "I'd like to see the cabin while I'm here sometime."

"Sure. You don't need my permission," Bo said gently, as if he considered Ella somewhat fragile. He told her where to find the key. "But it would be cool if we all went together, as a family." He said this to Ella, not Max.

It was a reminder of her place. Max swallowed and took a half step back.

"Thanks so much." Ella's gaze fell to the sleigh. "Bryce told me about the challenge."

"And about me losing, I suppose," Bo said, sinking once more into glum territory.

Max poked him in the back. "I'm getting weary of this glass half-empty attitude of yours."

"I'm going to win this year," Bo said with what sounded like complete sincerity. "Win or lose, I *love* the challenge and my team."

"So much better," Max murmured.

"For the record, Bryce didn't mention who won or lost." Ella's smile was bittersweet. "He talked about how fun it was to play as if you weren't the high and mighty Monroes. He said those trips you all took and those challenges at the holidays made him feel like any other kid, not one in the spotlight." She drew a labored breath, eyes bright. "Bryce was always able to slip into a tuxedo as if it was a second skin, but deep down he wanted to be an everyday Joe. I think he had Grandpa Harlan to thank for letting him know how that felt, instead of just living life with a silver spoon in his mouth."

Max blinked back sudden tears and she hadn't even known Harlan Monroe.

But he seemed like a good man, one who

would have stepped up and raised his granddaughter if she'd been orphaned.

Bo's gaze turned distant and his farewell to Ella was barely a murmur, as if he, too, was touched.

Adam scampered in, followed by Luna. He circled their sleigh in less than ten steps, before striking a lofty pose at the back, propping his fists on his hips. "Our sleigh is bigger than your sleigh."

"We know," Bo nodded, gradually returning to the present.

"Aunty Em is going to sparkle our horse and sleigh." Adam was full of information and more than willing to spread it. "Mom and Papa Shane are going to have a matched set of horses pull their sleigh across the meadow. And Ashley…" Adam pouted. "Their team wouldn't tell me what they were doing."

"They said it'd be pretty," Luna piped up. "Like Cinderella's pumpkin."

Adam was scornful of this information. "What does Cinderella have to do with sleighs? Besides, they're already married." He butted his boot toe against one of their bent rails. "This is tiny."

"Like me," Luna said brightly, ever the optimist. "It's just my size."

Max's gaze flew to Bo's and she knew he was thinking what she was thinking.

Their sleigh was a child's sleigh. Just Luna's size.

"Why overthink it?" Max murmured with the beginnings of a smile.

Bo returned that smile and upped her an eye twinkle. "My thoughts exactly."

WHY OVERTHINK IT?

Maxine's words to Bo stayed with him long into the day and well into the evening. He tossed and turned on the couch seeking sleep and disturbing Spot.

Her words had been spoken in regard to the sleigh, but the sentiment lingered for other reasons. Were his plans to become a good marriage candidate overthinking things? He kept circling around that idea every time he was with Maxine. And when he wasn't with her, the security of plans took firm hold on his thoughts.

Bo gave up on sleep and headed toward the kitchen where someone was banging around as if dinner was being made. Spot padded behind him.

They found Gertie in the kitchen. Short gray hair askew, she had three large, steaming pots on the stove and something cooking in the oven. She wore a frilly red apron that said, Retired But Still Baking. And she didn't seem to care that it was steamier than a sauna in the kitchen.

"What are you doing in here so late?" Bo went to open a window while Spot retreated to the kitchen doorway, panting.

The old woman swatted at Bo with a dish towel trimmed with appliqués of fall leaves, giving a hint as to her prickly mood. "Have you ever fed a crowd of forty? I bet not or you wouldn't be asking me what I'm doing in the kitchen days before Thanksgiving."

"You're not boiling turkeys, are you?" Bo peered into the steaming pots, but they were all liquid.

"I'm making the brine for the turkeys. Plural. As in three." Gertie thrust out her chin and blew a breath upward, ruffling her short bangs.

"Can I help? Or roust Franny or Emily out of bed." Surely, someone should be helping the ranch matriarch.

"Too late for that." She gestured to several small canisters of seasonings on the counter. "I'm about to add salt and my secret blend of seasoning to each pot. Then all I have to do is keep them at a slow boil so everything dissolves and blends together."

"Okay. I can make coffee and help you put the turkeys in the brine." This seemed like a marathon task.

"Pfft." Gertie swatted Bo's leg with her dish towel. "I won't put the turkeys in the brine until Wednesday. Go back to bed."

"No. Why are you making brine in the middle of the night days ahead of time?"

Gertie crumpled the dish towel in her hands, expression giving way from playful annoyance to stress. "Because there's people to be fed, the challenge going on and everything that needs to be organized for it. I'll start making pies tomorrow, Wednesday the turkeys start their soak and I'll make rolls."

He leaned against the end of the countertop, reaching over to pat Spot's head, considering Gertie's reaction if he tried to give her a supportive hug. "That sounds like a lot of work. Why won't you let anyone help you?" He was certain Emily or Franny would pitch in if the old woman let them.

Gertie huffed, shaking herself the way a chicken did after its feathers had been ruffled. "After having a stroke and fighting my way back, I'm thrilled to be cooking. It may be labor, but it's a labor of love. Nobody's going to take that from me."

Spot sniffed the air and apparently decided his bed was calling. He disappeared, heading toward the living room and the couch they shared.

"Now, speaking of *love*..." Gertie gave Bo a sly glance. "The L-word and having you here brings Max to mind. You took her house hunting yesterday."

Bo leaned back and gave Gertie an incredulous look that he hoped said, *You're going to go there?*

She chuckled and opened the oven door, revealing sheets of what smelled like gingerbread.

"Don't tell me Shane wrangled you into making gingerbread for the houses?" Bo was shocked. "Franny and Emily could have made that. Or Cam and Ivy down at the diner."

Gertie scoffed. "Those gingerbread houses have to be put together before Wednesday and no one else volunteered." She closed the oven door and faced him, so much determination in the furrow in her brow that he held up his hands in surrender. "Don't feel sorry for me because I'm busy. I have a talent in the kitchen and with the knitting needle. People still want me around and..." She narrowed her eyes as she considered him. "You understand about pride, don't you?"

He nodded, not that he'd admit he'd been given more than his share. "But Gertie, pride gets in the way just as much as it lifts a person up and drives them ahead." He pointed at the time on the microwave. It was near midnight. "Much as I appreciate this heart-to-heart, six a.m. comes awful early in the morning at a ranch, honey. It's time to call it a day."

"Honey?" Gertie rolled her eyes. "Shouldn't you be calling Max honey?"

Wasn't it too late for an inquisition?

"You—and everyone else—need to slow down on the Max thing." Bo ran a hand over his face, wanting to heed his own advice. "There's a reason we spend a lot of time together. Maxine volunteered for my team. And as for the house hunting, it was the polite thing to do. A host keeps their guest entertained."

"Ha!" Gertie twirled her kitchen towel as if contemplating giving Bo another playful swat. "Shopping for a home is very personal. Not the kind of activity you bring a guest along for. And I've seen the way you two look at each other."

Bo knew how he looked at Maxine, but he was unaware anyone else was picking up on those signals.

"By her decree, Maxine and I are just friends." Without time or privacy to explore anything else. "I value her opinion. She's got three degrees, you know."

"Yes, she's told me." Gertie peered in her steaming pots. "But for all that book learning, Max lacks a worldview. A man like you can break her heart without realizing it."

"A man like me..." He'd been trying to go slow, to respect her boundaries and honor his plans. To keep in mind that she wasn't looking for more than a place to enjoy the holidays and pine over the dynamics of a large, close-knit family.

"You know what I mean." Gertie turned, playfully swatting Bo's leg with a dish towel. "For a Monroe, you're sluggish on the uptake. Max is here today and gone tomorrow unless you do something about it."

"That's my cue to head back to bed." Bo confiscated the dish towel when the old woman made another pass at him. "Promise you won't stay up much longer. You're getting loopy and swinging this towel too much."

He folded the dish towel and laid it on the counter.

"You may be right about the dish towel." Gertie put a hand on his arm, staying his exit. "But about you and Max… I don't want to see you get hurt."

Bo did a double-take. "I thought you were concerned with Maxine's heart, not mine."

"That was before you were so emphatically denying everything." Gertie tapped his chest with her fingers. "You two can say there's nothing between you, but those feelings inside won't go away."

"They won't go anywhere if those feelings aren't in sync." He gave Gertie's hand a squeeze. "Maybe it's better this way. I've created my vision, my plan, for falling in love. The when. The where. And the who."

And sadly, Second Chance and Maxine didn't meet any of his criteria.

Not a one.

CHAPTER ELEVEN

"WELCOME TO THE scarecrow making competition." Holden was getting into the swing of being emcee. He held up both arms by way of greeting.

Bo stood with Maxine, Luna and the other Monroes. It was Monday morning, Day Two of the competition, and the teams were assembled in the breezeway of the Bucking Bull's barn. A couple of hay bales had been brought down from the loft to use as stuffing and they'd all been given leather work gloves.

Bo hadn't seen much of Maxine or Luna that morning. He'd been working on making the shed into an operational sleigh workshop, running extension cords from the barn and tracking down tools he'd need, along with a heater.

"Thanks to Gertie, Odette and Flip, our notable seamstresses, for making the scarecrows." Holden held one up.

The scarecrow had a head made out of a

burlap sack with friendly features sewn on its face—triangular eyes, a button nose, a broad smile. The burlap sack was stitched to the collar of a long sleeve shirt, the tails of which in turn were sewn to the waistband of a pair of blue jeans.

"Cute," Maxine said.

Bo supposed the stuffed scarecrows would look interesting decorating a porch or a field next spring.

Holden handed his example scarecrow to Adam. "Each team will stuff the scarecrow with straw, button up the chest and tie its wrists and ankles closed. When your scarecrow is finished, you'll hang him on the horseshoe outside of a stall. Any stall. But listen up. This is important. Although anyone can button up a scarecrow's shirt, the youngest person on your team *must* do all the stuffing. One adult can hand their stuffer straw but can't put it inside the scarecrow. If anyone is caught cheating, they'll need to remove four handfuls of straw."

A few Monroes griped about the harsh punishment, but Bo thought it was fair.

He and his team walked to their stuffing station.

"You know what to do, right, Luna?" Maxine picked up a handful of straw and pretended to stuff it inside the scarecrow's unbuttoned shirt and then down a pants leg. "It's just like when you stuff your dirty clothes in the laundry bag back home."

"What a great way of putting it." Bo gave one of Luna's curling pigtails a gentle tug. "It's just you and me this time." He and Maxine had come to an agreement on their strategy a few minutes ago. She'd wanted to compete with her daughter but he wanted to redeem himself. "If you work fast, you can beat all your cowboy friends."

"What about her?" Luna pointed to Gabby, who was the oldest of the child competitors at twelve.

"Gabby?" Bo scoffed. "You're going to leave her in the dust."

"You wish." Gabby tossed her strawberry blond hair over one shoulder. She may only be a Monroe by her father's marriage, but the tween had the Monroe swagger down.

"Are you sure you don't want me to feed Luna handfuls of hay?" Maxine's brow was lined with worry.

"Look." Bo held up one hand, fingers splayed. "My hands are bigger than yours. They hold more straw."

"More isn't better, you know," Maxine whispered. "They didn't say anything about fullness or density." She glanced around as if to make sure she hadn't been overheard. "A thin scarecrow can win in less time than it takes to stuff a plump one."

"Excellent point," he whispered back, pleased to see that no one seemed to have noticed her advice. "Now we have a strategy. You really are good at this."

"Thanks." Maxine kissed Luna's cheek. "Have fun, honey."

"Have fun and play hard," Bo said to the little girl. "I'm going to be feeding you lots of straw, real fast, over and over again."

"Got it." Luna gave him a thumbs-up.

"It's not just about..." Maxine cut herself off, drew a breath and righted her round glasses. "Okay, for you, it is about winning. But just remember though that we're here for the fun. You should have fun, too."

"I'll try," he said, thinking if she was in his life more things might be fun.

"Players, take your positions." Holden clapped his hands.

Bo got down on his knees next to Luna. Maxine moved back to give them room.

"On your marks. Get set. Stuff those scarecrows!"

Cheers rose up from the spectators. At the swelling of noise, the horses in the barn backed deeper into their stalls.

Bo piled straw into Luna's little hands. Half the straw fell, fluttering onto the scarecrow's shirt. But Bo had accounted for that. He shoved his hands into a hay flake and pivoted back to Luna. "Here you go."

Bless her heart, she had her hands cupped and ready.

Again, just as much straw stayed in her little hands as fell on their scarecrow.

Luna's features were scrunched. Her movements quick. "Stuff. The. Laundry."

"Stuff the laundry." Bo took up his partner's mantra. Grabbing more straw. Pivoting back. "Stuff the laundry." Just not too full.

They stuffed the head first, and then the pant legs. He let Luna continue putting straw in while he tied the ankles and wrists. And then it was on to the scarecrow's torso.

Bo spared a glance at their competition. Gabby was over-stuffing hers and still working on the legs.

"Keep going," Maxine called. "Stick to the plan."

And they did. Luna was a miniature cowgirl on a mission.

Bo fastened all the buttons and then leaped to his feet, dragging the scarecrow to a hitching hook and hanging him by a loop at the top of his head. "Done. We're done!"

Maxine came forward to hug Luna.

Bo swept both of them into his arms and twirled them around. "We won!"

The other teams spared them little attention. They continued to stuff.

"Your scarecrow is thin." Holden shook one blue sleeve.

"There's no stuffing standard," Bo was quick to counter, setting Maxine and Luna down.

"I suppose." Holden didn't look pleased.

"Stupid buttons!" Shane cried, attacking the task. "Why didn't we use Velcro?"

"Don't close it, Papa Shane. I haven't finished stuffing." Davey shoved straw past Shane's fumbling fingers.

"Thin scarecrows work," Shane reassured him. "Look at Bo's. Trust me."

"Nobody likes thin scarecrows." Gabby tossed a handful of straw toward Bo. "Gah!"

The remaining four teams closed up their scarecrows in seconds.

Shane and Davey came in second.

Wyatt and Gabby came in third.

Jonah and Adam came in fourth.

Rhett and Charlie came in last.

Bo couldn't have been happier. He reached for Luna and Maxine again, intending to swing them around in a second victory lap of sorts. But Luna had moved away, congratulating Adam on finishing his scarecrow. Only Maxine filled his arms.

Only Maxine.

Something panged inside of Bo, something that wanted to disregard plans and reasons they shouldn't be more than friends.

Maxine didn't seem like an only. Or a friend. Nothing like what he'd claimed she was, last night to Gertie.

And despite the cautions Gertie had made. Despite all his good intentions. Bo set Maxine down but didn't immediately release her, letting emotion guide him. "Do you feel like ice cream? Winning deserves ice cream." He pressed a quick, joyful kiss on her nose.

Was it too much?

His arms fell away, and he looked deep into her eyes, wondering if she'd think he'd crossed a line. "Hey, um. There's a rumor about an empty chalet south of town. We should get a milkshake, Maxine, and take a look. What do you say?"

"YOU SHOULD BE HAPPY, BO." Max slurped her pumpkin spice milkshake, the one they'd picked up at the Bent Nickel, which made milkshakes from real ice cream. She was trying not to dwell on one thought: *Bo kissed me!*

Because it had been a chaste kiss. And a kiss he'd obviously regretted since he'd run on afterward as if he was nervous. But still...

Beauregard Franklin Monroe kissed me!

Max drew a calming breath. It was vitally important for her peace of mind that she act like his lips on her skin was no big deal. "You won, Bo. Have you ever won an event before?"

"Never." Bo's French vanilla milkshake sat untouched in the drink holder of his truck.

It might have been her imagination, but he seemed to be leaning away from the center of the truck and away from her. That seemed at odds with his celebratory peck.

Luna was in the back seat chattering with Spot as they drove toward the chalet Bo wanted to check out. He'd been quiet most of the drive. Or more accurately, since he'd planted that wisp of a kiss on her nose.

A kiss every Monroe in the competition seemed to have noticed, because after Bo walked off, Jonah had said to no one in particular, "Bo is more complicated than he seems."

And Shane had told Gabby, "You should always pay attention to what a man does, not what he says."

And Gertie had taken Max's hand and given it a squeeze. "Stay grounded."

Stay grounded? Max's feet had barely touched the ground since.

But to let Bo know she'd been moved? That would only lead to embarrassment and awkwardness. Max had to treat him the way she'd been treating him since that mix-up in the airport.

She turned in the passenger seat. "Are we going back to the cabin we saw first?"

"No. Different place." So curt. So grumpy. "It's around here somewhere."

Max smiled. "Are you going to tell me what's wrong with you or should I guess?"

Do you have kissing on your mind?

Max sucked on her milkshake to keep from grinning.

Bo cast her a look that seemed to say she knew what was bothering him and shouldn't bring it up.

Oh. Max swallowed nervously. But still… She had to keep Bo engaged because… because… Max wasn't sure why she couldn't let him sit and think about what had happened. She just knew that silence wasn't acceptable. "I'm guessing you're worried about skiing tomorrow."

"No, Mama," Luna piped up from the back. "Bo thinks our scarecrow is too skinny. Even Adam said so when they put them around the porch."

The five scarecrows had been placed around the front porch, as if they were hanging out together—on the steps, on chairs, and one was propped and tied on a porch railing. It made everything feel like fall and Thanksgiving, even if the entire ranch was blanketed in snow.

"I'm not worried about our scarecrow," Bo reassured Luna. "Or the competition tomorrow."

"We need a strategy for skiing." Max chewed on her bottom lip, all thoughts of kisses fading. "Do I have to ride Rabbit?" The big, brown, skittish horse.

Bo glanced at her. "You're scared to ride fast."

"Obviously." She felt heat flood her cheeks. She wasn't used to trying things so far out of her element. "I'm also scared of falling off."

"We'll get you a riding helmet," he assured her, less uptight than before.

That didn't make Max feel any more confident. "We should practice snowman-making somewhere."

"Why?" He reached for his milkshake, leaning an elbow on the center console.

"Inexperience?" Max was torn between being pleased that Bo was loosening up and being anxious about the challenge tomorrow. "The last time we went to the snow and tried to build a snowman, Luna sat on a sled while I did the work." That was last winter.

"But I'm a big girl now, Mama."

"Yes, you are," Bo agreed. "Just look at how well you stuffed a scarecrow."

"I'm the best-est," Luna agreed. "Right, Spot?"

Spot panted. Luna yawned. And finally, the glow of Bo's innocent kiss faded, giving way to logic.

I live in another state. I have no future with this man.

How demoralizing was reality? Very. Max heaved a sigh.

"I think we're lost." Bo pulled over, checked traffic and turned around.

Max set her milkshake in the drink holder between them. "Here's the thing, Beauregard. That peck on the nose meant nothing to you or me." It helped to say it out loud.

Bo slowed the truck.

"I'm glad we're in agreement," Max said, resorting to her usual tactic of speaking first and setting boundaries.

Bo turned into what might have been a narrow lane or just space for a vehicle to drive through thick trees. Regardless, there were no tire tracks. If there was a house back in the woods, no one had been there in a long time.

"Bo?" He still hadn't answered Max about the kiss, and it was important to be realistic. "Bo?"

"There it is." He pointed.

A small house came into view. It had once been painted brown, with bright blue, gingerbread trim, but the paint was fading and chipped. In her mind's eye, Max could see it with bright colors and clean windows. There was just something about it that called to her, something hopeful and cheery.

They got out of the truck. Spot bounded ahead toward the door. Bo carried Luna.

We're like a family.

Max stopped in her tracks.

Family was something she longed for, but something she'd never been able to keep.

Bo was making plans for a family of his own. There was more to him than just his pretty face. He was generous and kind. Clever and driven. He'd never be satisfied with a meek mouse like Max, who was afraid to ride a galloping horse.

"Are you coming?" Bo set Luna down on the covered front porch, and turned back toward Max.

He was something, cowboy hat, strong cheekbones and broad shoulders aside. Although... He'd also be something in slacks and an ugly Christmas sweater. He'd be something when his hair was gray and his face wrinkled with age. He...

What am I doing?

Max clenched her hands to keep from naming the feelings barreling through her. She'd fallen under the spell of a man with whom love wasn't possible. What good was it to acknowledge longing and want?

Snap out of it.

"Maxine?" There was concern in Bo's voice. He retraced his steps through the snow to join her in front of his truck. "Is everything okay?"

Max knew she should nod and smile. She knew she should make her feet move forward and pretend nothing was wrong. But she couldn't. She couldn't move forward or back because...

"You kissed me," she blurted in a half-whisper when he was within touching distance.

"I did." He looked her up and down. "I got carried away by the win and I shouldn't have."

Right. This is good.

Max was able to nod and lick her lips, preparing to speak.

His gaze landed on her mouth and her heart thudded in her chest, and things that should have been straightforward suddenly became knotted and clogged. Arguments slowed to a stop in her brain. Words jammed to a halt in her throat. But she had to say something.

"I don't date," she whispered in a sluggish, heavy cadence. "I was hurt before."

His nod was slow, maybe even slower than hers had been a moment earlier. And his gaze was still on her lips as if he couldn't look away.

She wanted him to look away. She wanted all the pendulum-swinging feelings he created in her to settle and return to her control.

"I have a place in Missouri," she said when her wishes about feelings weren't obeyed. But as explanations went, that was lame. So she tried again. "I found a safe place. I'm appreciated there." At the university. Around town.

His brow wrinkled and his gray eyes darkened, but he continued to stare at her mouth, and she continued to be nervous about it.

"That's the thing. The... The thing that Clive didn't understand." Max swallowed, her mouth suddenly dry. "In Springfield... At Missouri State... They aren't going to wake up one morning and cast me out." She was welcome there, a sought-after graduate assistant who was eager to please.

Bo's gaze lifted to hers. "I understand."

Did he? Max struggled to draw a breath because she wasn't sure he did. "It's why—"

"It's why you keep getting degrees. That university is your family." He said it without derision or sarcasm. He spoke her truth as if cast-off orphans found their place in the world as continuing education graduate assistants all the time.

Speechless, Max nodded, staring into the

most beautiful pair of eyes on the planet and ruing the fact that in a few days she'd never look into those eyes again.

"Someday…" Bo said, in a voice as gentle as a caress. "Someday, you're going to realize that there are other families happy to take you in and keep you in the fold."

Max swallowed thickly, unable to express her disagreement—either verbally or with a headshake. That was how powerful a masterpiece Bo was. He made her want to agree with him, to believe that a man with everything—looks, connections, education, money—could be interested in a woman who was…who had…who was nothing like him.

Somewhere deep inside of her, in a place unrattled by things like physical masterpieces and all sorts of kisses, big and small, a teeny, tiny voice whispered a very small doubt: *this will end badly.*

But the rest of her… The rest of Max's entire being was hoping that wasn't true.

"You need to breathe, Maxine." Bo touched her cheek, barely a sweep of his finger over her skin. "I've been thinking about this thing between us, and I believe we need to let it breathe to see what it is, the way you do with fine wine."

She did shake her head then, a slow back and forth. There was a thing between them? She knew that already. Her surprise was that he felt it, too. That was too much to contemplate. *He* being interested in *her* was too much for her brain to process.

"Mama, are you all right?" Luna stood on the porch, frowning at them. She was bundled up in a borrowed blue jacket and wearing a borrowed straw cowboy hat, looking like she belonged.

It's me that doesn't belong.

Not here. Not with Bo.

"We'll be there in a second," Bo told Luna without turning. And then he lowered his voice so that only Max could hear, "I've got an idea, Maxine. I'm going to take your hand in mine and we're going to explore…"

Her breath hitched in her throat, hard, as if she was going to get a bad case of the hiccups.

"…that chalet."

She'd thought he was going to say explore a relationship, an idea that was stupid and hopeful and all wrong for two people with less than four days left to spend between them.

"This is like spring break," Max murmured, watching his hand find hers, feeling his fingers curl around hers, and still feeling lost in this detached sense of reality, like the world was slowing down because she needed to pay careful attention to what happened next.

"Spring break? It's November," Bo said softly, the way she recalled him talking to Rabbit when the horse had spooked for no reason.

Max was spooked, too. By whatever tenuous thing was unfolding on this crisp, sunny day.

Suddenly, words and thoughts pressed forward, demanding release. "When college students go on spring break, they look for love, hopeful they'll find a romance. One that might last even though they know it won't. It's temporary. This… This is exactly like spring break, except it's Thanksgiving."

"We're too old for spring break." He walked slowly backward, bringing her with him one deliberate step at a time.

"But we only have four days." The words escaped her in a near-shattered tone. She blinked back tears of unfortunate longing.

"Breathe," Bo instructed, gaze mesmerizing.

"But your plans…" Her defenses were as thin as the scarecrow he and Luna had stuffed, because she was reaching for straws—excuses to keep her heart safe, to keep it from being broken the way Clive had smashed it when he'd divorced her.

"Breathe," Bo said again as they reached the chalet's stairs.

And Max did breathe. She breathed in. She breathed out.

But try as she might, she still felt dazed and unsure.

Because she let Bo hold her hand as they walked through the house.

And not once did she heed the little voice in her head that warned her that all holidays came to an end.

CHAPTER TWELVE

"IS THIS OUR HOUSE, MAMA?" Luna called from upstairs.

The little girl and Spot were exploring, running about as if they had to be first in each room on the off chance that there were Easter eggs to discover.

Bo smiled a little, having discovered his surprise outside the empty house. There was nothing inside that interested him other than Maxine. His feelings for her ran deep. And he suspected hers did the same.

He kept her small hand enclosed in his as they drifted through the kitchen and into a small family room. The house was closed-off, boxy, brown. Thin, scalloped wood trim tried its best to carry off the impression the craftsmanship outside had made—that this was an authentic Swiss chalet.

He'd known two steps in that the house wasn't for him, a pace quicker than him knowing Maxine might be what his heart was searching for.

The logical part of his brain, the lobe he used to solve puzzles and mechanical problems, was reluctant to put a name to such feelings because he lacked proof. His theorem had been lined with check boxes—a house in Houston, a home in Second Chance, a steady job. All the outward trappings that a husband and good provider should have.

Maxine wanted none of that. She wanted family, emotional security, unconditional love. Things that couldn't be measured or checked off on a spreadsheet.

That fact scared him. Why? Because he wasn't sure he could convince her that he could give her what others had failed to provide—unconditional love.

His pulse was pounding quicker than it should.

But there was something about holding Maxine's hand in his that promised calmer times ahead.

If only...

He wasn't sure what their *if onlys* were or how to reassure her—and himself—that this connection between them would flourish and last. He'd dated and been in relationships where the initial attraction sparkled, then fizzled. This felt different. This felt real.

He stopped in front of the sliding glass door and looked outside. Snow piled on a wooden porch and its rails. Snow rolled across a broad backyard and over a swing set to the trees reaching toward the sun. There was no view of the mountains. No impression of grandeur. And yet, he didn't turn away.

Because Maxine's hand is in mine.

Above them, footsteps pounded across the floor.

He smiled and faced Maxine, taking in the delicate angles of her face, the ones mostly hidden behind her overly large glasses. "Who knew a little girl and a big dog could make so much noise?"

"Only everyone who has a little girl and a big dog," she retorted, having regained some of that sass he enjoyed so much. "You don't like the house."

He shook his head.

"I don't like it either." She gave her hand a tentative tug, a meager attempt to draw free.

He held on, reluctant to let her go. "We should lock up, get back on the road and finish our milkshakes."

Maxine nodded, gaze roaming the room

and skipping over him. "We should pick up sleigh decorating supplies at the general store before we go back."

"Are you breathing, Maxine?" He knew she was, obviously. But he wanted her to settle in to this test of his, the one he hoped would prove there was substance in these new feelings.

Her lips twitched, as if she'd managed to contain a smile before it broke free. "I was listening to the sudden silence."

No sound came from upstairs.

"Luna, get down here. We're leaving." She tugged at her hand again, glanced down at their physical connection and then turned, towing him along after her. "You should always worry when kids are too quiet."

"Coming, Mama."

And the thundering sound of footsteps on the stairs proved that to be true.

The foursome converged in the entryway at the base of the plain staircase. Maxine took inventory of Luna. Luna took inventory of them. Spot shook himself, twisting the stretched, maroon sweatshirt out of place. The bear emblem on the back rested on one side.

"Did you get lost?" Luna stared up at them,

righting her glasses. "Mama always holds my hand when I get lost."

"Mostly when you're at risk of being lost." Maxine tugged her hand a little before turning to Bo. "I'm not lost. I'm right here. Breathing."

Tug. Tug.

"If I let go, you won't run?" Back to Missouri and the safe little life she'd built for herself.

"Run where?" Luna righted Spot's sweatshirt. "Is this another Monroe thing?"

"No," Bo said.

"Beauregard." Maxine drew their joined hands up between them and laid her free hand over the top of their entwined fingers. "We're here in town until Friday. We're on your team. There's no need to hold on so tight."

Oh, but he thought there was. Because he was willing to bet that once their grip loosened, Maxine would find an excuse to retreat. Maybe not back home. But to a place he couldn't reason with.

Not that he could hold on to her like this forever. So he loosened his hold.

And he was right. As soon as his fingers relaxed, Maxine stepped back, free.

And completely without plan or coherent

thought, Bo stepped forward, drew her into his arms and kissed her on those tart lips the way he suddenly realized he'd been dreaming of, practically since the moment they met.

THERE WAS HEAT in Bo's kiss.

A warmth that seeped into Max just like a fresh-brewed cup of tea did first thing in the morning, satisfying and welcome.

But that wasn't all his touch communicated.

There was wonder in his gentleness. Longing in his restraint. Curiosity for kisses different than this one or the whisper of a kiss he'd graced her nose with earlier.

I wonder what it would be like to wake up to this. To him.

A thrill bolted through her.

"What are you guys so happy for?" Luna yanked on their arms. "Did you see the swing set?"

Not to be left out, Spot wormed his way between them.

Luna stepped into the gap and stared up at them with wide eyes. "Did we win something?"

"Yes." Grinning, Bo lifted Luna into his arms, chuckling when Max pressed her palms to her hot cheeks. "We won more ice cream before vegetables."

"Yes!" Luna clapped her hands and called to Spot as Bo carried her through the front door.

"Don't get ahead of yourself." Max was about to follow them when she remembered how quiet Luna had been on the second floor. Instead of heading outside, she hurried upstairs where she found three bedrooms and a bathroom, all as empty as the rooms below.

At least, she thought they were empty. The smallest bedroom's closet door was open and inside was a child's white shoebox with the lid off. Luna had obviously poked around the contents, which were scattered on the brown carpet.

There were several square photographs. One was dated 1954. A couple stood together on the front porch beneath the bright blue gingerbread trim. There was another photo of the same couple in front of a tinsel-draped Christmas tree, each holding a small, wrapped package. Then one of the woman in the kitchen stirring something in a pot. Their smiles in that era were self-conscious.

Like the feeling I get when I think about Bo. Or he holds my hand. Or kisses me.

Time-faded, rectangular photographs chronicled the couple's history in the next two decades. Pregnancies. Babies. Gap-toothed smiles from children sitting on swings. A girl in a pretty, white Easter dress. A boy wearing a too-big cowboy hat. A black and brown mutt dragging a stick taller than he was. The mom and dad graced the camera with more casual poses and ease, their love for each other communicated with a touch, the tilt of the head or an embrace.

Glossier, newer photographs documented the activities of two teenagers and the home-owning couple's entry into middle age, many taken in front of that backyard swing. Their expressions were more joyous and carefree, uncaring of gray hair and lines on their faces.

Envy gathered in Max's chest, clenching around her heart. Envy for loving parents. Envy for a devoted husband and father. Clive had washed his hands of Luna when he'd landed that Dean of Education job on the East Coast.

Max sighed, sifting through the photographs, preferring them to her personal memories.

There were a few pictures of the couple in their sunset years, sitting at holiday dinner tables, carving turkeys, serving pie, or posed in front of a Christmas tree. They glowed with happiness over a good life lived.

Do I have that glow? Will I?

She didn't think so. She was too scared to earn it. The risks of heartbreak were too high. Suddenly, she knew with certainty that come Friday she wasn't looking back.

The decision she hadn't made was how to spend those hours before she returned to her safe life. She could bask in Bo's affection and kisses, knowing it, like a spring break vacation, wouldn't last. Or she could end things before they went any further.

A horn honked, a brief tap that reminded Max of where she was. *Who she was.*

A woman who wasn't meant for a storybook life, especially with a beautiful man from a prominent family.

Sadness filled her, sorrow she had to hide from Luna and Bo.

Breathe.

Saying a silent farewell to the couple who'd made the little chalet their home, Max carefully put the pictures back in the shoebox. She went downstairs, locked the door and replaced the key in the clay flowerpot, which seemed to be the key-hiding system in Second Chance.

Spot poked his head out of the back window, giving her a doggy grin.

Bo stuck his head out of the driver's window, concern in his eyes. "Everything okay?"

"Yes," Max reassured him, climbing in the truck, buckling in and taking Bo's hand to give it a squeeze. "For the record, we're not having ice cream twice today. That would be too much of a good thing."

And too much of a good thing might just break her heart.

"I CAME TO check on you since you missed dessert." Jonah closed the door to the shed and then stood staring at the mess Bo had made. "Dude, you no longer have a sleigh. You have kindle for a bonfire."

Bo didn't want to agree, but the evidence was hard to refute. "I started out trying to replace stripped screws to strengthen the structure." And he'd ended up with nothing but loose boards and bent rails, all of which had happened after he'd given Maxine a chaste good-night kiss.

She'd taken Luna and Spot and left him alone to work.

He should feel happy. Why didn't he feel happy?

Because it felt like Maxine was holding back.

"It's snowing again. Really coming down." Jonah came to stand next to Bo, thrusting his hands deep in his parka pockets. "You have no luck when it comes to the holiday challenge."

"Nope."

"You'll need to build a sleigh from scratch."

"Yep."

"And decorate it by Thanksgiving morning."

"I know." Bo let annoyance creep into his voice. "Now would be the time to look on the bright side." The way Maxine could about everything but a romance between them.

"Huh." Jonah glanced around the shed. "How about this for optimism? You've always done your best work on little sleep and lots of caffeine."

Bo grunted, not sure that was true.

"Of course, a blank slate will probably look better than what you had." Jonah's gaze settled on Bo's face, mildly inquiring. "Fresh starts are always up your alley."

The implication of his cousin's words sank in. Bo scowled. "You think that's what I'm doing with Maxine? Making a fresh start after Aria?"

"I didn't say that." But Jonah didn't protest enough. After all, he was a screenwriter and always careful with his words. "Whatever you build here…" Jonah let that phrase hang for a bit. "…will probably make you happier than you were yesterday, or last week, or last year."

"It depends." Bo began stacking the thin wood into piles, thinking of Maxine and how she was back to being her chipper yet prickly self after being told they should let things blossom between them. "This is going to require a new set of plans and resources." And he didn't mean the sleigh. He needed time to think, to journal, to make lists of how to make Maxine fall in love with him.

Bo kicked a warped board at his feet. If only now wasn't a time that needed action. He had no time to sit and strategize.

"Hmm." Jonah took a step back, giving Bo room to abuse or organize his discarded parts. "You do appreciate a good plan. But, as we've noted, time is running out."

Bo swore. "You're enjoying this, aren't you?"

"Me? Enjoying seeing you struggle to win…*the competition*?" Jonah grinned, clearly pleased with himself and reveling in Bo's situation on multiple levels. "I think it'd be grand if you came out on top this year."

"Grand?"

"Epic." Jonah headed toward the door. "Let me know if you need any advice on how to pull this off."

"I don't need your advice." Not when it came to building and not when it came to matters of the heart.

A few minutes after Jonah left, Shane blew in on a gust of wind and a flurry of snowflakes.

"It's really blowing out there." Shane surveyed Bo's workspace. His empty workspace, since he no longer had a sleigh. He sat down on the bench next to Bo, raising his gaze slowly, revealing an unusual amount of sadness. "And here I thought I was in trouble. Your sleigh has completely disappeared."

Bo had been sketching ideas for a new miniature sleigh, one that didn't need much more material than he had or knew was lying around the ranch. But he wasn't a designer like his cousin Bentley, and all his sketches stank. So much so, that his mind had wandered and beneath a crossed-out sleigh sketch he'd written: *How do I make sure Maxine has good memories this Thanksgiving?*

Because things hadn't been the same between them since they'd left the chalet.

And now, things weren't right with Shane.

Bo set the notebook aside. "What's wrong?"

"I…uh…" Shane set his elbows on his knees and leaned forward, wringing his hands.

"You can tell me." He obviously wanted to or he wouldn't have come all the way out here.

"It's the sleighs." Shane opened his mouth to say more. Closed it. And then turned to Bo. "It all started with Ashley wanting to make her sleigh more…glamorous."

"The Cinderella theme? I think you mean romantic."

Outside, the wind whipped past, shaking the shed walls.

Shane winced. "Franny started talking about romance and weddings."

Bo nodded. "Makes sense. Your wedding is coming up next month, right? New Year's Eve?"

Shane rubbed the creases in his forehead. "Is that what I told you?"

"Yes. Maybe," he added when Shane's frown deepened. "But what do I know? I'm just a guy who goes where he's told when he's told."

"Exactly what I said to her." Shane dragged his fingers slowly over his face. "I told everyone we were getting married on New Year's Eve and she sent out wedding invitations for New Year's Day." He swore. "I can't believe we got our wires crossed. And now, she's not even speaking to me. Much."

They sat in silence. The wind whipped past again, gusting with what felt like increasing strength.

Bo ran a hand behind his neck. "When you say you got your wires crossed, you really mean—"

"I messed up." He stared at Bo with a haunted expression. "I might have started out saying the right thing and ended up saying the wrong thing. Or I may have been wrong from the beginning. But what does it matter? The groom isn't supposed to make this kind of mistake. I'm in the doghouse."

Bo clapped a hand on Shane's shoulder. "I'm sorry. If I can do anything—"

"Yeah, well. About that." Shane gave a hollow laugh. "Can I kick you off the couch tonight?"

Another big gust of wind shook the shed while Bo wondered where he was supposed to sleep.

"They say it's really going to be nasty tonight," Shane said. "I hope the tarps stay on the sleighs. If you end up staying down at the campground in one of those cabins, maybe you could check on them?"

"During what feels like a blizzard?" Bo suddenly had no desire to give up the couch. Unless... "Shane, this might be your lucky day."

"Not hardly."

"Help me shut everything down here." Bo stood, taking inventory of what was plugged in and turned on. "And then I'll need you to be my sidekick at the bunkhouse."

CHAPTER THIRTEEN

"Is Spot going to spend the night with us?" Luna sprawled next to the big white dog on her bunk. She'd been reading him one of her picture books.

"I don't think he's staying." Max sat at the small table flipping through several pictures she'd taken on her phone during their trip.

There was snow, horses, children, dogs. But no pictures of Bo. No selfies of them as a couple.

Yet.

She turned her phone over and set it on the table. *Yet* was a dangerous word. A word that implied hope that things would be different for her this time.

The wind outside howled as if it was gathering strength. A lone shiver went down her spine, making her wish for a pair of strong arms around her and a deep voice to tell her there was nothing to worry about.

"Come on, Max," she mumbled to herself. "This isn't Missouri." It wasn't Tornado Alley.

But she couldn't ignore the tension between her shoulder blades or how her neck stiffened with each ensuing gust. The mountains weren't supposed to feel like this. She had to be calm for Luna, but she felt like she was failing. Failing miserably.

A soft knock at the door had her running to answer, and throwing herself into Bo's arms. "I'm so glad it was you."

"That's what every man likes to hear." He half carried her inside, making room for Shane behind him, who closed the door, shutting out the gathering storm.

Reluctantly, Max squirmed out of her cowboy's arms. She didn't want to give her overactive imagination—or Shane—the wrong impression. "To be honest, I would have leaped into Gertie's arms if she'd been at the door. I'm…uh…scared of storms."

"I feel offended that you didn't mention my name." Shane's smile lacked its usual luster.

"Your arms would do, too," she rushed to reassure him.

"What about Adam?" Not to be outdone, Luna had hopped off the bottom bunk. Somehow, she'd managed to loosen her pigtails.

"I draw the line at adults," Max said briskly, busying herself with tidying Luna's wayward curls.

Spot was giving wiggly greetings to Bo and Shane. He paused to sniff the air in front of Max.

"Just because my hands are working doesn't mean they have food." Max spared a hand to give the dog a pat. It was amazing how much more confident she felt with two more bodies in the room. "What brings you guys here?"

"Other than my dog and my…" Bo captured Max's gaze. "…good friend Luna?"

Shane's cough sounded suspiciously like it had begun as a laugh.

Bo's smile said he didn't care. "Shane kicked me off the couch for tonight. I thought I might bunk down in here."

"Wha-at?" Max snapped the band around Luna's pigtail.

"Admit it. You need a security blanket during the storm." Bo extended his arms, too full of himself for Max's liking. "I'm just what the doctor ordered."

Max did a quick inventory of the one room shack. "There are only two beds."

"I'll sleep on the floor." Bo's arms came

to rest in a crossed position, emphasizing his lowered brows. "Don't worry about me."

"You can't sleep on the floor because…" She mentally flailed about, searching for a reason. "…because you have to compete tomorrow. You're skiing behind the horse I'm riding. I bet Shane would like it if you were stiff and sore from a night on the floor."

"I would," Shane agreed.

"You wouldn't." Bo swung the back of his hand into Shane's chest, not that he connected with much more than Shane's jacket.

Shane…

Max turned to him. "Why did Bo lose couch privileges?"

Shane explained how he'd upset his fiancée by being insensitive enough to forget what day they were tying the knot, and how Franny had kicked him out of the house.

"Hang on." Max held up a finger. "You just said out of the house." She looked from Shane to Bo to Spot, as a feeling of relief swept through her. "You guys are sleeping in here tonight. Luna and I will take the couch."

"What?" Now Bo was in shock. He tilted his head toward Shane in what seemed a silent plea to reject Max's idea. But none was forthcoming.

The wind howled outside.

"This is perfect," Max went on, thinking the main house would do a better job of muffling the wind noise. "I've been wanting to get up early and help Gertie prepare breakfast."

Bo drew himself up, making noises that sounded like upset protests.

Max laid a hand on his arm. "If you want, we can play cards in the house until it's time to turn in. But you two will sleep out here. And tomorrow, Shane will have figured out how to make up with Franny."

"Thanks for the vote of confidence," Shane said without a single note of self-assurance.

"Hush." Max moved about the room, packing things they'd need for the night. "Don't be so pessimistic."

Several minutes later, Luna was lying in a sleeping bag on one end of the living room couch with Spot curled up on the other end, trying to convince Bo to allow Spot to sleep there, too.

"Trust me, honey," Bo told Luna. "There's not enough room on the couch for your mom, you and Spot."

"But he'll be cold in the bunkhouse," Luna

pouted and said in a small, tired voice. Ranch life was wearing her out.

"I'll keep him warm." Bo ruffled Spot's short fur. "He can stay here as long as you're quiet and try to go to sleep."

"Okay." Luna tucked her swaddled baby doll in her arm and closed her eyes.

Max and Bo moved toward the dining room.

There was noise outside, sounds of the wind blowing past, although it wasn't nearly as noticeable as it had been in the bunkhouse. Here, there was noise upstairs as the young cowboys brushed their teeth and prepared for bed. There was noise in Gertie's room, located on the other side of the kitchen, where a sitcom played on the television.

Bo set a deck of cards on the dining room table. "What do you want to play?"

"Gin rummy, of course." Her game. Her rules. Finally, something that was more certain than what was brewing between them.

They sat across from each other.

Max shuffled and dealt the cards. "I'm assuming you know how to play."

"Yeah, but I'm better at other games." He sorted his cards. "As kids, Jonah and I would spend hours playing War. Or Hand Slap."

"Hand Slap?" Max sorted her cards, frowning at a hand that had absolutely nothing. She held them one-handed in a fan. "I'm not a fan of violent games. Who thought putting their hands over someone else's and being fast enough to pull them away before they got slapped was a good game?"

"It's a game of timing and intuition." Bo held his cards in a single stack, as if he didn't need to be reminded of what he had.

"If they had Hand Slap in the Monroe Holiday Challenge, I'd bow out." She peered at the card that was face up between them—the queen of hearts. "Are you going to take that?"

He was staring and smiling, paying more attention to her than the game. "I'm not drawing the queen."

Max took it happily and discarded an eight of spades in its place.

The wind whistled past, pushing snow in a horizontal rush outside the window.

She crumpled in on herself, rubbing her arms from the sudden chill.

Bo drew a card and discarded a two of diamonds without any thought. "Where were you during the storm? The one that took your parents?"

Max pressed her lips together. She didn't like to tell people about that night. She reviewed her hand, forcing her mind to work through point-earning strategies and…

The wind wailed once more.

…she felt the urge to wail along with it.

Instead, she started talking. "I was there with them. My dad was renovating the basement. He'd torn out the bathtub and the bathroom walls the weekend before." Down to the studs. "The alarm sounded in the middle of the night. I remember Dad carrying me downstairs to the space that was the bathroom. They made a bed for me in the corner and I…" She glanced toward the living room where Luna slept peacefully. "I fell back asleep. It was just another tornado warning to me." One of many she'd lived through in her lifetime. "I woke up when it hit. I didn't even…" She stacked her cards and laid them face-down, having lost the desire to play. "I don't know what happened to them. I woke up alone with the world caving in on me."

She hadn't seen Bo get up from his seat and come around the table. She'd been lost in the memory of that nightmarish night. But she was aware of him drawing her to her feet, of his arms coming around her and him guiding her head to his shoulder, even as she was aware of a tightness in her chest, the familiar feel of heartache that she associated with loss. Loss of her parents. Loss of family support.

"It's okay. I'm here." Bo's arms tightened around her. "I'm not going to disappear."

Max clung to him without thinking of the future, needing only to be in the here and now.

"WELL, HELLO, FRANNY. COFFEE?" Max was in excellent spirits the next morning.

Or so she told herself.

"Yes. That's so nice of you, Max." Franny accepted the cup Max poured in the kitchen, looking like she hadn't slept well. Her gaze was dull. Her normally neat braid had a stray loop. "Did you make breakfast, too?"

"I did. Emily and Jonah have already eaten." Max had woken up early, dressed and made her way quietly to the kitchen, where she'd fried bacon and scrambled eggs for breakfast. For the first time in days, she felt as if her holiday was normal. She was mostly alone and helping others get their day started. She rinsed a sponge in the sink and began wiping counters. "I should have insisted we sleep on the couch from the beginning."

She should have stayed in the main house the majority of the time like a housebound, old lady whose time for receiving kisses and tenderness from a man had long passed.

Bolt, the gray-muzzled family Labrador, whined softly, staring up at Max with big brown eyes that pleaded for a bit of bacon and reminded her of Spot, which reminded her of Bo, which reminded her of…

Shoot.

Her excellent mood threatened to crumble like a strip of overly crisp bacon.

Bo had picked her up when she'd broken down last night, bringing her into his embrace and eventually onto his lap. She'd felt safe in his arms, comforted by his kisses and tender caresses. He'd left late, taking Spot with him. And she'd fallen asleep holding the idea of a future with Bo close to her heart.

But dawn had arrived, as it always did, and with it, the reality of her life firmly front and center. Yes, being with Bo felt right, like coming to a long-awaited home. And yes, he said he wasn't going anywhere. But that was just the flip side of what everyone who'd ever offered her love had told her, everything experience had shown was her normal.

This is your home now.

Until it wasn't.

We love you.

Until they didn't.

So here she was. Hiding in the kitchen, wiping down everything in sight, hoping to keep Bo at literal arm's length. Today would be different. There'd be no kisses, no embraces, no confessions of the past on her part. She wouldn't allow her feelings or his to breathe and grow and turn into something both of them would regret.

"Have you seen Bo this morning?" Franny asked too innocently, filling her plate with eggs.

"Have you seen Shane?" Max countered without thinking, hand pausing mid-wipe across the counter. Where had that retort come from? She hadn't meant to be snippy to her host. Her hand continued its slow, circular motion across the countertop as she mumbled a soft, "Sorry."

Franny took a good long look at Max. "You think I should forgive Shane for getting our wedding day wrong?"

"It seems like an honest mistake." Max searched the kitchen for something else to do. Gertie was showering and due out any minute, at which time she'd told Max she had to vacate the premises. "You love Shane, don't you?"

"I do. I really do. Thanks for pointing that

out." Franny gave her a joy-fueled grin that was a testament to her patience with temporary houseguests and the love she had for Shane.

"Then it's a good story to tell your grandkids someday on your wedding anniversary." Max opened the drawer where the hot pads and dish towels were kept. She stacked the hot pads and shook out a dish towel dotted with smiling turkeys.

Franny didn't take a fork from the nearby silverware drawer and move into the dining room. Instead, she moved next to Max and bumped the hot pad drawer closed with her hip. "Cleaning never solved anything, Max, including helping a woman decide if she loves a man or not."

Heat crept up Max's neck, flooding her cheeks.

Franny's gaze searched hers. "I don't know what's going on between you two. And frankly, it's none of my business. But I do know that Bo isn't the type of man to play with your emotions."

"I know that," Max whispered. "But what if I'm not the one for him?" He was larger than life in personality and presentation. And she was meant for quiet corners and an unassuming life.

"How will you know if you hide in here?" Franny rolled her eyes, moving away. "Isn't that the point of hanging out and making out and filling the quiet moments with secrets you don't normally share with anyone else?"

"Y-y-yes." Max leaned against the counter, needing the support.

"Scary, right?" Franny grinned, finally plucking a fork from the silverware drawer. "That's how I fell in love with Shane, which was after I was widowed and had decided I'd never find love again, by the way. At some point, Max, you have to decide if love is worth the risk of trying again. It's your decision, not Bo's." She left the kitchen with her plate and coffee mug. "Why is no one eating? Boys, last call for breakfast before this morning's challenge. You, too, Luna."

Footsteps echoed throughout the house. In a blink, the kitchen was filled with hungry children and Gertie, who shooed Max on her way.

If only Max was sure of the direction she should take.

"I HEAR YOU ran into a problem with your sleigh."

Max turned at the words, eager to learn who

was having problems with the final challenge, which was still two days away.

She and Luna were getting out of Franny's truck, having taken a ride down to the campground and meadow where the day's skiing challenge was going to take place. The storm blew through with less snow overnight than expected, but still left several inches of fresh flakes on the ground.

Luna hurried to join Adam and the other young competitors, following the path of trampled snow to reach them.

Max glanced around, having yet to identify whose sleigh was problematic.

"You should have taken one of the mid-sized sleighs." A tall man walked toward Max. He shared Bo's dark hair and solid build. Instead of a cowboy hat, he wore a blue knit cap, and instead of cowboy boots, his boots were the metal toe, lace-up kind.

She recognized him as one of Bo's cousins, not that she could remember his name. "Uh, hi…"

"Bentley." He gave her an unassuming, patient smile. "Where's Bo? I thought I'd offer to help him with sleigh-building after this morning's competition."

"I haven't seen Bo yet this morning." Admittedly, she had mixed feelings about that. He hadn't shown up for breakfast. "But about the sleigh... We just need to decorate it." And accent a red holiday Christmas dress of Luna's to have more bling, something Gertie had ideas about.

Bentley's brow quirked and he gestured toward a group of Monroes nearby. "Jonah just told me your sleigh fell apart last night."

"What? Where's Bo?" Max turned and stared up the winding drive that led to the ranch proper, hoping to see Bo riding toward her, preferably on any horse other than Rabbit and bearing news about their sleigh. But the road was empty. "I had no idea. He didn't say anything to me." His team member. The woman he'd comforted and kissed last night. His...

The familiar, unwanted pressure that warned her of emotional danger, the heartbreaking kind, returned.

"I didn't mean to worry you," Bentley said evenly. He moved closer, steady and calm, which in turn calmed her. "Jonah would have said something if Bo was injured."

Max bit her lip. *He should have said something to me.*

"If Bo didn't tell you, he might not have

wanted you to worry." Bentley seemed to want to say more. Instead, he draped his arm hesitantly over her shoulders, as if comforting people with a touch was a new thing for him.

"It would be just like Bo, wouldn't it?" Trying to carry a burden she could help him bear.

"It would be," Bentley agreed, moving to give them both space.

There was still no sign of the riders, but the young competitors were making their way across the snowy meadow to the tree line where they'd be assembling their snowmen bases. Their pace was slow given the amount of snow on the ground. Luna was already lagging behind.

"I need to help my daughter cross the meadow." Max started walking. "Thanks for letting me know."

Bentley nodded, turning toward the road while she veered toward the meadow, passing Emily and a stack of basketball-sized pumpkins, and Wyatt with a collection of skis.

She followed the path the kids had made in the snow, catching up to Luna. Together, they made their way across, joining the other kids at the tree line.

"Being a cowgirl is hard, Mama." Luna raised her hands, a plea to be picked up. She wore a borrowed pair of black snow pants and matching boots, and the bright orange knit cap that Gertie had made for Max. "Did you bring cookies?"

The other kids looked hopeful.

"I didn't. Sorry." Max picked her up and carried her a few feet away to remind her of the job ahead. "Do you remember how we practiced making snowmen last night?"

Luna nodded, tucking her head in the crook of Max's neck, chill fingers tangling in Max's hair.

"Where are your gloves?" Max took one of Luna's cold hands and blew on it for warmth.

"I left them at the ranch." Luna sat up and offered Max her other hand to warm.

"You'll wear the riding gloves Franny gave me," Max told her, setting her down and making sure of just that. They were a horrible fit. The leather fingers were twice the length of Luna's little ones.

Luna didn't seem to care. She called to Adam, "Look. I have scarecrow hands." She bent over the empty glove fingers and giggled.

Adam thought this was hilarious and ran over. "Let me try."

The kids each exchanged one glove. They

spent the next few minutes messing around, the way kids did when they had spare time on their hands. Their gloved hands created everything from squawking chickens to bear claws.

Bo called for Max from the other side of the meadow. "We're getting ready to start."

"Good luck, my darling." Max hugged Luna and then made sure both gloves were on her. "Stay warm. Have fun."

"Stay in the saddle, Mama." Luna gave her a precious, sunny smile.

Max started the long walk back.

Stay in the saddle.

Why did Max suspect that was going to be the hardest part of the challenge today?

A few minutes later, she wondered if the hardest part of the challenge was getting back to the starting line. The meadow was easily the length of a football field. Between the high elevation's thin air and her hasty pace, she was sweating when she reached Bo's side at their station.

Holding Rabbit's reins in one hand, Bo laid the other on Max's shoulder and drew her close while Holden began his announcements.

"Welcome to the horse-pulled ski and snowman event." Holden stood at the front of the assembled Monroes. "Each rider will have a tow rope and pull a skier behind them. Each skier will carry a pumpkin. Across the meadow, your team member will start making a snowman base when the race begins. Horse, rider, skier and pumpkin must all cross the finish line—no stragglers allowed. Time will be called when you place your pumpkin on the snowman's body. Judges, you need to make your way to the finish line. Contestants, you've got a few minutes to mount up and get ready."

"Bo." Max stepped back, putting distance between them. "Why didn't you tell me the sleigh fell apart?"

"Yeah, about that..." Still holding Rabbit's reins, Bo picked up a riding helmet from its resting place on his skis. He fit the helmet on top of her curls. "It broke while I was trying to make it safer." He fastened the strap beneath her chin, easing a finger between it and her skin to make sure it wasn't too tight. Her pulse quickened. "Better it fail in a shed than with Luna on it."

He was right about the sleigh, of course. "But we were supposed to decorate it today."

"We will. After Bentley and I are done rebuilding." Bo drew her to Rabbit's left side, walking stiffly in a pair of black ski boots.

The tall brown horse swung his head around to look at them. Maybe he didn't like what he saw. He pivoted, moving around so that Bo and Max faced him.

"He doesn't want me riding him any more than I do." Max rubbed at the short swirl of hair on the horse's forehead. "I'm sorry, fella."

"Rabbit doesn't like much of anything other than running." Bo held the reins beneath Rabbit's chin with one hand and curled his arm around his neck with the other. "I'll keep him in place. You get on."

"Right." Like balancing in inches of snow on one foot while raising the other in the air was going to be easy.

"Hang on." Bo somehow drew Max back enough to brush his lips against hers. "I wrote my morning affirmations, but we need a kiss for luck."

They'd need more than luck today. Still, Max soaked in the warm look on his face and wished that he could be hers forever.

"Riders should be mounting up." Holden clapped his hands, encouraging action.

"You can do it, Max," Laurel called from a

safe distance away, jiggling a baby in a pink snowsuit.

"Hey, Laurel." Ashley hefted a pumpkin. "Aren't you supposed to be rooting for me? Your sister?"

"Go, Ashley," Laurel said with less enthusiasm.

With Bo steadying Rabbit, it only took Max two tries to climb up in the saddle. Her borrowed cowboy boots were wet, her toes and fingers cold, and she had no confidence in her ability to stay in the saddle all the way across, but she was determined to try. For Bo. For Luna. And maybe—if she could get past her trepidation—for her own competitive self.

There was a blue nylon rope knotted around Rabbit's saddle horn. It went under Max's leg and over Rabbit's haunches, which the gelding didn't like. He swatted Bo and the rope with big twitches of his long tail, pivoting his tail-end as if anxious to rid himself of a pesky fly.

What if he decides he wants to get rid of the rope and his rider?

A wave of panic struck. It was a long way down from atop that horse. "Bo, I think we should change places. Rabbit likes you so much better than me."

"Don't panic, Maxine." Bo snapped his boots onto his skis, then bent to pick up their pumpkin and the end of the nylon rope. "All we have to do is get across together. You and the horse. Me and the pumpkin."

"But you say that like…" *We'll all be dragged across.*

The judges had reached the other side of the meadow and were positioning kids across from their counterparts. Max surveyed the field and her competition.

Petite Olivia and Ashley were going to be skiing for their teams. Their pumpkins were too large to fit snugly beneath their short, jacketed arms. There was hope in that.

As for the riders, Max was the only one with the rope threaded beneath her leg. The others had their ropes running over their thighs and held on to it with an underhand grip. That was worrisome.

"Bo, shouldn't our rope be on top of my leg?" Max half turned, her movement causing Rabbit to shift sideways. The tension in the rope raised her leg a little. "Bo?"

"It's the best position for you, Maxine. I didn't think you'd be able to hold the reins, hang on and manage a tow rope." Bo didn't look up. He was too busy shifting his grip on the pumpkin and wrapping the nylon rope a few times around his wrist.

"This isn't safe," she told Bo, and anyone else who was willing to listen. Where was Gertie? She was the voice of reason.

"The danger is what makes it fun." And to prove it, Olivia laughed.

"Kids, do not try this at home," Jonah called back.

And then it was too late to protest because Holden was raising his arms and getting things rolling. "On your marks. Get set. Go!"

Five horses leaped forward, including Rabbit, towing their skiers across the starting line. Max might have cried out. Who could tell? Everyone seemed to be shouting.

Sensing this was a race, Rabbit lunged forward with speed and power, just as Bo had hoped and Max had dreaded. The momentum created tension in the rope beneath Max's leg and half lifted her out of the saddle.

She screamed, dropped the reins and clung to the saddle horn, practically standing on one leg.

"That's it," Bo cried. "Keep going."

To Max's right, Jonah fell face-forward in

the snow and was dragged a few feet before Emily pulled her horse to a stop.

What if Bo fell and got hurt? Max started to turn and look over her shoulder, which made her tilt farther to the right.

Rabbit slowed down.

"Don't look back," Bo shouted.

Max jerked herself to a front-facing position. "How will I know if you fall?"

Her question was lost among the shouts of the audience and competitors.

To Max's left, Ashley dropped her pumpkin, shouted at Wyatt to stop and tumbled sideways when he did.

On the other side of Ashley, Rhett's horse hesitated, perhaps daunted by the increasing depth of the snow. And then without warning, he leaped forward. The sudden acceleration had Olivia falling backward. One of her skis slid free.

"This is bananas!" Max shouted. At any moment, Rabbit could turn skittish and send her tumbling. She held little hope of making it all the way across without being dumped.

Beyond Rhett, Franny slowed her horse into a steady walk, a pace that allowed her horse to find its footing and keep Shane on his skis.

Slow seemed like a great strategy about now. Max gathered her courage and snatched at the reins. It took her a couple of trics, but she was able to capture the thin strip of leather and pull back, slowing Rabbit to a steady pace, which created slack in the rope and allowed her more balance in the saddle.

"Bo, we're doing it."

There was no answer behind her.

Max turned. She'd lost Bo twenty feet back. "Oh, no." She sawed on the reins. "Rabbit, be reasonable. We have to go back." She managed to turn the horse around.

"Didn't you hear me yell at you?" Bo stood at the ready when they neared, pumpkin under one arm.

"Who could hear anything with all this shouting? It's mayhem." Max took this as an opportunity to move the rope on top of her leg. She tossed the end to Bo. She must have been getting a handle on horse steering because Rabbit turned much easier the second time.

They set off at a slow pace and were immediately overtaken by Emily and Jonah. Ahead of them, Franny and Shane were approaching the finish line.

"Go faster," Bo called.

"No. Quit being a back seat driver."

Rabbit's ears swiveled around.

"Pay attention to the road, boy. Slow and steady," she told the horse.

"Faster!" Bo was beginning to annoy Max. "They're pulling away."

"Our new strategy is to take it slow." At a slow and steady pace, they'd both make it safely to the finish line.

Ahead of them, Jonah face-planted again. This time, Emily noticed his fall right away.

"Yay for strategy," Bo cried. "I'm still upright and behind you, Maxine."

"Yay for strategy," Max muttered when they crossed the finish line, hopping off and hurrying to Bo in order to transfer the pumpkin to Luna since it would take too long to wait for Bo to clip out of his skis.

And bless her heart, Luna had a snowman base made. It was over a foot tall, and she'd stuck Max's gloves in the sides so they looked like hands.

Dropping to her knees, Max set the pumpkin, noticing that someone had drawn a big, toothy smile on the orange gourd. "You did great, honey."

"We did great!" Bo brought them to their feet and into his arms. He jumped up and down, spinning their little group around. "Second place. Second place." He tilted his head back and laughed.

All the stress of the race dropped away at the sound of his laughter. Along with it, all of Max's fears that she'd fall or he'd fall or someone would get hurt dropped away, too. Her cares evaporated in the glow of Bo's joy.

"Hey, smile for the camera." Cam snapped a picture with his phone. "You guys did great."

"Send me a copy of that." Max leaned into Bo's chest, drinking in the sense of belonging and storing it deep in her heart for when this holiday was all over.

CHAPTER FOURTEEN

"Do you know what I like about your sleigh?" Bentley bent down, sifting through the pieces of Bo's broken sleigh.

"Nothing?" Bo ventured a guess, half-distracted by the morning's afterglow—coming in second in the skiing competition and celebrating with Maxine and Luna. He smiled every time he thought of those two Holloway females and the possibility that he wasn't going to be this year's biggest loser. That is, if he could fix their sleigh. He'd thought it was possible. But now, the thrill of the morning's victory evaporated like a puff of air in a snowstorm.

"That's right. I don't like anything about your sleigh." Bentley stood, nudging the debris to the side of Bo's workspace with his foot. He was slightly taller than Bo and a whole lot smarter when it came to creative fixes. "This is all trash. But the good news is that a blank slate is freeing."

"Free but blank." It was demoralizing since he needed something to compete with on Thanksgiving. "Any ideas?"

"As a matter of fact, no." Despite his cynical pronouncement, Bentley laughed and grinned, which wasn't unusual these days coming from his cousin. Bentley used to dole out emotion as if it were in scarce supply. "Funny thing about helping my fiancée and her family restore antique carnival rides." He glanced toward the rest of the shed and the piles of boxes, random tools and ranch equipment. "I've learned there's always something to inspire me in these old ranch buildings."

Bo followed the direction of Bentley's gaze. All he saw was rusted old equipment, cardboard boxes and plastic tubs. He didn't see inspiration anywhere. "Are you suggesting we dumpster dive in the rubble back there?"

Bentley nodded, still grinning. "Think of this less like a place where old things come to die and more like a place filled with hidden treasures waiting to be repurposed."

Bo had heard about the carnival rides being in pieces and stored in an outbuilding at the Bar D, but he wasn't convinced this musty old shed held anything of use. "This is a gamble." He gestured toward a nearby stack—a small microwave draped in what looked like snow chains, a ripped, blue saddle blanket and a plastic tub labeled "Christmas lights."

His cousin laughed again. "Lately, everything in my life has been a leap of faith. Sometimes, doors open and you aren't exactly certain what that door leads to but you have to step through because you want to, more than anything."

For a man who planned that sounded rough and Bo said so.

Bentley clapped a hand on Bo's shoulder. "As a fellow engineer, I know it's habit to follow a logical plan. There's safety in blueprints and standard processes. But sometimes, you have to embrace the unknown and trust that your ability to creatively problem-solve will lead you to a more satisfying result."

That seemed a bridge too far, Bo thought.

"Save the high-level rah-rah oratory for another audience." Bo tipped his cowboy hat back. "What are you trying to say about me and my sleigh problem?"

His cousin began poking in a cardboard box on top of a rickety barrel. There was another barrel behind it with some kind of saw on top. "I'm saying that we'll find something here to save your sleigh entry. It probably won't be what you envisioned as your ideal. But you'll be happy, nonetheless."

"Right." Not entirely bought in, Bo dragged an old bathroom vanity clear of a stack of boxes labeled "outgrown snow boots." The shed went back another ten feet or so but it would be a challenge just to work their way through. "If there's any treasure to be found, we'll need to dig for it."

"Hold on." Bentley stopped him again, his eyes bright. "I'm also saying that sometimes you need to trust your gut and your heart. Just look at me. I'm engaged to a woman I've known less than a year and I'm going to open my own workshop here in Second Chance. If I'd approached these life changes like an engineer, I'd want to crunch numbers and probabilities and weigh the financial viability."

"We both know you did a little of that anyway," Bo grumbled.

"Yeah," his cousin laughed. "But not much."

They moved the first row of junk out of their way, finding nothing of use.

Bentley picked up an old carburetor. "Do you remember that time Grandpa Harlan's motor home broke down in the Catskills?"

Bo nodded. "It was pouring down rain and

we were the only ones willing to poke around the engine with him."

"You and Grandpa Harlan fixed it." Bentley set the carburetor back in a cardboard box. He inched between the stacks of junk and swept cobwebs out of his way. "I wanted to be like him...and you. To be able to fix things that were broken."

"You surpassed us both. I fix things on oil rigs while you modify engines and boats for speed and efficiency."

"Just because I have ideas in my head for inventions and improvements doesn't mean I'm a genius." Bentley moved deeper into the back of the shed, inching between stacks and piles, poking around. "If I've learned anything in my professional life, it's that you need a good team around you. I wouldn't mind having a workshop partner up here, someone with mechanical engineering experience that can help me bring my visions to life." He dragged a blue plastic tarp off a section, balling up the cover and tossing it aside.

"Are you offering me an open door?"

"Yes. And look." Bentley dragged an old pull sled from behind a wooden rocking chair. "Problem solved. People used to pull little kids in this, although I don't see the sides anywhere."

"It's a sled," Bo said dejectedly. It wasn't much better than what he'd started out with.

"It's a factory-made sled compared to the homemade one you used to have." Bentley hefted it up and handed it to Bo. "It's a classic. Built fifty or so years ago, I bet."

Bo carried the sled to what remained of their workspace. It was solidly put together and, admittedly, had some old school charm. "Luna would look awfully cute in this. We can rebuild the side rails easily enough."

"Things are looking up." Bentley navigated slowly back through the maze of junk.

Bo blew out a breath, suddenly relieved. "And all because you opened a door."

"THIS IS OUR new sleigh." Bo pushed back the shed doors so that Maxine and Luna could see what he and Bentley had spent the past two hours working on.

It was Tuesday afternoon. They still had plenty of time to decorate the sleigh, especially since it was so small. And Bentley had given Bo plenty of things to think about. His cousin was setting up shop in Second Chance, planning to continue his work designing and building things. He left the door open for Bo to join him. The offer was unexpected, like a gift, and yet didn't fit his carefully laid-out life plan.

Luna and Maxine rushed in, another pair of unexpected gifts, full of praise for the miniature sleigh.

"It looks just like Santa's." Luna ran around it, followed by Spot. "It's red. All it needs is a place for toys and reindeer."

"We're working on that." Bo put his arm around Maxine, fitting her next to him. "Do you like it?"

"Can I just say how happy I am that the other one collapsed?" She stared up at him, laying her palm over his chest, brown eyes sparkling. "It's beautiful."

He enjoyed receiving her praise. "We took some short-cuts inspired by the original sleigh. The base is an old pull sled we found tucked away in the back of this shed. All we did was rebuild the back and sides, then painted everything."

Maxine's attention shifted to their sleigh. "You don't worry that it's too small to impress the judges in the competition?"

"I have a secret weapon." Bo picked up a pair of cloth antlers attached to a padded headband. "I have a harness and long leash that I put on Spot when we go for runs in the city. He's going to pull Luna in the sleigh. And when he wears this…" Bo called his dog over and put the antlers on over his broad head. "He'll be her reindeer."

If dogs could look dubious, Spot did.

Luna laughed and Spot shook himself before trotting over to give her doggy kisses.

"How will Luna steer?" If Maxine had a job title on their team, it would be Chief Safety Officer.

"This isn't the ski pull, honey," Bo reassured her. "We'll walk next to Spot. I'll keep hold of his harness."

"You thought of everything." Maxine hugged Bo, and then stepped back, righting her glasses. "And with Luna in a Santa costume, your entry will be sure to melt hearts. You just might win this."

"*We*. We might just win this." He stared into Maxine's eyes and hoped that he had a chance to win more than the family challenge. He wanted to establish something with Maxine, but he had no idea how to do that in the two days they had left together. He smiled as if he had it all figured out anyway. "Tomorrow is the gingerbread decorating contest. Are you sure you don't mind that Luna and I will do the honors together?"

"Are you implying that I, as a woman, would be a better choice to frost a cookie house?" Maxine waved her hands in front of her chest. "I am not into fine lines and precise little accents made with frosting."

"Adam says there's going to be candy." Luna removed Spot's antlers and tried them on herself, putting them on lopsided but mugging for them anyway. "Can I have vegetables for breakfast, Mama? That way, I can have candy."

"Maybe we'll bend the rules this one time." Maxine straightened Luna's antlers. "Maybe you can have candy before vegetables."

"Because it's the holidays?" Bo asked, grinning.

"Because it's the holidays." Maxine nodded, looking as happy as Bo felt.

"I like the sound of that." Bo picked up a box of small LED lights. "Why don't you two head back to the house to help Gertie make pies? I'm going to attach these lights to the sleigh and then I'm done."

Luna tugged on Bo's jacket. "Can I tell Adam about our sleigh?"

Bo got down on his knees and took Luna's

small hands in his. "Can you wait until Thanksgiving to talk about it, honey? Our sleigh is going to be a surprise, like a Christmas present."

"Oh." Luna hung her head. Her glasses slid down her nose. And the antlers bobbed toward the floor.

With a gentle touch, Bo lifted her chin and then restored her glasses to their proper place on the bridge of her little nose. "Do you know what kind of house you want to make tomorrow? The gingerbread one?"

Luna shook her head, shaking the antlers in the process.

She made him smile. Bo couldn't stop grinning. "We can make a log cabin or a chalet or—"

"Santa's house." Luna's eyes widened.

"What a great idea." He tapped her nose with his finger. "Now that's something you can go talk to Adam about."

"Santa's house." Luna skipped out the door. "Come on, Spot."

His big, teddy bear of a dog trotted after her, heart as lost as Bo's to Luna and Maxine.

"You're good with kids," Maxine said, standing a short distance away.

Bo got to his feet and went over to her, placing his hands on the gentle curve of her hips. "Do you consider that an asset in a man?"

"I think…" She hesitated, ruminating over her words for too long. "I think we should be careful with the way we explore things. I'm leaving on Friday and…"

His hands dropped away. "Why do you do that?"

"What?" She smiled, but it seemed forced.

"You leap ahead to the end when this might be an open door to something that isn't short-lived." Bo took a breath, tried to center himself because the unknown made him nervous, too. And then he smoothed a lock of Maxine's thick, curly hair over her shoulder. "Who knows? This thing between us might surprise you. We might grow old together."

She adjusted her glasses, gaze skittering away from his. "In… In my experience…"

"I think we can both agree you've had more than your share of bad experiences trusting someone to love you the way you should be." Oh, it took effort to keep the anger from his voice. Because he was angry. At all those relatives who'd passed Maxine along. At her ex-husband for not realizing her confidence needed bolstering and supporting her.

"Bo, I…" Maxine clasped her hands together. "When you think about this exploration of yours, do you see it lasting beyond Friday? Beyond Second Chance? Because try as I have been, I can't see how we could have a future."

"But you have tried." He'd noticed that slip in her admission.

She nodded, curtly. "And I wish…" She extended a hand, placing a palm on his cheek. "I wish that I could see a way to make things last, but I can't."

"PLEASE TELL ME we can help in the kitchen." Max gave Gertie her best smile, the one she used on crotchety old professors and difficult administrative assistants. "I know you're making pies. I can cut fruit, mix ingredients, roll out dough." Anything to hide away in the kitchen so that she wouldn't have to face Bo or her own cowardice.

Luna was in the living room working a puzzle with Adam. Spot lay in front of the hearth. Any moment, Bo would be done lighting the sleigh and come inside. He'd want to talk.

Gertie tsked. "I've already glued the gingerbread houses together on the dining room table. Emily and Franny filled a container with diced apples. There are blueberries defrosting in the sink. And we've only got one bit of counter space here to roll out dough." She reached into a flour canister and then sprinkled the flour onto the countertop. "Cam volunteered to make me some pumpkin pies. And truth be told, I was glad of the help there. I'll stick to fruit pies. And you should stick to enjoying that man of yours."

"I can…" *I can stop being a chicken.* "I can wash the dishes. I'll stay out of your way." Because it was clear that Gertie liked things run just so.

"Those dishes are always multiplying." Gertie scoffed. "But Emily washed them earlier."

"Oh."

"I can see you'll be morose if you never get a chance to help." Gertie floured her rolling pin. "There are some garden clippers in that drawer on the end and a bucket on the back porch. We'll need greenery to decorate the table and mantel for Thanksgiving. There's not much about the garden to cut since snowfall, but there are all kinds of evergreens about the yard."

Max perked up. "Greenery. Decorations. On it."

After checking that Luna wanted to stay indoors and that Gertie would keep an eye on her, Max bundled up and headed outside. She'd never been much of a gardener and didn't know what most plants were called, but that didn't stop her from cutting lengths of greenery. She filled the bucket with enough to make more than one grand centerpiece.

"There you are." Bo stepped out on the back porch. "I thought you might like to come on a walk before the sun sets."

"Is that wise?" Max climbed the back porch steps slowly.

He shrugged, but he couldn't shrug away the hurt in his gray eyes. "About matters of the heart, is anything wise?"

Oh, how she wanted him. Max tapped his chest, giving in a little. "You, sir, are a determined man."

Bo opened the back door, standing aside to let her in first. "I'm only determined where you're concerned. Gertie said to leave the bucket on the back porch."

"Okay. Let me just get Luna." If she was going to give in to temptation, the least she could do was recruit a chaperone.

"Luna's asleep." Bo pointed to the living

room where Luna was snuggled next to Spot on the rug.

Someone had laid a blue crocheted afghan over her.

"Come on." Bo took Max's hand. "You know I don't bite. We don't even have to talk."

That's what I'm afraid of.

But she allowed him to lead her out the door and into the fading sunlight. They walked around the house and strolled to the driveway, heading toward the main road.

"You might know this," Bo began, after they'd been walking in silence for several minutes. "You being an expert and all on the subject. But people tend to take on roles in large families."

"You mean, like the clown or the leader?"

He nodded. "You've probably already identified the leadership committee—Shane and Holden. And the family jokester, Jonah. My sister, Kendall, is like the princess, although up until a year ago, Ashley would have given her a run for the title role."

Max liked the sound of his deep voice and how it blended into the sound of the wind whispering through the tall trees. She liked the broad curl of his straw cowboy hat and that it emphasized the breadth of his shoulders. She liked the feel of her hand in his.

Bo cleared his throat. "You're probably wondering where I fall in the Monroe family tree."

It was a guessing game. And she loved games. "Are you the book smart one?"

"That would be Bentley."

"Are you the jock? No." She course corrected, hyper-aware that she wanted to say Bo was the playboy in the family but somehow knowing he'd be offended if she did. "That can't be. Is it the kitchen whiz? No, that would be Cam."

Bo chuckled. "Why do I get the feeling that you're toying with me?"

Why is it that he can read me so well?

She shoved that thought to the back of her mind.

Bo sighed. "You can say it. I'm the family rogue, the confirmed bachelor, the…" He glanced down at her with that mischievous smile she liked so well and perhaps a glint of sadness in his gaze. "Do I need to go on?"

"I get the idea." And that he didn't like to be pigeon-holed by labels.

"You know, these good looks are pure luck. And because of them and the roles my parents, grandparents, aunts and uncles would as-

sign us, even if it was only in conversation…
they shaped me." He paused, helping her navigate an icy patch on the drive. "My mother used to worry that I'd never date because I was prettier than the girls at my school."

"That's extreme."

"My mother worries too much," he said gruffly. "But you get the idea. Growing up, I noticed that girls couldn't be themselves around me because my looks were too intimidating and because I was the silent type."

"You were never the silent type." He chattered more than Luna.

"I was when I was a kid." Bo nodded gravely. "I rarely spoke up in class. One of my high school teachers didn't think I did my own work."

"Are you saying you were stereotyped because of your good looks?" Max glanced up at him, first incredulously, and then with acceptance. Because she'd judged him by the same yardstick. "I apologize."

"For what?"

"For thinking you were a turkey man."

He laughed again and she couldn't believe in a few days this beautiful guy would be part of her history. "You never really be-

lieved I was a plain turkey and mashed potatoes man."

"I didn't," Max went on, forcing herself to
speak when all she wanted to do was wrap
her arms around Bo and never let go. "Although admittedly, your good looks confused
me at first, but now that I've heard about your
incredibly *difficult* childhood, I know exactly
who you are. You're honey ham, vegetarian
stuffing and pumpkin cheesecake with a sug-
ared, graham cracker crust."

He beamed at her. "Pretty good, Maxine
Marie."

"I try, Beauregard Franklin."

They continued down the drive, joined
hands swinging slowly between them. And
Max couldn't help but think about the little
chalet on the end of town and the loving couple who'd made a lifetime of memories there.

"I used to date. Before Clive, I mean," Max
admitted slowly. "I had a rule though."

"Of course you did." Did nothing she said
surprise this man?

"Three dates." She spared him a grin. "Any
more than three dates, and it felt like people
expected us to get married with a future all
laid out ahead of us."

"Which you refuse to allow yourself to

see." Bo lifted her hand to his lips and placed a kiss on her knuckles. "You won't even let yourself plan out a career." A second kiss softened his insight.

"I know what you think." It was what her ex-husband had thought, too. "I'm smart enough that I should be able to get past this." Her past.

He nodded.

"But putting my heart in someone else's hands, having to build a new community of love and support… It overwhelms me. It drives me backward. It puts me on the defensive."

"You won't find love with your guard up," he said gruffly. And he should know. He'd put thought behind finding love and made a list.

"That's why I've stopped looking."

Snow fell from a tree branch ahead, sliding onto the ground with a hiss of movement.

"Is that what you want for Luna?" Bo asked. He might have been walking and moving forward, but he sounded still. So still. "You think she should grow up and live her life in limbo."

"No." Never. "That's why we spend holidays with others." But it wasn't the only reason. "She's so much braver than I am. And it's because of these experiences. We come at a time when people are at their best. And we leave before things go back to normal." Before Max had a chance to love and be left behind.

"Maxine Marie." Bo stopped and faced her. He caught her other hand and brought both up to rest next to his chest, over his heart. "You can have what Luna has. And I think your parents would want that for you, too."

And then he closed the distance between them and kissed her.

And if Max could muster up the courage, she'd have agreed with him.

Instead, she enjoyed his kiss and waited for the other shoe to drop.

CHAPTER FIFTEEN

"WHERE DID THIS crowd come from?" Maxine stopped inside the doors of the Bent Nickel Diner, Luna propped on her hip.

We look like a little family.

Bo beamed at everyone and anyone, enjoying the feeling of being part of a family unit, of belonging with Maxine and Luna.

It was Wednesday morning. Tables had been set up at the back of the diner for the gingerbread house decorating. Folding chairs in neat rows made for good viewing by an audience that was already filling seats. The diner was buzzing with conversation and excitement.

"These are all locals." Bo slipped out of his jacket and indicated Maxine do the same. "The whole town heard about the Monroe Holiday Challenge. More and more people were asking if they could watch. Shane and Holden thought this was a great public relations opportunity." Because changes were coming to leases at the end of the year, and it would help if townsfolk thought fondly of them when finances were discussed.

But…an audience. His competitive streak awakened.

"What's that look?" Maxine poked his chest and sidled closer. "This is a decorating competition and suddenly you look like it's a national championship game."

Bo blinked, smiled, told his ego to check itself at the door. "Cookies and frosting. Got it."

"You'd better." Maxine set Luna down and busied herself removing their coats. She wore the orange knit cap Gertie had made for her. Her long brown curls rippled over her back just begging for his touch.

He took their jackets, pausing to tweak one of Luna's pigtails and smooth Maxine's hair over her shoulder before taking Maxine's hand and leading his team to the back of the diner.

Luna ran past them to join Adam, who was talking a mile a minute and gesturing wildly about pumpkins, skis and snowmen as he talked to several other little boys.

Behind Bo, Maxine dragged her feet.

Bo stopped and turned to face her, bringing

her within kissing distance. "Are you embarrassed to be seen with me?"

"No." But a blush painted her cheeks a soft red.

Bo leaned closer, whispering in her ear, "If you aren't embarrassed, then I guess you wouldn't mind giving me a kiss for luck. It worked so well yesterday." He drew back a little to catch her expression.

Her brown eyes widened, then swept across the room, perhaps registering the fact that they'd attracted attention from some of the assembled.

"That's right." He touched his forehead to hers, brim of his cowboy hat hovering over her knit cap. "You may be in a supporting role for this challenge, but you're not invisible to the crowd. It's not so bad, is it?" He'd tossed down a bite-sized challenge. "Being seen with me." As his significant other.

"You're impossible." She rose up on her toes and kissed him briefly anyway.

Bo had never grinned so wide in his life.

There was hope in that kiss, hope that Maxine would realize her heart was safe with him. He tugged her toward the tables that Ivy and Cam had set up, tossing their coats into a booth that was already overflowing with competitors' jackets, hats and scarves.

One of Gertie's gingerbread houses sat on each table near the wall, as well as tubes of brightly colored icing and plastic containers filled with small cookies, licorice, chocolate chips, sprinkles, candy canes and peppermint rounds. And probably other goodies he couldn't see.

"Have you thought about what Santa's house looks like?" Maxine wasted no time getting down to business.

"I made a sketch." Bo produced a folded piece of paper from his pocket and handed it to her. "You know me and my plans."

"Lists, lists, lists." Maxine tsked, studying his drawing. "You do understand that Luna is four and not one to strictly follow something like this?"

"Why wouldn't she? The theme was her idea. She'll get on my page." He only hoped that Maxine would get on the same page as Bo so things could develop. All Maxine had to do was get over her fear of being hurt. "I'm meeting Ella and some other family members this afternoon at the cabin, the one with the fantastic view of the valley. Want to come?"

"Are you going to look for proof it was your

grandfather's?" Her brow clouded. "If it's just family, I shouldn't go."

"Or maybe you should." He couldn't help it. He drew her into his arms. "Could be that cabin is where we come to vacation when we visit family."

She heaved a sigh, wrapping her arms around him.

"Mixed signals coming at me, Maxine Marie." He set her away from him. "Maybe you need one of my convincing kisses."

She handed him his gingerbread plans instead, then righted her glasses. "Maybe you should focus on the competition right now."

"Max!" Gertie waved to her from the other side of the room. She had a small sewing kit laid out on a table alongside what looked like Luna's bright red dress. "I need your input."

"That's Luna's costume for tomorrow." Maxine kissed her fingers and pressed them to Bo's lips. "Go brief Luna."

Bo didn't want to brief Luna. He wanted to gather Maxine in his arms again and hold her there. Because there were still things they had to learn about each other.

He frowned. That wasn't quite right. Because...

There were still things he needed to say to her. Because...

"Bo, explain to me what I just saw." His sister joined him. Kendall wore a black cashmere sweater, rhinestone accented jeans and the homeliest pair of fringed, hot pink cowboy boots he had ever seen. Come to think of it, she'd been wearing those boots a lot lately.

"You were mooning over Max," she continued. "You've never been one for public displays of affection."

"Or one to bring your dates to family events." Olivia joined them, crossing her arms over her gray yacht club sweatshirt. "How did such a nice girl-next-door win the heart of the family's playboy?"

"I know you're ready to settle down, Bo." Kendall inched closer, lowering her voice. "But you shouldn't snap up the first woman who fits that list of requirements you have."

Bo clenched his jaw. "It's not like that."

"Tell us what it's like." Olivia closed ranks, and when he didn't immediately answer because she'd caught him off-guard, she added, "Do you think about her all the time? Wonder how she could fit in your life? Or what you'd sacrifice to fit in hers?"

He nodded.

Kendall took hold of his arm. "Does she

make you laugh? And the thought of life without her steal your breath?"

He nodded.

Kendall and Olivia exchanged looks. And their looks turned into amused grins.

"You're in so much trouble," Kendall said.

"More trouble than this next competition," Olivia added. "You're falling in love."

Love? Bo's gut reaction was rejection of the concept. Love took time. Love had to develop and fit plans. It had to be proven. What he had with Maxine was still fresh and new. Sure, he felt like he knew her greatest strengths and biggest fears. And sure, Maxine understood him, from his competitive nature to his need to plan his future.

Their future.

Our future.

Our open door.

He blinked. *I love her.*

He loved her stubbornness and her kindness. He loved her vulnerability when it came to belonging and trusting. He loved that she wanted to put Luna first even if it made her uncomfortable. He loved that she'd found a way to create her own family—an academic one. He loved how she felt in his arms and how tenderly she kissed him.

But my plans... My timeline...

They'd have to be tossed. It was clear to him now. The oil rig job wasn't the right fit for a life with Maxine and Luna. He'd need to relocate where Maxine felt comfortable and where he could have work that satisfied him. They'd still need a house in Second Chance. And—

"Do you see that?" Kendall asked Olivia. "It's like we can see the gears in Bo's head working."

"He looks off-kilter, which is only to my advantage in today's challenge." Olivia laughed.

The challenge... Winning...

He could organize his feelings and plans later. "Decorating a gingerbread house isn't going to be that hard."

Olivia laughed again. "Do you know who's going to win this challenge? Ashley, Wyatt and Gabby."

Bo scoffed.

"I'm right." Olivia turned toward the tables filled with gingerbread. "You're competing with a pre-schooler on your team. Shane, Jonah and I all have to decorate with elementary school boys. Gabby is twelve. She and

Ashley are going to make a pretty gingerbread house while the rest of us end up with gobs of icing and clumps of candy." Olivia swung back around. "You and I hate to lose. We'll be lucky to escape last place today."

She was right.

Kendall confirmed it by rubbing his shoulder consolingly. "And the worst of it is that you have to be gentle with little Luna and allow her some creative freedom or you'll hamstring whatever you've got going with Max."

She was right.

"But…" He wanted to say, *"I have to win."* Because for once, he was in the running to bring home the trophy. "But…" He didn't want to hurt Luna's feelings or earn Maxine's wrath.

He washed a hand over his face, hoping to wipe away emotions that didn't serve him when it came to love, and not completely succeeding.

"It's okay. I don't need to win," he told them anyway. "It's enough to escape last place."

But he didn't really believe that, because the wound of too many loser trophies had soured him to anything but triumph. And he was so close to triumph.

"You've got a glow today." Gertie spared Max a glance before spreading the little red dress she was adding sparkle to for Luna out on the table.

Max touched her warm cheeks, self-conscious of the attention her affection for Bo was bringing.

Two older women sat across from Gertie. Their gazes took Max in with a sharpness that indicated opinions had already been formed.

The slighter woman chuckled. "I recognize your work, Gertie." She gestured toward Max's hat. "You couldn't have made a hat with red and white yarn for her for the Christmas season?"

"Oh, don't you start, Odette." Gertie smoothed the flare of the small skirt. "We haven't gotten through Thanksgiving yet. Orange is on trend, as the young folks say, at least until next week."

"I'll be wearing this hat through Valentine's Day," Max said, staunchly supporting Gertie. "I'm not much of a trend follower."

"Oh, Flip should like to hear that." Gertie clapped her hands. "She's the town trend-setter or trend-bucker when it comes to crafting and such."

Gertie… Flip… These were the women who'd sewn the scarecrows for stuffing.

Flip wore a camouflage-patterned hunting vest. She angled her face up toward Max. "What I'd really like to hear is how you nabbed our Bo. He's been cooler than an icicle to the ladies hereabouts. And he's clearly smitten with you."

Max's cheeks heated once more. "Oh, I didn't trap him."

"More importantly," Flip went on as if Max hadn't spoken. "Are you going to settle here in town? We're currently experiencing a population increase and a baby boom, which is good for business. My artwork sells in Sophie's boutique alongside Odette's baby quilts and Gertie's knitting."

"All these babies… It makes a nice reason to work on baby things," Odette noted, smiling almost dreamily. "I do so love to create baby quilts. Would you like to have another baby?"

"Oh…" Max's cheeks felt warm enough to steam milk. "Did you want my opinion or help with Luna's dress, Gertie?"

"Yes." Gertie held up one long, red sleeve. "We think we should trim this with white, but none of us has any faux fur on hand. The best we've got is white bias tape."

"Bland," Flip pronounced with a wave of her hand.

"We want to do better," Odette explained.

"Oh. I hadn't realized Gertie had recruited you to help." Max fingered the thin red material. "I don't want to be any trouble. Luna needs to wear this tomorrow, which means we don't have much time."

"Maybe we don't need to trim the dress." Flip stared at the ceiling, frowning slightly as if collecting her thoughts. "Didn't Emily win some kind of princess cape in one of her rodeo competitions? Or was that some other girl?"

Gertie gasped. "It was Em. But it wasn't a cape. It was a little faux fur jacket, more like a shrug with white trim."

"Do you think she'll let Luna borrow it?" Max glanced around, searching for Emily. "She's not on our team."

"Sometimes it's better to ask for forgiveness than permission." Gertie carefully folded up Luna's dress.

"Oh, no. I can't let you do that."

But Gertie shooed her away and from the

look in her eyes, the old woman's scheme was already set.

And before Max could locate Emily to ask permission, Holden announced the challenge was about to begin.

"AS THIS YEAR'S Grand Poo-Bah of the Monroe Holiday Challenge, I'd like to welcome everyone, especially our new audience." Holden was warmly pompous, entirely in his element as ringmaster. "No, let me rephrase. Everyone seated here in the diner isn't just a spectator. Today, you'll be judges, casting votes for the best gingerbread house."

"What?" Bo hadn't factored this into his plans. Since his conversation with Olivia and Kendall, he'd been quietly circulating through the Monroes who weren't competing, leading Luna by the hand and letting her win them over with her cuteness. He'd been banking on sentiment to win some votes. But now...

Bo surveyed the crowd of townspeople, worried. He didn't like surprises. This changed things, because little Adam was a local favorite.

"Smile and wave," Bo said to Luna.

The little girl was tugging at a loose string

on her purple sweater. She glanced up, fiddling with the set of her glasses. "To who?"

"Everyone."

The little girl raised both hands in the air and waved, like she'd just completed a gymnastic vault perfectly and attention was her due. And maybe it was, because she earned applause and waves in return.

She's going to be a handful when she gets older.

If Bo played his cards right, he'd be around to enjoy it.

"The rules of the gingerbread house decorating event are simple." Holden rubbed his hands together, looking like one of Second Chance's resident cowboys with his hat, brown leather vest, jeans and boots. "Each house has walls and a roof that are glued together. The house, in turn, has been glued to a square of cardboard to serve as a yard. The youngest team member is paired with any adult on the team. Each team member must contribute to the embellishments. Teams have thirty minutes to decorate their house and yard with anything on their table. No stealing from someone else's table." Holden shook his finger at the contestants.

"Luna, honey." Bo picked her up, settling

the little girl on his hip so he could whisper instructions. "I'm going to frost the roof. And while I'm doing that—"

"I'm going to make elves," Luna said excitedly. "You can't have Santa without elves."

"Right. Sure." Bo scanned their candies for anything that might look like an elf. "I'll cut some red licorice."

Luna put her hands on Bo's cheeks. "Don't worry. I can make elves by myself." And the way she said it was more a command than reassurance. This little girl was going to do it by herself.

And all Bo could do was try and control the damage.

His gaze landed on Maxine. She sat at the lunch counter with her hands clasped in her lap. She looked nervous. In fact, he'd go so far as to say she looked like a mama bear ready to step in if her cub didn't have a good time.

And now, even his metaphors were bad.

He set Luna down. "Okay. You work on the elves. I'll work on the house."

Thirty minutes was going to fly by.

"On your marks." Holden backed out of the limelight. "Get set. Go!"

Bo snatched up the tube of white icing and began drawing scalloped lines on the roof.

Luna grabbed a strand of red licorice and took a bite.

He had no time to discourage her from eating their supplies. There were two sides of a roof that needed embellishment. "Your mom is going to make you eat vegetables later."

Luna grinned, picking up scissors and trying to cut a strip of licorice while she chewed.

Bo's even scallops very quickly turned uneven. "I need to slow down." And stop worrying about what Luna was or wasn't doing.

"Can you help me?" Luna held up a piece of licorice and the scissors, thought better of it, and bit off another piece.

Bo kept scalloping, wondering if it would be okay to ignore her. He finished one side of the roof and moved to the other side of the table.

Luna followed him around, carrying her licorice and scissors. Eating, not decorating.

"Do you need help, Luna?" This from Maxine.

Bo took it for the warning it was. The correct answer to Maxine's question was that Luna needed help and shouldn't be ignored.

Bo set down the tube of icing and took over licorice-snipping duties. "I'm going to cut you some pieces for elf arms and legs, okay?"

"Okay." Luna tapped his arm mid-snip. "It's stuck in my teeth." She opened her mouth, revealing a glob of licorice on her bottom molars.

"You're going to have to swish that out." Bo waved to his cousin Cam. "We need some water over here." He reassured Luna everything would be fine and went back to work on scalloping the roof. He was fond of the kid but wasn't ready to stick his finger in her mouth.

"Looks like everyone's taking a different approach right out of the gate." Holden swooped back center stage as if this was one of those competitions on the food channel and required play-by-play. "Gabby and Ashley are creating a winter wonderland with snow everywhere."

"We decided to recreate the Lodgepole Inn," Ashley told him, not looking up. "I'm laying down icing and Gabby's spreading it across."

"Makes us wonder what you'll do next." Holden stopped at Jonah and Adam's table. "You've got a kaleidoscope of color. Care to explain?"

Jonah straightened, rubbing his nose, and leaving a stripe of yellow icing. "We're going for abstract art. Fall colors representing Thanksgiving."

"Abstract art." Bo scoffed, bending back to his work, reluctantly admiring Jonah's strategy of decorating to his young team member's level of skill.

"I'm done with the elves," Luna said from the other side of their gingerbread house. She'd laid out two red licorice stick figures and covered them with red icing.

"Great job, Luna. Have some more licorice." While Bo tried to figure out how to make that better looking.

"I don't like licorice." Luna wiped her hands down the front of her sweater. "We need candy cane trees."

"Go for it." Bo was almost done with the scallops.

Holden had moved to Olivia and Charlie's table. "This is a cookie paradise."

There were wafer cookies on the roof, perhaps meant to be shingles, and cookies attached to the walls of the house, perhaps meant to be shrubbery. Charlie's mouth was full of cookies, for no reason other than cookies were in reach.

Luna dropped a small candy cane on the floor, picked up the two broken pieces and stuck them on the cardboard next to her flat, licorice elf, using the red icing for glue.

Bo opened his mouth to give her alternative direction. He hadn't expected her to create in two dimensions rather than three. And her contributions were nothing like his plans. But Maxine was giving him the stink eye and Luna was humming happily. There was no way he could undo what she'd done without looking like a heel.

Except he didn't want to lose.

"Luna, honey, maybe you should replace the broken candy cane with a whole one."

"Can't." She crunched something, her lips rimmed with what looked like red candy cane stripes. "I ate the last one."

"We had a cupful." Bo glanced around their workspace.

"I gave the rest of ours to Davey." She pointed to the next table over where Davey and Shane were attaching candy canes to every side of their house.

"Why would you give them to Davey? He's on another team."

Luna shrugged and kept crunching. "He asked."

"He asked." And Bo hadn't noticed, probably because he'd been listening to Holden do his emcee schtick.

Luna wiped her hands on her sweater again, scanning their remaining candy stash. "He said please."

The crowd chuckled and laughed, repeating Luna's words and marveling at her cuteness.

Bo smiled, working it. He smiled at Maxine, whose raised brows said she knew exactly what he was up to.

"And what have we here?" Holden stopped at Bo's table, grinning like he enjoyed seeing Bo on a downward trajectory in the competition.

But there was hope. The audience loved Luna. All Bo needed was to summarize what they were doing with a theme…

"This is Santa's house," Luna said as if it should be obvious to Holden. "Don't you see the elves?" She opened a box of raisins and placed a couple near the broken candy cane.

It would be just like Bo's dry, sarcastic, superior-minded older brother to liken Luna's elf rendering to a murder crime scene. Bo had to think fast.

"We're creating a multi-dimensional, multi-media presentation of Old Saint Nick in the days leading up to Christmas." Bo dragged in a breath and kept on going. "Two D. Three D. You can see it, can't you? If you squint, you can tell that the elves are taking a break after their shift near the reindeer paddock." He gestured toward the raisins, stopping himself from explaining their similarity to reindeer droppings.

Luna did a double-take and set the raisin box back on the table. "We need to make Santa."

"Of course we do," Bo said with excessive gusto. "Move along, Holden. We're busy here."

CHAPTER SIXTEEN

"GREAT JOB, LUNA." Maxine picked her daughter up and smirked at Bo. "Your house is awesome."

"It is. No doubt. Luna did a great job," Bo gushed. If this had been a pre-school project, they'd be winners. "We did the best we could in the time we had." What with candy being eaten, given away or broken.

Time had been called. The teams were assembling behind their gingerbread houses while the judges came through for a closer look.

Maxine linked her arm through Bo's and whispered, "Be careful. Your disappointment is showing."

"It's true, I had a plan. But our project has character." Bo smiled harder at the passing voters, also known as Second Chance residents.

They milled about examining the gingerbread house entries.

"We should have written letters to Santa."

Luna lay her head on Maxine's shoulder but extended her arm to hang on to the collar of Bo's polo shirt, as if needing to touch both of them. "And had some toys to stack under my candy cane tree."

"All great ideas." Maxine rubbed Luna's back.

"Keep those in mind for next year." Bo covered Luna's little hand with his own. "We could even practice doing this again at Christmas."

"I like that." Luna closed her eyes.

"Sugar crash." Bo took Luna and settled her against his shoulder. "And I'm man enough to admit that this was a lesson in humility." He'd given up on his vision in order to keep up with Luna's creativity. Their roof was great. And they had a few snowmen made from stacked peppermint rounds. They'd decided Santa was inside the gingerbread house reviewing the naughty and nice list. "Take a look at our competition. All we really need to stay in the running is for Shane's team to get fourth or last and for us to be in the top two or three."

Maxine sighed, reaching over to rub Luna's back again.

Holden called for folks to take their seats, readying for the vote.

Bo spent a few minutes re-evaluating the playing field. He'd assumed their biggest hurdle would be Ashley and Gabby, but they'd had an overly optimistic plan. Covering everything with white frosting and smoothing it out had taken fifteen minutes. Their decorations were nice but sparse because they'd left a lot undone.

Jonah and Adam's house looked like a finger painting. And a black finger painting at that, since all their icing colors had been mixed and swirled together by Adam's little hands.

Shane and Davey had run out of candy canes, unable to get anyone else to donate theirs. They'd switched tactics to creating peppermint round columns on the house corners. Their rooftop and grounds were bare.

Olivia and Charlie had managed to cover a lot of surface with cookies, but in Bo's opinion, their entry lacked the character of Luna's licorice elves and peppermint round snowmen.

Paper was passed out and votes made. Cam collected the votes in a big bowl. Then he and Holden retreated to the kitchen to count ballots.

"Good luck to us," Bo murmured.

"Do you want me to take her?" Maxine held out her hands.

"No. She's fine." Maxine's daughter felt right in Bo's arms. She wasn't a burden and she somehow managed to make his heart feel fuller.

"Okay. If you're sure." Maxine smiled softly, as if she, too, was touched by him holding Luna. And instead of lowering her hands, she reached up and brushed the hair from Bo's forehead.

"The votes have been tallied." Holden returned from the kitchen a few minutes later and held up a piece of paper. "No sense dragging it out. We'll get right to it. Fifth place goes to… Jonah's team."

The crowd applauded. Jonah, Emily and Adam exchanged high fives in front of their blackened masterpiece.

Bo nodded. This was good.

Please give fourth to Shane.

"Fourth place goes to Shane's team."

Maxine found his hand and held on. She knew how important the competition was to him.

If we win tomorrow, we could win this thing.

"Third place." Holden turned toward the cookie house. "Olivia's team."

First or second. That was what they were looking at. Realistically, the smooth white frosting on Ashley and Gabby's house combined with their cute candy trees, licorice doors and windows showed more artistic talent than Bo and Luna's gingerbread house. But still, Bo squeezed Maxine's hand, hoping.

"And the runner up is… Bo and Luna." Holden swept his arm toward Ashley and Gabby. "Which means the winner is Team Ashley."

"Second place is awesome. We're number two. We're number two," Maxine said as the crowd pushed forward to congratulate the contestants. She glanced up at him. "You're happy?"

"I am. And I'll be happier if we win this thing tomorrow."

"Or you could just be happy with the experience itself," Maxine told him.

"The way you are with your holidays?" The question came out without Bo thinking. Immediately, he wanted to take it back.

But Maxine nodded. "I take what I can get."

Bo shook his head. She deserved so much more. "That's not good enough. You should want it all." He did.

The win, the title and her heart.

THE LOG CABIN was just as Max remembered it—a snow-blanketed cabin nestled in the pines with a breathtaking view of the valley. All it needed was smoke coming out of the chimney to make the scene Christmas card ready.

But since she and Bo had visited, more snow had fallen, in some places more than three feet. It had taken a call to Franny's father to bring his truck with a snowplow attachment on the front to clear the drive from the highway. And now there were a dozen Monroes and half a dozen vehicles stuck between the plowed drive and the cabin while Bo and Holden shoveled a path to the front door. They'd gone a good thirty feet and had another fifteen or so to go.

Max was glad she'd left Luna back at the ranch with Spot and the other kids where she'd be warm and fed.

"This has to have been where Grandpa Harlan lived," Bo's cousin Sophie was saying. "That cabin looks just like the one he had built on the back of his property in Pennsylvania, and this is a million dollar view. He'd have loved this."

"Does this mean there's going to be a scuffle over who can live here?" Max wondered aloud.

There was a chorus of dismissals.

"I like my place," Sophie told Max. "It's in town and just a walk away from the general store."

"I live at the Bucking Bull now," Shane said.

Similarly, others had already established themselves at various ranches and businesses in and around town.

Max was relieved that there wouldn't be any family drama over the property, especially if Bo wanted it. "If this place had more going for it, I bet Bo would be happy to take it."

"More going for it?" Shane gestured to the view. "Why would anyone need more when you have that?"

"Didn't you know?" Max asked. "Bo's got a list of things he's looking for in a house."

"Really?" Shane seemed interested.

"Yeah. Want to see?" Although Max couldn't remember all the items on the list, she knew where Bo kept it. She backtracked to Bo's truck with Shane.

Bo's was the last vehicle parked in the lane. Once there, Max climbed in the driver's seat while Shane stood just outside the door, taking a phone call.

She reached into the center console. Only

instead of pulling out one folded sheet of lined paper, she pulled out several. Turned out, he'd made lots of lists. The Perfect Job. The Perfect Home Base, which was different than the list for a vacation home. And then she opened a sheet of paper with a surprising heading. The Perfect Woman. "Now, why doesn't that surprise me?"

She read through the list.

Sophisticated. Gorgeous. Elegant. Nothing messy in her past relationships. Knows what she wants at all times. Knows where she's going in life.

Max dropped the paper as if burned. Nothing on that list described her. Nothing.

This is the other shoe.

How could Bo kiss her like she meant something to him when she was nothing like the woman of his dreams? How could he tell her to breathe and explore the feelings they had for each other when he clearly had no intention of getting serious with her?

I have to pack my bags and leave.

She couldn't. She had no way to get to the airport, not to mention that Luna was excited about being the main attraction in their sleigh tomorrow.

Max wrapped her arms around her waist,

hurting inside, feeling as small as when she'd been a girl.

At least then, they'd had the nerve to tell me to my face.

"What's wrong?" Shane opened the truck door wider, having completed his call. She'd forgotten he was there. "Can't you find it?"

"No. Gosh, Bo is a pack rat." Max folded the list and shoved it into Bo's center console along with all the others, struggling to regain her composure. "I… I remember now. Um… An open floor plan. Move-in ready. A three car garage."

Shane laughed. "He won't find what he wants around here."

You got that right.

That was why he must have settled for her.

"But Bo should take this place, especially if it was our grandfather's." Shane moved back to let her out. "Sometimes, I don't think he knows what he wants. I think that's why he makes all those lists and plans. Half of them never come to fruition."

And now Max knew why. His expectations were lofty.

Across the snowy meadow, Bo opened the door to the cabin.

Shane looked toward the cabin and then back to Max. "Are you coming?"

"No. I've seen it before." And experienced rejection too often to play the game. "I'll wait here."

"If that's the case, you should start the truck and run the heater." Shane gave a little wave before heading off.

Max drew a shaky breath. Bo had left his keys in the cup holder. She started the truck.

She meant to wait there for Bo, she really did.

But instead, she put the truck in Reverse and backed away from Beauregard Franklin Monroe.

It was always easier to leave than to be abandoned.

THERE WERE MORE Monroes swarming about the log cabin looking for clues about who had lived there than there were ants on a potato chip dropped at a summer picnic.

They all wanted to know if their grandfather had stayed here during his visits.

The problem was that whoever had lived or stayed here last had cleared out almost everything. But Bentley had a theory that built on Ella's and had recruited Bo to help him prove it. While others walked around looking for things, Bentley and Bo moved at a slower pace, studying the building's structure.

"I found a bottle opener." Bo's cousin Sophie held up her find, having rummaged through a kitchen drawer. "He always preferred bottled beer."

"I found a straight razor in the bathroom." Holden came out with his prize. "He didn't like electric razors."

Jonah stared out the bedroom window. "If the snow wasn't so thick, we could poke around the yard. There might be something out there he left behind."

"People come first." Olivia stood in front of the hearth, reading the cross-stitched message on the framed sample hanging above it. "He used to say that, right?"

"Yeah, he did." Shane stood in the middle of the living room, arms crossed and brow furrowed. "Face it, we have no real proof that Grandpa Harlan was ever here. Anyone might have left these ordinary objects behind."

"That's why Bentley and I are looking for signs that the house was moved." Bo tried opening a bedroom window. It fought him all the way, only allowing him an inch at a time. "The front door sticks and so do most of the windows. That's usually an indication that a house has shifted on its foundation or has been moved." He struggled to slide the window closed.

"I found it," Bentley called from the other bedroom. "The crawl space is in the closet under the carpet." He'd pulled the carpet back and opened a narrow trap door that Luna would have had trouble fitting through.

They all crowded into the bedroom, feeling the cold draft coming from below the house.

"What are we looking for down there?" Shane put his hands on his knees, peered into the crawl space.

"More importantly, how are we going to get down there?" Holden leaned against a wall as far away from the closet as one could get and still be in the bedroom.

Bentley took out his cell phone and put it in flashlight mode. "I'm going to look at the foundation. If it's original to the cabin, that'll be a clue."

"How do you know it's original?" Sophie turned to Bo.

"Newer materials versus something shoddier." Bo shrugged. "If Grandpa Harlan moved the cabin in the last decade or so, he'd have a concrete foundation."

"Which this is," Bentley said in a muffled voice, his head inserted in the crawl space. "And there are milled beams and modern metal brackets down here, which imply recent work." He sat back on his knees.

"But what if this log cabin was built recently?"

"I saw some square nails used in the eaves," Bo said. "No hobby builder is going to use square nails. Those were made by hand."

"Still, we can't just assume this was the cabin Harlan was born in, the one that used to be near the Bent Nickel Diner."

"After Bryce died, Harlan let me stay in the cabin at the Monroe compound in Philadelphia." Ella placed a hand on the round log wall, patting it fondly. "He had a plaque outside the front door. It was made of wood, and it said something like…'This is where your story begins.' And then there was a big *M* carved beneath it."

"I remember that," Holden said.

Bo didn't. "I didn't see a plaque outside when I came the other day." And the snow on the ground had been lower. "But I wasn't looking." He'd been distracted by the unexpected view and the enigma that was Maxine.

He still remembered vividly the feel of her in his arms and the soft sound of her crying.

"Why would you look for the plaque? You were looking at a house, not Grandpa Harlan's home." Bentley got to his feet. "And now the snowdrift is nearly five feet high. The front door faces west, which is where the storms have been coming the last few days. Maybe it's hung below the snowdrift. Or maybe it's come off."

They all traipsed to the front door.

Bo pried it open and stepped outside, looking around the door. But nothing hung there above the five feet or so of snow banked against the house. He took a shovel and began digging snow away from the outer wall on one side. Holden took up the task on the other side.

"Nothing," Bo said after a few minutes of work.

"Nothing," Holden agreed, stepping back. "Not even numbers to indicate an address."

Bentley joined them on the porch, bringing his face close to the log walls. "There are holes here, as if something was nailed in. If there was a plaque, maybe it fell off. I don't think Grandpa Harlan visited the last two years before he died."

Holden and Bo took turns shoveling snow from the wall and foundation.

It wasn't long before Bo's shovel connected with something. "Here." He hoped it wasn't another empty flowerpot.

Bentley bent over and shoved aside snow with his bare hands. When he straightened, he had a carved wooden plaque in hand. "Grandpa Harlan. You old dog." He turned the plaque around and displayed it for all to see.

This is where your story begins.

A bold *M* was carved below it.

They all began to laugh and hug, as if somehow this one sign brought them closer to their grandfather, the old man who'd indelibly left his mark on each of them by spoiling them, loving them and eventually challenging them to be better people by writing an unorthodox will and leaving them Second Chance.

Bo glanced around, looking for Maxine.

But she was nowhere to be seen.

And neither was his truck.

CHAPTER SEVENTEEN

THE HARDEST PART about Max knowing she was leaving was not letting her heartbreak show.

She went back to the Bucking Bull Ranch and tried her best to smile as if nothing was wrong, when in fact everything was wrong.

She'd let herself begin to fall for a man who wasn't serious about her. And as if that wasn't bad enough, he'd led her on when she wasn't even close to being his romantic ideal. All she wanted to do was curl into a ball in a dark corner and have a good cry.

Instead, she climbed the stairs to the farmhouse and forced her lips into an upward position when Luna and Spot ran to greet her at the front door. The Great Dane still sported Max's college sweatshirt.

Will Bo look at that and remember me with regret? Or laugh at how gullible I was?

Max tended to think the worst. And those thoughts knotted her insides. She might have retreated to the bunkhouse if not for Luna. Dear sweet Luna and her ever-loving optimism.

"Mama, Granny Gertie let me set the table." Smiling and babbling, Luna grabbed one of Max's hands and led her inside. "Wait 'til you see. It's so pretty. Even Adam says so."

I have to be strong for Luna.

Max drew a ragged breath and blinked back unwanted tears, not that there was anyone to notice her upset. Luna was trundling ahead of her, and the Clark boys were playing a video game in the living room, ignoring them as they passed. Spot trotted by the boys and then trotted back to Luna and Max with that endearing doggy grin, lightening Max's mood just by his presence.

I can do this.

Max paused to bestow some love to the gentle giant, rubbing his ears and whispering endearments. It wasn't the dog's fault that his owner was callous.

Luna and Spot love me unconditionally.

And as she'd expected, like so many of her well-intentioned relatives, Bo couldn't love her enough. The list detailing his ideal woman was proof.

"Mama, come on." Luna gripped Max's hand once more, pulling her toward the dining room and the beautifully set table. And then her little darling was climbing into a chair at the head of the table. "Look how pretty." She held up a delicate china plate that had purple chrysanthemums and delicate gold accents.

"It's beautiful." Max admired the plate and set it back down.

The table had a maroon tablecloth draped over it. Jewel tone cloth napkins had been rolled and slid through gold napkin rings, placed above each plate next to purple water glasses. Ornate silver framed the setting—a knife and spoon on one side, two forks on the other. A large silver candelabra with golden candles sat in the middle of the table with evergreen branches flanking the base.

"And Granny Gertie has turkeys." Luna pointed to a pair of ceramic turkeys that were salt and pepper shakers. "She has Santa and Frosty shakers, too, but she said those are for Christmas." Luna raised her smiling face toward Max. "Can we come back for Christmas?"

"Of course you can," Gertie called from

the kitchen before Max could begin to make excuses.

Max helped Luna down from the chair and joined Gertie in the kitchen where she was wrapping potatoes in aluminum foil. "Please tell me I can help." If Max kept busy, she could stop thinking, stop feeling.

"No, thank you, Max," Gertie sing-songed. "Luna and I have everything covered."

Max sighed, glancing back at the festive dining room table. "Your Thanksgiving table is perfect, but we've got dinner and breakfast to eat before then."

"The table is set for tonight. Rancher fare. Steak and baked potatoes." Gertie ripped off another piece of aluminum foil. "We'll be setting up tables and portable heaters in the barn breezeway tomorrow for Thanksgiving dinner. There's just not enough room in the house for everyone Shane invited."

"Makes sense." And it also meant that there'd be tables to set up and decorate in the morning. Max was rather desperate to stay busy and away from one handsome Texan.

"Emily and Franny are out checking on stock." Gertie snuck Max a quick smile. "I poked through Emily's closet and found just what we need to complete Luna's costume for the sleigh ride."

"I tried it on." Luna clung to the countertop, nose barely reaching her fingers. "I make a good Mrs. Claus. It's because I'm cute." She grinned up at Max.

"And clever," Max told her. "Mrs. Claus isn't just another pretty face."

"I don't hear the others." Gertie opened the oven and began putting her foil-wrapped potatoes inside, cautioning Luna to keep clear because of the heat. "Did everyone come back together from the cabin search?"

"No. I took Bo's truck." The admission messed with her steady intake of breath. There was a reckoning coming and Max needed to be ready for it.

"You know, I could have told them it was Harlan's cabin." Gertie continued to load the oven with potatoes.

"Really. Why didn't you?"

"They don't ask me. But just you wait. Shane will come back with a million questions." Gertie tsked. "Those Monroes. They don't always think things through."

"Tell me about it." Even the ones who jotted their intentions down in notebooks every morning.

Gertie closed the oven and set a timer. "I've got the steaks for tonight marinating in the refrigerator and the turkeys for tomorrow soaking in the brine. Pies and rolls are made. And yet, I feel like I'm forgetting something."

"I know what it is." Max moved to the door that led to Gertie's room. "You need to put your feet up and take a rest. No sewing or knitting. No cooking or prep work."

Without warning, Gertie hugged Max, chuckling. "Thank you for saying that. Your presence here has been a blessing." She stepped back, holding Max at arm's length. "And what I said before was true. You're welcome to come back for Christmas. I know Bo would love to have you."

Max didn't have the courage to tell her she was wrong.

"I THINK YOU should move into that log cabin," Shane told Bo on the drive back to the Bucking Bull.

"That's entirely up to Maxine." They had a lot to talk about.

"I expected you to say something about the cabin not meeting the criteria on one of your lists." Shane took the last hill to the ranch at a snail's pace, driving carefully through the slush and ice.

"Maybe I need to make a new list." With Maxine, whom he hoped he'd find at the ranch. For some reason, he suspected she might have left him on purpose. She hadn't been pleased with his attitude during the gingerbread competition. What had he missed?

"Do you ever wonder why you make lists?" Shane's question came out of the blue.

"No. I've been making lists forever." Bo spotted his truck, relieved since that meant Maxine had come here. He put a hand on the door latch, ready to get out, eager to check on Maxine, to see her smile and reassure himself that she was okay. That *they* were okay. He would have called her, but he'd only just realized that he didn't have her cell phone number.

"Yeah, but why do you make them?" Shane parked in front of the farmhouse next to Bo's vehicle. "When did you start? I was thinking about it today when Maxine was hunting down your list of your requirements for a home in Second Chance. I remember you having your nose in a notebook on some trip we were on with Grandpa Harlan." When Bo would have opened the door, Shane caught his arm. "Did he suggest it?"

Bo frowned. "Why does that matter?"

"He knew what each of our weaknesses were," Shane said earnestly. "And he was good about taking the time to give us the tools we needed to feel better about ourselves or succeed in life." He withdrew his hand. "He left us Second Chance for the same reason. For us to find our own center of gravity, rather than entrenching us in the businesses he'd created."

Maxine walked in front of the living room windows, carrying Luna. Bo wanted to join her. He needed to join her.

"Shane, I—"

"I had a lot of time to think after my accident in September," Shane went on in that listen-to-me way of his. "Life in Second Chance is slower than the life I had in Las Vegas running Monroe hotels. It frustrates me sometimes, but on a personal level my life is infinitely richer now."

"I'm happy for you but—"

"You need to think about what Grandpa Harlan has given us. And I don't mean this town or a cabin with a spectacular view. I mean the life he wanted us to live."

"Shane," Bo said through gritted teeth. "The life I want to live is with Maxine."

And she was currently walking down the porch steps and heading to the bunkhouse, carrying a sleepy-looking Luna. She was probably going to put her down for a nap.

He hopped out and hurried after them. "Maxine. Luna. Wait up."

Maxine's steps faltered, but she didn't look back. "We're going to rest, Bo. We'll see you at dinner."

Luna waved at him over her shoulder.

His steps slowed. Something wasn't right. He felt it in his gut.

But he respected her wishes, so he turned around and followed Shane inside the farmhouse. He found a seat in the living room, a pen and scrap of paper, and he started writing. His heading was: *The Perfect Life*. The first thing he wrote beneath the heading was: *Maxine*. The next thing was: *Luna*.

Spot came to sit next to him, resting his big muzzle on Bo's thigh.

Spot.

And that was as far as his list went.

"You've been avoiding me," Bo said in a voice that sounded carefully neutral.

Max was washing dinner dishes in the kitchen. She glanced at Bo, registering the note of sadness in those gray eyes, before looking about, trying to find someone else to act as a buffer, just like she'd been doing throughout dinner.

Bo picked up a dish towel and began drying the fancy dinner plates she'd washed. "Everyone's going to watch one of those kid-friendly movies in the living room. You can tell me what happened today."

"Nothing happened." The words felt forced, even to Max. "I was the only non-Monroe at the cabin, and I didn't want to intrude."

"And…" He opened a cupboard and put the plate he'd been drying on a shelf. He may not have lived at the ranch, but he knew where things belonged. He belonged here.

She did not. "There is no *and.* I just needed… *wanted* to give you some space." Max drew a deep breath, trying to hold herself together when all her parts wanted to shatter.

"My space is your space." Bo picked up another plate. "You seemed okay with that this morning."

Max had spent the afternoon thinking about how she should handle this conversation. She'd run through lines, choosing her words specifically. But practice didn't always make perfect, especially where Bo was concerned. "I think it's for the best if we stop right here." She rushed on, "There's no future and it's time that you admit it."

"You? You mean we?" He put the dried plate away and took her wet, soapy hands in his, forcing her to face him. "We need to talk about this."

The last thing she wanted to do was run through a litany of shortcomings she had when it came to his ideal woman. "The year after my parents died, I lived with my uncle Todd and his family. Everyone thought that was best. They had two toddler girls and I guess my family assumed the situation would be mutually beneficial." *Why am I telling him this?*

Bo didn't question why. He waited for her to continue.

So Max kept talking. "But I was grieving and all I did was stay in my room reading books and feeling like no one understood me. I don't think I was surprised when they told me I'd be going to live with my paternal grandmother. She was widowed and had an active social life. She taught me how to cook, clean house and play gin rummy. I did everything I could to be a help to her. And when the family discovered that she was leaving me at home alone to take weekend bus trips to a local casino, I was sent to my aunt Kate's."

Bo's mouth pressed into a thin line.

"I don't know why Kate volunteered. Her marriage was falling apart. Her kids walked around like I did, trying not to upset anyone." She'd never felt welcome. "When they divorced, I wasn't surprised that I was sent to live with my grandpa Norm, who no one realized had dementia."

Bo's hold on her hands tightened.

"Grandpa used to call me by my mother's name, but I didn't care. He gave good hugs, appreciated my cooking and taught me how to drive." It didn't matter to him that she was only fourteen and underage. And she quickly became a better driver than he was. "But then came the doctor's diagnosis of dementia. And the family decided I should live with my aunt Bea, Nathan's mother."

"Why do I feel like you're leaving a lot of gaps in this story?"

She was. "The gaps don't matter. Don't you see? What matters is that I didn't fit in anywhere, not the way I did with my own parents. It's never the right time or the right fit."

His jaw ticked. "We fit, Maxine. We fit perfectly. You've stepped out of your shell to compete with me. My family loves you. I love you."

I love you.

How Max wished she could embrace those words and embrace him. But it wasn't real. It couldn't last. Nothing in her life ever had.

She shook her head, pulling her damp hands free. "You don't. You can't. I saw your list for the perfect woman. I'm not it."

He flinched. "You saw... I make lists all the time. And throw them away just as often."

She wasn't going to let him talk her out of this. "We had a good time together, Bo. I think Nathan knew we'd hit it off. But you shouldn't toss around the L-word as if what we have is something that can endure."

"You're scared."

She didn't justify his remark with as much as a blink. She was terrified.

"You're scared," he said again, hurt coloring those two words. "And finding those stupid lists was an excuse. You were looking for an out, and people who look hard enough always find what they're looking for."

He was right. But only half right. She had to look for an out. She had to keep her heart from being smashed by rejection. And someone as handsome and smart as Bo was sure to reject her sooner or later.

"I'm going to go to the bunkhouse." Max took a step back. "Can you finish the dishes for me?"

"Maxine…" He reached for her.

She backed away, feeling like she was about to miss the last train. "We can make it through to Friday, Bo, if we're civilized adults. And I've asked Emily to drive us to the airport Friday morning, so we can say our goodbyes on Thanksgiving."

"Nothing about the way I'm feeling right now is civilized," he said darkly.

Max didn't know what else to say. So she left him in the kitchen and Luna in the living room, and practically ran to the bunkhouse, where she let herself have a good cry.

Bo STOOD IN the kitchen, numb.

What happened? Max saw his lists. So what? He made lists whenever, wherever.

A sound at the end of the kitchen had him lifting his head.

"I didn't mean to eavesdrop." Gertie moved toward him, pity in her gaze. "But I happened to overhear since my room is right here and…" She hugged him.

Bo was slow to raise his arms and return the embrace.

They stood like that for longer than some might feel necessary.

"Do not think of this as the end. She's just scared, like you said." Gertie stepped back, clinging to Bo's arms as if what she had to say was important and difference-making. "I heard what Max said about her childhood. You're right. She's been looking for any sign that you aren't serious about her."

He nodded, feeling like he'd been standing outside in a snowstorm for too long. He was cold and frozen to the core. "She found my lists. It's a stupid habit."

"Habits aren't stupid if they're done for a purpose." Gertie stepped up to the sink and picked up plate washing where Maxine had left off. "You've always talked about your lists when you talk about your future."

On autopilot, Bo picked up the dish towel and returned to the task of drying. "I make lists about everything. Lists of what I want in a couch. Lists of what I want my day to feel like. Lists of what I need to do on a daily basis. Shopping lists. Workout lists. Bucket lists."

"Lists of what you want in a wife?" Gertie gave him an apologetic glance. "I heard that, too."

"Yeah, well, it was… No one ever knows who they'll fall in love with, I guess." He knew that now. He should have thrown all his lists away. But if he had, Maxine would have found something else she considered proof that they weren't meant to be.

"Then why make a list?" Gertie asked softly, staring up at him.

He shrugged. Shane had essentially asked the same question earlier.

"What do you think all those lists give you?" Gertie no longer looked at him. "If you find the answer to that question, you may find what you need to win Max back."

Her words didn't hearten him. "You're assuming she'll listen to me."

"Oh, she'll listen. You still have the sleigh decoration competition ahead. She won't disappoint Luna by backing out. She plans to stay until Friday."

Bo nodded. "I'm just so blindsided by her rejection that I can't think." He'd told her he loved her. And she'd walked away.

Gertie gestured out the window toward the backyard. "Emily always does her best thinking out at the firepit."

Bo glanced outside. It was dark, but the light from the kitchen illuminated a bit of weather. "It's starting to snow."

"Which is why you'll need to light a big fire."

"You're sending me out in the cold?" He was acting like his dog, preferring the warm indoors to the mountain elements.

Gertie nodded. "The cold will help you come to your senses. Don't give me that look." She tsked and nudged him with her elbow. "Isn't that what good grandparents do? Even surrogate ones? Give you a little time out to think about things?"

He supposed that was true. That was certainly what his Grandpa Harlan would do.

Bo sighed. "Let me help you finish the dishes first."

"You're a good man, Bo. A keeper."

If only Maxine thought so.

CHAPTER EIGHTEEN

"THIS MOODINESS OF yours is a problem." Bundled in his parka, Jonah plunked into the folding chair that Bo had intended to use. "Gertie said you shouldn't be out here alone."

"Really? She sent me out here to think. Alone." Bo had finally gotten a big fire going and his opinionated cousin had taken the seat he'd shaken snow off of earlier.

"Think-schmink. Everyone's snuggled up inside watching a movie with a guaranteed happy ending, including your dog." Jonah propped his feet on the stone lining the firepit. "Spot's adopted Luna. I know who your new dog-sitter is."

Frustration vibrated up Bo's spine. "Go back inside, Jonah."

His cousin dropped his feet and lifted his gaze to Bo's face. "I recognize that look. That's the tell-tale sign of a broken heart."

"Go back inside. I don't want to talk about it."

"I promise not to joke." Jonah sank back in

his seat, shrugging deeper in his parka. "No. I can't promise no humor. But I do promise to tone down the sarcasm."

Bo grabbed another folding chair covered with inches of snow. He banged it on the ground, knocking the snow off the way he wanted to knock the obstacles to a happy ending with Maxine out of his path.

"Frustration over the possibility of losing the Monroe Holiday Challenge?" Shane joined them, handing two beer bottles to Jonah, and claiming the chair Bo had just finished clearing of snow while retaining a bottle for himself.

"I doubt it's the challenge that's upset him," Jonah told Shane. "Look at that face. It's Max."

Grumbling, Bo set about removing snow from a third chair. "Her name is Maxine." He refused to give her less than her due.

His cousins remained silent, drinking beer, and reeking of domestic bliss.

Finally, Bo sat down.

Jonah handed him a beer.

The snow fell. The fire crackled. Presumably, the earth continued to rotate on its axis. Surprisingly, his cousins kept their commentary to themselves.

"It's the lists," Bo admitted when he couldn't stand the silence anymore. "Maxine saw one of my stupid, stupid lists and it scared her."

Shane leaned forward, elbows on his knees, questions in his eyes. "Because…"

"My plans never included someone like her," Bo said baldly, agony so raw in his voice that it sounded like nails dragged across a clean chalkboard.

"What did you do? Describe Aria?" Jonah's gaze connected with Bo's. He must not have liked what he saw there because he immediately apologized.

"About those lists…" Shane was still studying Bo intently.

He wanted to know why, the same as Gertie. Bo shrugged. "It started with the challenge, I think." Where had that impression come from? Bo drew a calming breath, took a sip of beer, watched snowflakes fall, trying to calm himself and follow the trickle of a memory. "I think I told Grandpa Harlan that I wasn't good at anything."

"Typical childhood complaint," Shane said.

"But there's more pressure to be a so-called good Monroe." Jonah should know. He'd had health challenges as a child that had given his self-confidence a big hit.

"Yes, but…" Bo closed his eyes. It felt like there was more to this than just making a list. "Grandpa Harlan told me to make a list of what I'd done the day before. We…we went over it. He must have praised me for things I'd done. He had me write down what I thought I needed to do to have a more successful day." In his mind's eye, Bo could see the list he'd made.

Run fast. Play hard. Pick myself up when I fall.

"Confidence builders." Shane sat back in his chair. "You know, mantras and stuff."

Bo did know. He'd embraced positive affirmations. He thought about the plaque they'd found at the cabin.

This is where your story begins. How he wished that was true.

"I think I remember that day." Jonah frowned. "I was jealous that you got something from Grandpa Harlan and I didn't."

Bo smiled a little. "Is that why I found my notebook the next morning with scribbles in it? Was that you?"

"I'm a writer." Jonah harrumphed as if miffed, but a smile played at the corner of his lips. "If it was scribbles, it was a complete scene with stage direction and character motivation."

"We were a competitive lot." Shane lightly slugged Jonah's shoulder. "Admit it. As kids we all felt pressure to be a Monroe, whatever that meant."

Bo drew a belabored breath, acknowledging there had been pressure, realizing there still was. "How did you know, Shane? About the lists, I mean? You asked me about them earlier. Did Maxine say anything?"

"No. I've been watching you struggle though, as a couple. And I knew that Grandpa Harlan left his imprint on you somehow, just like he did on the rest of us. Helping us find our way." Shane leaned forward again, gaze earnest. "Sophie retreated to anything quiet and collectible. Cam found a place in the kitchen, I rebelled. Olivia sailed out on the ocean. Ashley stepped into the spotlight of acting."

"What about me?" Jonah asked, grinning.

"You wrote," Shane replied without hesitation. "You wrote stories about our adventures when we were together. Thinking back, that was the two of you, playing cards or sticking your noses in notebooks."

"I'm never making a list or writing an affirmation again," Bo moaned. "I'm a grown man and look how much trouble that stupid, thoughtless habit caused. How am I going to win Maxine back?"

"I have an idea about that," Shane said, which shouldn't have surprised Bo. Shane was always full of ideas.

"Oh, no." Jonah shook his head.

But Bo leaned forward, ready to listen.

He was that desperately hopeful.

THANKSGIVING MORNING DAWNED clear and bright, the way every morning in the Idaho mountains had during her stay.

Before Max put on her glasses, she knew the world outside would be beautiful, sparkling with snow. And she knew the laughter and love she'd witness among the Monroes would be beautiful, too. More so because she was looking from the outside in.

"Mama, is today the day I'm Mrs. Claus with Spot as my reindeer?"

"Yes, honey. It's Thanksgiving." But Max couldn't think of a thing to be grateful for.

"I hope there's bacon for breakfast and pancakes and cowboys." Luna put on her glasses and went to stand at the window. "Lots and lots of cowboys."

"I hope so, too." For her sake. Max sat up carefully and just as carefully prepared Luna for their goodbyes. "Today is the last day for cowboys. We go home tomorrow."

Luna spun around and Max didn't need her glasses on to see her daughter's displeasure. "I don't wanna."

"Luna, you know we don't live here," Max said gently, forcing the words past a throat thick with emotions. "All your toys and your friends are back in Springfield."

"But I have a pony here, Mama. And cowgirl friends." Luna crossed her arms over her chest. "I eat my vegetables and I help Gertie."

Max made her way from the top bunk, found her glasses and got down on Luna's level. "Sweetheart, I know you like it here. But just wait until Christmas. We'll be somewhere else and you'll make new friends and find new favorite things."

Luna's body was rigid. "I wanna come back here at Christmas."

We'll see.

That was the standard line of every parent that led kids along when in reality, "we'll see," meant no. Max refused to say those two words. Instead, she set about getting ready for the day, physically and mentally.

Luna's mood lightened when she put on her red dress over a pair of gray leggings. "I am Mrs. Claus."

Max hoped that role would keep Luna in good spirits for a while.

When they finally made it over to the farmhouse, all was quiet. The house was empty, except for Gertie. Even the dogs were gone.

"Hello?" Max called out.

"Breakfast is ready," Gertie replied from the back of the house.

"Where is everyone?" Max checked the time as they made their way to the kitchen. "Are we late?" She didn't think so.

"Oh, you know this crowd." Gertie set two plates full of food on the dining room table. "They were excited about getting to their sleighs. Last minute decorations and such. They left me here to get you fed."

Max wanted to ask how Bo was doing. He'd be stressing about winning the sleigh competition and the entire Monroe Holiday Challenge. He had a lot riding on their tiny sleigh. But he no longer gambled on a future with Max.

She'd expected him to stop by the bunkhouse last night or catch her when the movie was over and she'd returned to the farmhouse to collect Luna at bedtime. But he hadn't sought her out. Her trepidation had turned to sadness.

Why not me?

"Such a pretty dress, Luna." Gertie paid Luna some special attention. "After you eat, we'll try on that pretty jacket and Santa hat again."

After breakfast was eaten and the dishes done, they loaded up in Bo's truck with Max driving.

"Isn't it beautiful up here?" Gertie twisted and turned in her seat as she took in the snow-covered trees and blue sky. She was bundled up in a thick brown jacket with a brown felt cowboy hat on her head. "All this snow reminds me of the day my husband proposed. He was so nervous that he dropped the ring in a snowdrift."

"Oh, no. What did he do?"

"He?" Gertie laughed. "Honey, I dove into the snow like a fox after a rabbit. He may have been rough around the edges and in possession of two left feet, but he was mine, faults, and all. I knew he couldn't afford to replace that ring and I wasn't going to let my chance pass me by."

"Is that a true story?" Because it sounded

suspiciously like a hint that Max shouldn't walk away from Bo.

"Every word." Gertie laid a hand over her heart.

They arrived at the meadow. The sleighs were on display outdoors, decorated with greenery, sparkly ornaments and bright lights. Horses had been hitched to four sleighs and one big white dog to a fifth.

Max parked near Shane's truck, pausing to collect her courage.

"Everything I told you is true, Max. Just like this is true." Gertie opened Bo's center console.

Gone were the stack of folded papers stored inside. There was only one piece of folded paper now. And Max's name was written on it: *Maxine Marie Holloway.*

"I don't want that." Max shifted toward her door, away from Gertie and the note.

"What is it, Mama?" From her car seat in the back, Luna squirmed as if trying to get free. "Chocolate? Chewing gum? Show me."

"No. It's…" Max didn't know what it was. But she felt deep down in her bones that it was life changing. She just didn't know if it was her life the note would change or Bo's.

"It's a love letter from Bo to your Mama,"

Gertie said in a chipper voice. "What do you think about that, Luna?"

A love letter? Max couldn't breathe.

"I love Bo," Luna said dreamily. "I wish we could stay here."

"Go on, girl." Gertie nudged Max. "Read it."

Reluctantly, Max picked up the paper and unfolded it.

How to prove to Maxine Marie that I love her now and always, no take-backsies.

Ask her to look deep in her heart and trust what she finds there.

The back door of the truck opened. Max's heart scaled up into her throat.

"Bo!" Luna cried happily. "Is it time for my sleigh ride?"

"It sure is, sweetheart." Bo smiled tenderly at Max before bending to the task of unbuckling Luna. "Are you ready, Mrs. Claus?"

"I am, Mr. Bo."

He lifted Luna into his arms, shut the door and walked toward the sleighs.

Without even talking to Max!

"He didn't say a word to me," Max marveled.

"Maybe he thought he'd said everything he needed to in that love letter." Gertie got out of the truck, pausing to look back at Max. "Maybe he thought you'd dive into the proverbial snowdrift, like I did." She closed the door behind her, leaving Max alone.

With nothing but a love letter from Bo.

Max read the letter again.

Love. He'd said he'd loved her last night.

But words were easy. It was actions that spoke the truth.

Images passed through her mind. Bo taking in the surprise of Max being Maxine at the airport. His laughter when she tried to guess his preferred menu at Thanksgiving. How quick he'd been to offer her comfort when she needed it. The gentle way he looked at her before they kissed. How his brow arched when she tried to tug her hand free of his.

When she recalled those moments, a sense of peace stole through her. She didn't feel like he found her lacking, as if he'd settled for what was in front of him instead of his romantic ideal. She felt seen. Cherished. Appreciated. Loved.

Loved.

She breathed in the idea that she could allow herself to be loved by Bo and trust that she was enough, have faith that he understood her so well that they could build something real and lasting.

She had work to do to make that happen. Confidence to build. Courage to be grasped.

Starting with making a move.

Max got out of the truck and went to find the man who understood her better than anyone, who knew her weaknesses and faults, and loved her anyway.

She found him standing next to Spot, who wore antlers and was hitched to their small sleigh.

"Mrs. Claus, you have the reindeer's reins," Bo said to Luna. "But I'm going to walk next to Spot in case he gets nervous."

Luna beamed, fussing with the too-large, plush shrug Gertie had borrowed from Emily and a cute red Santa hat. "Mama, the parade is about to begin."

"Great, sweetheart." Max tried to catch Bo's eye, but he was fiddling with Spot's harness. Max still had his note in her hand. The message was clear. If she wanted him, she was going to have to ask for him.

She moved closer to Bo and spoke quietly. "You know, all those times, all those places that I bounced around to, I wondered why not me? Why can't they hold on to me regardless of the other stuff that was going on? I thought if I kept quiet and was a help that I'd prove keeping me was the right choice."

Bo kept his gaze down.

There were lots of people around, but no one seemed to be talking.

Max drew in a fortifying breath. "My childhood wasn't picture perfect, but it led me to you. And you may think I haven't been listening to what you've been putting down, but I have. At some point, I can't live a life in a bubble, not the life I want to lead, not a life that includes you. Because I love you, Bo. I love you and it terrifies me and it shouldn't. I love you and I wonder how my life will change because of it and it shouldn't. I love you and—"

"Nothing has to be decided right now." Bo's arms came around her. "I'm here. And nothing about us being together should ever be scary."

"It's just that you have everything," Max said in a small voice, fingers fumbling with the snap on his jacket. "And I can't understand why you'd need me."

"Can't you?" He rolled his eyes. "I don't have everything. It's why I made those lists. And

I didn't know what I wanted, which is why I made new lists. And you were the first woman to look at me and see beyond the exterior, to see the man I am inside. The imperfect, work-in-progress man who lacked direction until you walked up to me in an airport and gave me the business."

Max breathed easier for the first time that day, slipping her arms around him. "You deserved the business. You can be a little full of yourself."

He nodded.

"And you're too competitive."

He nodded.

"But you're wonderful with me." She nodded toward their sleigh. "And with Luna and Spot."

"We love Bo," Luna chimed in.

"I love him, too," Max said levelly, meeting Bo's gaze, no longer scared by what she saw there or what the future might hold, as uncertain as it was.

And then Bo kissed her sweetly with a promise of more to come.

It was a perfect moment, even if neither of them was perfect.

A horse harness jingled. Someone coughed.

"Happy Thanksgiving!" Holden's voice

rang out across the meadow. "Everyone, we're ready to begin the parade."

"Finally," Adam huffed. "The kissing should stop now!"

"There's always too much kissing," his brother Charlie said.

"And lovely-dovey talk, Papa Shane," Davey added.

Max and Bo eased apart, smiling at each other while the rest of the assembled laughed at their heckling.

Bo had a look in his eyes that said he wouldn't mind another kiss.

"We have to complete the competition first." Max was brimming with joy, but she knew Bo had unfinished family business.

"Always the responsible one." Bo tsked.

It only took a few minutes for the sleigh parade to begin. There were horses and ponies, glitter and costumes. She and Bo brought up the rear of the parade with Spot pulling Luna in their little sleigh.

Luna had a ball but by the end of their short parade, they were all cold and ready to head back to the ranch proper. All they needed was for the winner to be decided. And yet, there seemed to be a heated debate among the judges.

Bo didn't wait to free Spot and let him run. Or to pick up Luna and try to keep her warm. But it was the pacing through the snow that gave away his obvious nervousness.

Max let him pace, giving him a smile when he looked her way. She knew how important making his mark on the challenge was to Bo.

Finally, Holden separated himself from the crowd. "We all knew when we resurrected the challenge that this year would be different. Competing in Second Chance is truly unique for more than just the little romance that we've witnessed." Holden gestured for Bo to join him. "You need to come over here, brother."

Bo glanced at Max, who shrugged. She had no idea what was going on.

Carrying Luna, Bo joined his brother. Spot trotted along with him.

"We thought it would be appropriate for you to announce the winner of the sleigh parade." Holden handed Bo a slip of paper.

"You wrote it down?" Bo glanced toward Max apologetically.

She shrugged.

Bo looked at the paper he'd been given. And then he turned to Max with a glowing smile. "The winner of the sleigh parade is Team Maxine."

The crowd cheered.

Max ran over to join Bo and Luna, slowed by the snow. "You mean Team Bo."

"No." Holden smiled at Max. "We wanted you to feel like part of the Monroe family. This is our way of making that statement."

Touched beyond belief, Max found her eyes filling with tears. She wrapped her arms around Bo and Luna, burying her head in his chest.

"Who came in second?" Bo asked in a gruff voice. "Or third? Or—"

"They all dropped out of contention for this event," Holden told them, smiling like he knew something they didn't.

"But that means..." Bo's eyes widened. "We won? Who won the whole thing?"

"You did, Bo." And then Holden was hugging them. "You did it at last."

Max took Luna and gave the two men space.

"Wow," Bo managed to say, still wrapped tight in his brother's hug. "I don't know what to say."

"You don't need to say anything." Holden held him at arm's length. "If we've learned anything over the past year, it's that making family happy is a top priority."

The Monroes surged forward to congratulate Bo, Max and Luna. There were plenty of hugs to go around and well wishes for Bo and Max.

"I need to get back to the turkeys," Gertie said, walking toward the vehicles. "You all can figure out how to get the stock home."

"Can you believe it?" Bo had his arm around Max. "We won."

"Like there was any doubt after we got in our groove." Max couldn't stop smiling.

But the truth was that the deck had been stacked in their favor, all in the name of family. And Max thought Bo had the best family ever.

"HOW ARE YOU holding up?" Bo asked Maxine as they sat down for Thanksgiving dinner later that day.

"I'm good." Maxine's smile said she was so much better than good.

Bo had to kiss her.

They'd spent the latter part of the morning setting up tables, chairs and heaters in the breezeway of the barn. The tables had been decorated with greenery and candlesticks, each setting with a sturdy paper plate and plastic utensils. Maxine had also tried to help in the kitchen but had been chased out a time or two by Gertie. There was a large buffet set up and the barn was buzzing with conversation about all that had happened that week. Holden said grace and then the kids rushed the buffet line.

Bo put a gentle hand on Maxine's shoulder, keeping her in her seat. "Let Luna get her own food."

"You think I was getting up to help fill Luna's plate?" Maxine scoffed, placing her hands on the paper plate in front of her. "The food is always the best part of the holiday."

Bo moved his hand below her hairline at the back of her neck. He loved his family but he wanted to spend time alone with Maxine. "The best part of the holiday for me was when you changed your flight to Sunday."

"I can't just tell you I love you and then fly home." She rolled her eyes, which necessitated an adjustment to her glasses. "Besides, we needed to extend our stay and help eat all the leftovers. I wouldn't want to disappoint Gertie."

"I should have known it would all come

back to the beginning." Bo brought his lips to her ear. "To food."

She snuggled closer. "Hey, I still need to know what you'll be eating today and what you'll eat when the leftover train begins tomorrow."

"What he eats?" From across the table, Holden laughed. "Don't you know? Bo will eat anything. Ham, turkey or turducken. Stuffing done any which way. Rolls, croissants, French bread. Pumpkin, apple, mince or pecan pie. You'll never have to worry about what he'll eat because he'll eat it all."

Maxine turned to look at Bo. "Is that true? Was I wrong about everything?"

"Maybe." Bo shrugged. "Or maybe you were right about everything. Let's head to the buffet and you can decide which it is."

CHAPTER NINETEEN

"WE ARE GATHERED here today…" Shane made the most of an audience, standing in front of a roaring fire in the lobby of the Lodgepole Inn. "…to vote on the future of Second Chance. I officially call this meeting of the Second Chance Monroes to order."

Or at least, he tried to.

Bo chuckled, amused by his cousin's optimistic sense of authority.

In addition to the twelve Monroes who'd inherited Second Chance, the lobby also contained their significant others and children, plus a select number of trusted residents, like Tanner, who was a distant relation, and Mackenzie, who ran the general store. Shane wasn't going to command the room with anything less than a loud voice and a shrill whistle.

Or one loud-mouthed cousin with better things to do.

"Let's get this meeting over and done with," Bo shouted above the din. He sat in a

nook by a front lobby window with Maxine.
He was going to Missouri with her tomor-
row, leaving Spot in the care of family at the
Bucking Bull.

"I don't know why we're having this meeting," Jonah said from a chair next to Bo.
Emily sat on his other side, braiding Luna's
hair, concentrating on taming the springy
curls. "We voted on what to do with Second Chance yesterday. Has someone changed
their mind?"

Yesterday's vote had only involved the
principle twelve Monroes.

"No, not at all. This is just ceremonial."
Bo drew Maxine closer, thinking about other
ceremonies and traditions they might be participating in, everything from kisses under
the mistletoe to exchanged vows standing at
an altar. "A lot of people here knew Grandpa
Harlan or accepted his buy-out offer. They
need to hear it from us. And it might as well
come from Shane." His cousin was the family
figurehead in town, after all, and its unoffi-
cial mayor, although there was talk of voting
on and forming a more official town council.

"Four Monroes showed up in town last January," Shane was saying now that the crowd
had quieted. "Myself, Laurel, Sophie and Ella."

"Oh, man. He's going way, way back." Jonah rolled his eyes. "This will take forever."

Maxine shushed him. "I've never heard this."

Neither had a lot of the children. They acted as if he was about to recount a favorite bedtime story.

"We'd been told at the reading of Grandpa Harlan's will that he wanted us to find what made us happy, whether that be in the family business or not. But he knew he had to take away every silver spoon we'd been given, every advantage we'd been offered, or we wouldn't take the time to figure out what we wanted out of life."

"Wily old coot," Jonah said to Bo, who fist-bumped him. "Gotta love Grandpa Harlan."

"Quiet, you two." Emily spared a moment from braiding hair to roll her eyes at them.

"Grandpa Harlan may have bequeathed us his hometown, but what we found in Second Chance wasn't a straightforward business opportunity." Shane smiled out over the assembled, but it was an honest smile, a happy-with-those-around-me smile. A year ago, his smile had resembled that of a vacation time-share salesman. "It's hard to turn a profit, much less find yourself, when everyone who lives in town or runs a business here only has to pay one dollar a year for their lease. We were all at a loss, mourning and adrift, including me. And there were several Monroes that wanted to sell Second Chance to develop a luxury resort or a high-end property." His gaze found the eight Monroes who hadn't originally arrived in town, including Jonah and Bo.

Maxine glanced at Bo and frowned. "You wouldn't have."

He shrugged, because he would have. "That was before." Before he'd fallen for the charm of Second Chance, its people and a simpler, slower life. Before Maxine arrived and fell in love with it, too.

"And then a handful of us discovered lost stagecoach gold, and a new reason for people to stop at Second Chance. It was the opportunity all of us were looking for. It was something to build on." Shane glanced down at the crowd. "Come spring, a movie will be filmed here starring Ashley and Wyatt."

"And me!" Davey raised his hand, which set off a flurry of other children's hands up, since they'd been promised roles as extras, too.

Shane quieted them down. "Thanks to

Mitch, several locations in Second Chance are in the process of being designated as historical, protected landmarks. This means our town won't be easily changed."

The assembled gave Laurel's husband, Mitch, a round of applause. He was in the midst of handing one of the twin baby girls to Wyatt but managed a wave of acknowledgement.

"I almost forgot that we also found a member of a lost branch of the family—Tanner." Shane turned to the man who'd shown up claiming a Monroe heritage and a stake in town. "We're happy to call Tanner and his kids our family."

There arose a small, group cheer of appreciation.

"Yay, Mia." Luna applauded her friend.

Maxine gave her daughter a proud smile.

"But now, as the year draws to a close and ten of the twelve inheriting Monroes have decided to make their home here, at least in the near future, it's clear that we're keeping the town."

Someone whooped.

Shane nodded. "And now, it's time to make an official decision in regard to the properties we lease." Shane went on to outline a new lease structure based on square footage and lot size. The leases would still be incredibly low and affordable, but the money would go into a trust to provide services and salaries to run the town. The future was bright for Second Chance. The Monroes would always back the town they'd all come to love. "All in favor of the new plan come January first?"

Everyone raised their hands. Everyone, not just the twelve inheritors, but every man, woman and child.

"Great! The decision's carried." Shane waved a piece of paper. "I received this today from Grandpa Harlan's legal representation. You can all read it, but in a nutshell, it says that as of January first, an authorized biographer is coming to town. The non-disclosure agreements made with all of Grandpa Harlan's lease holders will expire on December thirty-first. This means that anyone who wants to, may speak to the biographer about their relationship or experiences with Harlan Monroe."

"That's exciting." Maxine glanced at Bo again. "I'd like to read more about your grandfather."

"Me, too." Bo nodded. Apparently, the old man had talked to this biographer for several years before he passed away. "Are we done, Shane?"

"Yes, meeting adjourned. We're done."

There was a mass exodus from the inn.

But before they returned to the Bucking Bull, Bo treated Maxine and Luna to a milkshake, because they had a sweet tooth and he wanted them to have an abundance of happy memories of Second Chance.

"YOU'RE RIGHT. THE VIEW from here is spectacular." Max stood on a snowy hill in Second Chance next to a white church with a tall steeple. "You can see the valley stretching all the way to the Sawtooth Mountains."

She and Bo had made the climb from the Lodgepole Inn to the snowy rise. It was Christmas Eve morning. They'd returned to town a few days ago and were staying at the Bucking Bull once more.

Bo stood behind Max, arms encircling her. "I know it was something of a hike a mountain goat would take what with the snow and all, but I thought you'd enjoy the view up here."

Max snuggled deeper into his arms. She was enjoying life with Bo very much. Not that she didn't appreciate the grandeur of the view. She just appreciated him more.

After Thanksgiving, Bo had traveled back to Missouri with them. While he'd explored career options in Springfield, Max had decided three college degrees was enough.

They'd spent the weekend after that visiting Houston, which allowed Max to evaluate if Texas was where she wanted their life together to begin. But it was Second Chance that felt like their place, like home. And now, Max had to figure out what that life might look like.

Luckily, Max had bumped into Second Chance's sole teacher yesterday and struck up a conversation. Their chat had taken an unexpected turn when she'd mentioned interest in enrolling Luna in kindergarten next fall. He'd talked about his increasing workload. In addition to Monroe children, there were film crew families coming in spring. Max had been thrilled when he'd asked her if she'd be interested in teaching. Apparently, she could apply for an emergency teaching certificate while earning her teaching credentials.

"You know how much I enjoy learning and teaching," Max had said when she'd told Bo, reminding him that she'd been a graduate assistant for years. "There's talk of wanting to open a brick-and-mortar school right here, rather than having a satellite program with independent study. Do you think I'll be a good school teacher?"

"I do," he told her, reinforcing his approval with a deep kiss.

I do.

They'd talked about their future, about places they wanted to visit in the world, about changes that were needed at his grandfather's cabin in Second Chance, about committing to a life together.

In fact, Bo was talking with Bentley about creating inventions at a workshop Bentley was building at a ranch north of town. It meant putting their engineering heads together, which was a little scary when Max thought about all that problem-solving power. Watch out, world. New inventions were going to be made in Second Chance.

Change was happening fast. But it didn't feel overwhelmingly fast, not to either one of them or Luna. Luna loved Bo, too. And she was thriving with a more permanent, extended family on the horizon. This morning, she was taking riding lessons at the Bucking Bull under Franny's expert tutelage.

From behind her, Bo pressed a kiss to the side of Max's neck. "This is where several Monroes have been married."

"I can see why. It's gorgeous." She turned in his arms. "But I'd rather look into your eyes." She still marveled at the love she saw there.

"Honey, you're the item that's been missing from all my lists, all my life." Bo released her and sank down on one knee in the snow, making Max gasp. "But now you're the last thought I have before I fall asleep and the first thought I have when I wake up every morning. I love you. And my love for you grows every day. Will you marry me, Maxine Marie Holloway?"

"Bo..." Max wanted to say yes. But she hadn't lost all of her carefulness when it came to love and trust. "Are you—"

"I'm sure, honey."

Of course, he'd known what she was going to ask. And he didn't look disappointed that she had done so. Instead, he stared up at her as if he'd be crushed if she didn't answer in the affirmative.

"I love you, Bo. My answer is yes," Max whispered. And then she fell into his arms and shouted, "Yes!"

EPILOGUE

FOR MAX, THE CHRISTMAS SEASON in Second Chance was the winter wonderland she'd been promised.

It snowed. And snowed. And snowed some more. But it never quite snowed enough to close the passes and isolate the town from the rest of the world.

It was as if Harlan Monroe was looking down on the town from above and making sure this holiday was the best the town had experienced in years. He was, after all, Second Chance's guardian angel.

The snow meant that life slowed down, but no one seemed to complain overly much about that, especially Max.

There were potlucks and gift exchanges, lots of decorating and numerous plates of holiday cookies. There were carols sung and stockings hung by the fire. And there was a feeling that this holiday was special because love was everywhere. Not just for Max, Luna and Bo, but for all the Monroes.

If Harlan was looking down on his hometown, he'd have smiled happily at the love he saw there, and the difference his last wishes had made upon his grandchildren.

He'd have seen love in the medical clinic where Dr. Bernadette gave birth on Christmas Day. Proud papa Holden Monroe couldn't stop smiling at his new daughter. They named the little tyke Christine. Max was lucky enough to have held the baby and imagine another one of her own, a boy with Bo's soft gray eyes and thick, dark hair.

Looking down, Harlan would have seen love in the Lodgepole Inn, where Laurel Monroe Kincaid was settling into life with two six-month-old twin girls, twelve-year-old Gabby and husband Mitch. Bo and Max had volunteered to help paint remodeled rooms at the inn after the new year.

Harlan would have seen love at the Bent Nickel Diner, where Cam Monroe was constantly changing the dinner menu with his fiancée Ivy's approval. They'd begun a meal delivery program for the town's older residents. Bo had bought a snowmobile and was mapping out trails to help make deliveries during the winter months.

Harlan would have seen love on local ranches like the Bucking Bull, where Jonah Monroe and Emily Clark finally settled on a wedding date for next year, as did Bentley Monroe and Cassie Diaz at the Bar D, and Olivia Monroe and Rhett Diaz, although they were preparing to create a new life at a ranch in Minnesota. Max bet the old man would have enjoyed the prospect of so many weddings because it meant more family gatherings.

Harlan would have seen love at a cabin in the woods, where Sophie Monroe Roosevelt and her husband, Zeke, were making ready for a little brother for twins Alexander and Andrew.

He'd have seen love at the McAfee Ranch, where Kendall Monroe was planning for the future and a special family of their own with Finn McAfee and his daughter, Lizzie.

And if he'd looked toward California, he'd have seen love where grandson Bryce Monroe's widow, Ella, was making plans to marry Dr. Noah Bishop, and Ashley Monroe had settled into a more grounded, satisfying life in Hollywood with husband Wyatt Halford.

He'd have been thrilled that Ashley was going to make a movie in his hometown.

Max often thought about Harlan Monroe and the impact he'd made on his family, Second Chance and herself.

She thought he'd be happy to see love bloom at a familiar rustic log cabin in the woods, where one day Bo along with his soon to be wife—her!—and Luna would fill the place with joy and laughter.

And, Max imagined Harlan was with them in spirit now on New Year's Day, when love would lasso the four corners of the Bucking Bull Ranch, where Shane Monroe was set to marry Franny Clark.

The Bucking Bull's barn had been transformed with swaths of ivory silk, satin ribbons and lush greenery for the event that would cap what had been a tumultuous twelve months for the Monroes. The folding chairs were adorned with burgundy bows and formed an aisle for Franny and her attendants to walk down. Guests smiled, laughed quietly and spoke in whispers as they waited for the ceremony to begin.

Shane stood nervously at the altar outside of the tack room in an elegant tuxedo. His brother, Camden, and cousin Jonah stood at his side. Cam had made the wedding cake and was worried the space heaters would melt the frosting. Jonah predicted instead that one of the Clark boys would bump into the table and tumble the cake to the ground.

Bo and Bentley had shored up the cake table's defenses with two large, oak barrels. Gertie had dressed the safety barriers with a flowing white tablecloth that had silver and gold trim.

Wherever there was a concern, there was someone to alleviate it.

Max wanted to pinch herself. She was lucky to be part of the Monroe family gatherings and events. She could also hear Gertie's voice in her head telling her the Monroes were lucky to have her and Luna, too. It went both ways. Family appreciated family.

"Thinking about what our special day will be like?" From the seat next to hers, Bo nudged her shoulder with his. He held an excited Luna in his lap.

"I'm thinking Shane looks so anxious. And how he's going to be floored when he sees Franny." Earlier, Max had seen Franny's wedding dress. It was lovely.

"Are you sure that's what you're thinking? You've been staring at the flowery altar for a while now." Bo arched a brow. "I know we talked about the meadow, but we could have our wedding here or—"

Max shushed him. "It's Franny's big day." She didn't want to detract from the bride's or the groom's special moment. It was why they'd kept their engagement a secret, even from Luna. "We have plenty of time to talk about when and where later."

"This is why everyone in my family loves you." Bo pressed a kiss to her temple. "And why I love you, too."

"One of many reasons," she teased quietly.

The wedding march began. Everyone stood and turned as the barn doors opened slowly and snowflakes gently floated in on a woosh.

Bridesmaid Ivy stepped from the snow and into the warm light. She wore a long burgundy gown. Her hair was piled in sophisticated curls at her crown. Carrying a single white rose, she walked down the aisle dusted in snowflakes, looking gorgeous and more like a wood nymph than the no-nonsense proprietor of the Bent Nickel Diner.

Maid of honor and sister of the bride, Emily, appeared next with a similarly elegant gown and hairstyle. She had more than a dusting of snow on her hair, shoulders and gown. But she sashayed up the aisle with her single white rose as if it was a warm summer's day.

Max started to worry about the bride, lingering out there in the falling snow.

But then Franny appeared, looking radiant on the arm of her father, who wore a black tuxedo and a white felt cowboy hat. Franny's dress was ivory and simple in design and structure, like a Grecian gown. Her hair was swept up and threaded with strands of tiny pearls. She carried a small bouquet of white roses. Her outward style and sophistication didn't matter. Franny could have been wearing her regular uniform of jeans and a button-down shirt. She radiated love and happiness, and that only came from within.

Max's hand drifted over her heart, where she imagined she felt something similar. So much love and joy. Happiness threatened to burst from inside of her. Instead, a tear slid down her cheek.

Bo gently wiped it away.

They were all seated, and the ceremony began.

Max's hand found Bo's, wanting to ground all the love in her heart. Love for these people and this town. Love for her child and for

Bo. And finally, love for herself because she hadn't loved herself for far too long.

She laid her head on Bo's shoulder and listened to the words she'd someday exchange with Bo.

To love, honor and cherish...

And she knew whatever the future held, she needn't worry. This was her place, her person, her family. For now and evermore.

* * * * *

For other charming romances in
The Mountain Monroes miniseries from
Melinda Curtis and Harlequin
Heartwarming, visit www.Harlequin.com
today!

Get 4 FREE REWARDS!

We'll send you 2 FREE Books plus 2 FREE Mystery Gifts.

FREE
Value Over
$20

Both the **Love Inspired®** and **Love Inspired® Suspense** series feature compelling novels filled with inspirational romance, faith, forgiveness, and hope.

YES! Please send me 2 FREE novels from the Love Inspired or Love Inspired Suspense series and my 2 FREE gifts (gifts are worth about $10 retail). After receiving them, if I don't wish to receive any more books, I can return the shipping statement marked "cancel." If I don't cancel, I will receive 6 brand-new Love Inspired Larger-Print books or Love Inspired Suspense Larger-Print books every month and be billed just $6.24 each in the U.S. or $6.49 each in Canada. That is a savings of at least 17% off the cover price. It's quite a bargain! Shipping and handling is just 50¢ per book in the U.S. and $1.25 per book in Canada.* I understand that accepting the 2 free books and gifts places me under no obligation to buy anything. I can always return a shipment and cancel at any time by calling the number below. The free books and gifts are mine to keep no matter what I decide.

Choose one: ☐ **Love Inspired**
Larger-Print
(122/322 IDN GRDF)

☐ **Love Inspired Suspense**
Larger-Print
(107/307 IDN GRDF)

Name (please print)

Address   Apt. #

City   State/Province   Zip/Postal Code

Email: Please check this box ☐ if you would like to receive newsletters and promotional emails from Harlequin Enterprises ULC and its affiliates. You can unsubscribe anytime.

Mail to the **Harlequin Reader Service:**
IN U.S.A.: P.O. Box 1341, Buffalo, NY 14240-8531
IN CANADA: P.O. Box 603, Fort Erie, Ontario L2A 5X3

Want to try 2 free books from another series! Call 1-800-873-8635 or visit www.ReaderService.com.

---

*Terms and prices subject to change without notice. Prices do not include sales taxes, which will be charged (if applicable) based on your state or country of residence. Canadian residents will be charged applicable taxes. Offer not valid in Quebec. This offer is limited to one order per household. Books received may not be as shown. Not valid for current subscribers to the Love Inspired or Love Inspired Suspense series. All orders subject to approval. Credit or debit balances in a customer's account(s) may be offset by any other outstanding balance owed by or to the customer. Please allow 4 to 6 weeks for delivery. Offer available while quantities last.

Your Privacy—Your information is being collected by Harlequin Enterprises ULC, operating as Harlequin Reader Service. For a complete summary of the information we collect, how we use this information and to whom it is disclosed, please visit our privacy notice located at corporate.harlequin.com/privacy-notice. From time to time we may also exchange your personal information with reputable third parties. If you wish to opt out of this sharing of your personal information, please visit readerservice.com/consumerschoice or call 1-800-873-8635. **Notice to California Residents**—Under California law, you have specific rights to control and access your data. For more information on these rights and how to exercise them, visit corporate.harlequin.com/california-privacy.

LIRLIS22R2

Get 4 FREE REWARDS!

We'll send you 2 FREE Books plus 2 FREE Mystery Gifts.

FREE Value Over $20

Both the **Harlequin® Special Edition** and **Harlequin® Heartwarming™** series feature compelling novels filled with stories of love and strength where the bonds of friendship, family and community unite.

YES! Please send me 2 FREE novels from the Harlequin Special Edition or Harlequin Heartwarming series and my 2 FREE gifts (gifts are worth about $10 retail). After receiving them, if I don't wish to receive any more books, I can return the shipping statement marked "cancel." If I don't cancel, I will receive 6 brand-new Harlequin Special Edition books every month and be billed just $5.24 each in the U.S. or $5.99 each in Canada, a savings of at least 13% off the cover price or 4 brand-new Harlequin Heartwarming Larger-Print books every month and be billed just $5.99 each in the U.S. or $6.49 each in Canada, a savings of at least 20% off the cover price. It's quite a bargain! Shipping and handling is just 50¢ per book in the U.S. and $1.25 per book in Canada.* I understand that accepting the 2 free books and gifts places me under no obligation to buy anything. I can always return a shipment and cancel at any time by calling the number below. The free books and gifts are mine to keep no matter what I decide.

Choose one: ☐ **Harlequin Special Edition**
(235/335 HDN GRCQ)

☐ **Harlequin Heartwarming Larger-Print**
(161/361 HDN GRC3)

_____
Name (please print)

_____
Address   Apt. #

_____
City   State/Province   Zip/Postal Code

Email: Please check this box ☐ if you would like to receive newsletters and promotional emails from Harlequin Enterprises ULC and its affiliates. You can unsubscribe anytime.

Mail to the **Harlequin Reader Service:**
IN U.S.A.: P.O. Box 1341, Buffalo, NY 14240-8531
IN CANADA: P.O. Box 603, Fort Erie, Ontario L2A 5X3

Want to try 2 free books from another series! Call 1-800-873-8635 or visit www.ReaderService.com.

---

*Terms and prices subject to change without notice. Prices do not include sales taxes, which will be charged (if applicable) based on your state or country of residence. Canadian residents will be charged applicable taxes. Offer not valid in Quebec. This offer is limited to one order per household. Books received may not be as shown. Not valid for current subscribers to the Harlequin Special Edition or Harlequin Heartwarming series. All orders subject to approval. Credit or debit balances in a customer's account(s) may be offset by any other outstanding balance owed by or to the customer. Please allow 4 to 6 weeks for delivery. Offer available while quantities last.

Your Privacy—Your information is being collected by Harlequin Enterprises ULC, operating as Harlequin Reader Service. For a complete summary of the information we collect, how we use this information and to whom it is disclosed, please visit our privacy notice located at corporate.harlequin.com/privacy-notice. From time to time we may also exchange your personal information with reputable third parties. If you wish to opt out of this sharing of your personal information, please visit readerservice.com/consumerschoice or call 1-800-873-8635. **Notice to California Residents**—Under California law, you have specific rights to control and access your data. For more information on these rights and how to exercise them, visit corporate.harlequin.com/california-privacy.

HSEHW22R2

COUNTRY LEGACY COLLECTION

19 FREE BOOKS IN ALL!

EMMETT
Diana Palmer

COURTED BY THE COWBOY

THE RANCHER AND THE BABY
Marie Ferrarella

Cowboys, adventure and romance await you in this new collection! Enjoy superb reading all year long with books by bestselling authors like Diana Palmer, Sasha Summers and Marie Ferrarella!

YES! Please send me the **Country Legacy Collection!** This collection begins with 3 FREE books and 2 FREE gifts in the first shipment. Along with my 3 free books, I'll also get 3 more books from the **Country Legacy Collection**, which I may either return and owe nothing or keep for the low price of $24.60 U.S./$28.12 CDN each plus $2.99 U.S./$7.49 CDN for shipping and handling per shipment*. If I decide to continue, about once a month for 8 months, I will get 6 or 7 more books but will only pay for 4. That means 2 or 3 books in every shipment will be FREE! If I decide to keep the entire collection, I'll have paid for only 32 books because 19 are FREE! I understand that accepting the 3 free books and gifts places me under no obligation to buy anything. I can always return a shipment and cancel at any time. My free books and gifts are mine to keep no matter what I decide.

☐ 275 HCK 1939   ☐ 475 HCK 1939

Name (please print)

Address   Apt. #

City   State/Province   Zip/Postal Code

Mail to the **Harlequin Reader Service:**
IN U.S.A.: P.O. Box 1341, Buffalo, NY 14240-8571
IN CANADA: P.O. Box 603, Fort Erie, Ontario L2A 5X3

*Terms and prices subject to change without notice. Prices do not include sales taxes, which will be charged (if applicable) based on your state or country of residence. Canadian residents will be charged applicable taxes. Offer not valid in Quebec. All orders subject to approval. Credit or debit balances in a customer's account(s) may be offset by any other outstanding balance owed by or to the customer. Please allow 3 to 4 weeks for delivery. Offer available while quantities last. © 2021 Harlequin Enterprises ULC. ® and ™ are trademarks owned by Harlequin Enterprises ULC.

Your Privacy—Your information is being collected by Harlequin Enterprises ULC, operating as Harlequin Reader Service. To see how we collect and use this information visit https://corporate.harlequin.com/privacy-notice. From time to time we may also exchange your personal information with reputable third parties. If you wish to opt out of this sharing of your personal information, please visit www.readerservice.com/consumerchoice or call 1-800-873-8635. Notice to California Residents—Under California law, you have specific rights to control and access your data. For more information visit https://corporate.harlequin.com/california-privacy.

50BOOKCL22

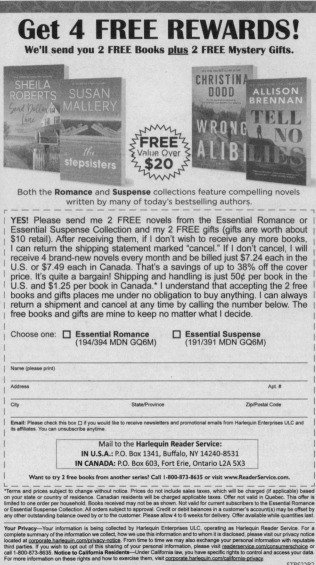

Get 4 FREE REWARDS!

We'll send you 2 FREE Books plus 2 FREE Mystery Gifts.

SHEILA ROBERTS
Sand Dollar Lane

SUSAN MALLERY
the stepsisters

CHRISTINA DODD
WRONG ALIBI

ALLISON BRENNAN
TELL NO LIES

FREE Value Over $20

Both the **Romance** and **Suspense** collections feature compelling novels written by many of today's bestselling authors.

YES! Please send me 2 FREE novels from the Essential Romance or Essential Suspense Collection and my 2 FREE gifts (gifts are worth about $10 retail). After receiving them, if I don't wish to receive any more books, I can return the shipping statement marked "cancel." If I don't cancel, I will receive 4 brand-new novels every month and be billed just $7.24 each in the U.S. or $7.49 each in Canada. That's a savings of up to 38% off the cover price. It's quite a bargain! Shipping and handling is just 50¢ per book in the U.S. and $1.25 per book in Canada.* I understand that accepting the 2 free books and gifts places me under no obligation to buy anything. I can always return a shipment and cancel at any time by calling the number below. The free books and gifts are mine to keep no matter what I decide.

Choose one: ☐ **Essential Romance**
(194/394 MDN GQ6M)

☐ **Essential Suspense**
(191/391 MDN GQ6M)

Name (please print)

Address   Apt. #

City   State/Province   Zip/Postal Code

Email: Please check this box ☐ if you would like to receive newsletters and promotional emails from Harlequin Enterprises ULC and its affiliates. You can unsubscribe anytime.

Mail to the **Harlequin Reader Service:**
IN U.S.A.: P.O. Box 1341, Buffalo, NY 14240-8531
IN CANADA: P.O. Box 603, Fort Erie, Ontario L2A 5X3

Want to try 2 free books from another series! Call 1-800-873-8635 or visit www.ReaderService.com.

*Terms and prices subject to change without notice. Prices do not include sales taxes, which will be charged (if applicable) based on your state or country of residence. Canadian residents will be charged applicable taxes. Offer not valid in Quebec. This offer is limited to one order per household. Books received may not be as shown. Not valid for current subscribers to the Essential Romance or Essential Suspense Collection. All orders subject to approval. Credit or debit balances in a customer's account(s) may be offset by any other outstanding balance owed by or to the customer. Please allow 4 to 6 weeks for delivery. Offer available while quantities last.

Your Privacy—Your information is being collected by Harlequin Enterprises ULC, operating as Harlequin Reader Service. For a complete summary of the information we collect, how we use this information and to whom it is disclosed, please visit our privacy notice located at corporate.harlequin.com/privacy-notice. From time to time we may also exchange your personal information with reputable third parties. If you wish to opt out of this sharing of your personal information, please visit readerservice.com/consumerschoice or call 1-800-873-8635. **Notice to California Residents**—Under California law, you have specific rights to control and access your data. For more information on these rights and how to exercise them, visit corporate.harlequin.com/california-privacy.

STRS22R2

COMING NEXT MONTH FROM

⑭ HARLEQUIN
HEARTWARMING

#439 WYOMING RODEO RESCUE
The Blackwells of Eagle Springs • by Carol Ross
Equestrian Summer Davies's life is on the verge of scandal, so an invitation to host a rodeo comes at the perfect time. But with event organizer Levi Blackwell, opposites do *not* attract! Has she traded one problem for another?

#440 THE FIREFIGHTER'S CHRISTMAS PROMISE
Smoky Mountain First Responders • by Tanya Agler
Coach Becks Porter is devastated when a fire destroys her soccer complex, and firefighter Carlos Ramirez, her ex, is injured. Their past is complicated, but an unexpected misfortune might lead to a most fortunate reunion this holiday season.

#441 SNOWBOUND WITH THE RANCHER
Truly Texas • by Kit Hawthorne
Rancher Dirk Hager doesn't have time for Christmas...or his new neighbor, city girl Macy Reinalda. But when they're trapped in a snowstorm, Dirk warms up to Macy and decides he might just have time for his neighbor after all...

#442 HIS DAUGHTER'S MISTLETOE MOM
Little Lake Roseley • by Elizabeth Mowers
Dylan Metzger moved home with his young daughter to renovate a historic dance hall in time for Christmas. When Caroline Waterson reconnects with a business proposal he can't refuse, Dylan finds himself making allowances—in his business and his heart.

YOU CAN FIND MORE INFORMATION ON UPCOMING HARLEQUIN TITLES, FREE EXCERPTS AND MORE AT HARLEQUIN.COM.

HWCNM0822

HARLEQUIN
PLUS

Announcing a **BRAND-NEW** multimedia subscription service for romance fans like you!

Read, Watch and Play.

Experience the easiest way to get the romance content you crave.

Start your **FREE 7 DAY TRIAL** at www.harlequinplus.com/freetrial.

HARPLUS0822